W9-AUY-327

HIDE YOURSELF AWAY

HIDE YOURSELF AWAY

MARY JANE CLARK

Doubleday Large Print Home Library Edition

ST. MARTIN'S PRESS ✠ NEW YORK

And again, for Elizabeth and David.
And for all those who struggle with
Fragile X syndrome, the most common
inherited form of mental impairment.
Please, God. Let us find a treatment or cure.

ACKNOWLEDGMENTS

The Ocean State.

I have been in love with Rhode Island since attending URI in the seventies. It's a state like no other, small in size, but large in atmosphere, history, and heart. As I returned again and again over the years, taking my children to Newport in the summertime, my Rhode Island connection only intensified. The sky was bluer there, the water sparkled more, the clean, crisp air wrapped itself around us, soothing us, renewing us.

So it only stood to reason that I would want to write a story that takes place in the setting that has blessed me with so many lifelong friends and happy memories. *Hide Yourself Away* is my valentine to Rhode Island.

Designing the valentine took help, of course. Now, here are Cupid's arrows to those people who helped along the way.

Jen Enderlin, editor extraordinaire, was key from beginning to end of this endeavor. It was Jen who suggested at the outset that the KEY News interns should be in competition, and it was Jen who broke the news that my original ending needed more work and gave me the time to get it done. To Jen and the enthusiastic team at St. Martin's Press . . . Sally Richardson, Matthew Shear, Ed Gabrielli, John Murphy, John Karle, Kim Cardascia, and Anne Twomey, my sincere thanks. And to copy editor Susan M. S. Brown, my gratitude for fine-tuning the prose and picking up those mistakes.

Susan Henderson, Preservation Society of Newport County docent, gave a fascinating tour of The Elms, offering insights on what life was like for the servants who staffed the fabulous mansion. Pointing out dumbwaiters and silver trunks large enough to stash a human body, Susan's backstairs tour provided some of the original grist for this mind's twisted mill.

Michelle Pin Seymour generously shared her idea and experience of having a tattoo engraved on her foot. Michelle's motive became the same as the character's in the book, as a loving tribute.

Anglophile Linda Lee Karas gave me pointers on what my character from Great Britain might think and how she would express herself. Leeb, you're "brilliant." Other CBS News allies helped as well. Michael Bass, B. J. D'Elia, Deborah Rubin, and Rob Schafer each came through with the fine points I needed.

Moral support and kindness poured in from many quarters. Liz Flock provided sympathetic companionship and a fabulous retreat in Maine, a perfect place to get focused and start writing. As the deadline loomed, Elizabeth Kaledin soothed and bolstered this worried author over many afternoon phone calls. Louise Albert, Joy Blake, and Cathy Haffler took over that task at night.

The Web site continues, with Colleen Kenny at the helm. Thank you, Col, for your creativity and devotion to www.mary janeclark.com.

Laura Dail, the world's most committed agent, offered her own, quite valuable, editorial observations in addition to her almost daily attention to my writing career. I know I am so very lucky to have Laura as my champion.

Every writer should be blessed with an independent editor like Father Paul Holmes but, unfortunately, there is only one of him. He is my treasured writing coach, offering his wisdom and keen insights, propping me up every step of the journey. There is no doubt in my mind that heaven sent Father Holmes my way.

My parents, Doris and Fred Behrends, and sister, Margaret Ann, continue to root for me and love my children, always looking out for their welfare. Knowing that they back me up enables me to get the writing done.

And now, it's finished. Till the next time, I don't have to hide myself away anymore.

HIDE
YOURSELF
—— AWAY ——

PROLOGUE

He wanted to have the light on, but she was just as glad that wasn't a possibility. Any illumination coming from the playhouse windows would beckon one of the staff to come and investigate.

He also wanted to have some music and had brought along his cassette player, but she insisted on silence. They couldn't risk the noise traveling out into the soft, night air. The only undulating rhythm coming from within the cottage this night would be the slow, steady rocking of their bodies.

She lay on her back on the wrought-iron daybed, thinking of the youngsters who had napped on the mattress. She strained at every cricket's chirp and skunk's mournful whine from the field outside. She wondered if there were animals in the condemned tunnel that ran beneath the playhouse. She

hoped not, since that was their predeter-
mined escape route should they ever need it.

She was having a difficult time letting herself go. He was having no such problem. He
was well into things. It was just as he was
becoming frenzied that she heard the voice
outside the cottage.

"Good Lord, it's Charlotte," she hissed as
she pushed him away.

They scrambled to collect their clothes. He
grabbed his cassette player as she slid
aside the wooden panel in the floor. Into the
darkness they lowered themselves, sliding
the trapdoor shut just as the playhouse door
above them opened.

The cold, hard dirt floor of the tunnel
pressed against their bare feet.

"What are you waiting for?" he whispered.
"Let's go."

"I'm getting dressed right here," she said.
God only knew what was in this tunnel, and
she would feel a hell of a lot better if she
were clothed as they made their way to the
water at the other end.

They sorted their clothes by feel and
dressed in the blackness as muffled voices
came from above.

"Who's that with her?" he asked.

"I can't tell."

Slowly they began to walk, arms out-stretched to the tunnel walls, feeling their way out to safety. She stifled a scream as she felt something brush her leg. A raccoon? A rat? God was punishing her for her sinfulness.

Eventually, the waters of Narragansett Bay glistened from the opening at the end of the tunnel. They stepped up their pace, the moon providing scant but precious light. As they reached their goal, he stopped.

"Crap."

"What's wrong?"

"My wallet. It must have slipped out of my pants pocket."

"Oh, sweet Jesus."

He grabbed her hand. "Don't worry, let's keep going. Maybe they won't see it."

"I'm going back for it." She was adamant.

"Tomorrow. You can get it tomorrow," he urged.

She wished she could follow him out, but she knew she wouldn't sleep all night knowing that his wallet might give them away.

"You go ahead. Go home," she said.

"I'll go back with you," he offered.

"No. You have to get off the property. They

can't know you were here. You have to go. Now."

"All right, but I'll see you tomorrow."

She swallowed as she watched him dart along the shoreline and disappear into the darkness. Taking a deep, resolute breath, she turned and stepped back inside, feeling gingerly against the side of the tunnel. Her fingers brushed against the hard-packed dirt and old brick, cold and clammy to the touch. She imagined what it must have been like for the slaves, running for their lives through this tunnel, inhaling deep breaths of the damp, musty smell that filled her nostrils now. Had they had lanterns to light their way? Or had they tapped blindly along in the blackness, not sure what was in front of them but willing to risk it, knowing only what horrors they had left behind?

When she estimated she must surely be close to the ladder that led up to the play-house, her hand receded into a large indentation in the wall. Pieces of earth broke away as she pushed against it. Her pulse quickened. Was the old tunnel safe? Could it collapse and trap her inside? Would anyone ever find her?

She prayed. If she got out of this one, she

vowed she would never, ever go to the play-house again. No matter how much he wanted her to, this was the last time. She promised.

She pushed on, sniffling quietly in the darkness.

Until she tripped over something and fell to her knees. Her breath came in short, terrified pants, her heart pumped against her chest wall as her hand groped over the form. It was covered with a smooth fabric of some sort, and it was large and intractable.

A human body, still warm, but lifeless.

She had had this feeling before, but only occasionally, in dreams. The urge, the ache, the need to scream, but somehow being frozen, unable to utter a sound. She pushed back from the body and cowered against the tunnel wall, trembling in the darkness.

Later, she would realize that she had been there for only moments, but then it seemed an eternity, the terrified thoughts spinning through her mind. She should go get help. She should summon people from the big house. But she couldn't. She wasn't supposed to have been here at all, and she was mortified at the thought of having to explain her forbidden tryst.

And, even worse, what if they blamed her?

What if they thought she had committed murder? She was rocking on her haunches, trying to soothe herself, when she heard the grating sound. The door was sliding open overhead.

She clamped her eyes tight, sure that this was the end. The murderer was coming to get her, too.

Instead, something fluttered from above, hitting her head, grazing her face. A piece of paper? A card?

She listened, shaking but undetected, as the door slid closed again.

Fourteen Years Later

The mining lamps that dotted the tunnel were powered by a generator, but that was one of the few nods to technology. The work was being done painstakingly, by hand. Just as the tunnel had been dug more than a century and a half before, human beings, not machines, scraped the clay and mortared the old red bricks now. Special care was being taken, inch by inch, foot by foot, to make sure that the walls were sturdy and firm. When the job was completed, thousands of tourists and historians and students would have the opportunity for the first time to walk the path American slaves had trod on their desperate flight to freedom. This tunnel had to be safe.

"We've got a soft spot here," called an expert mason, his words echoing against the walls of the underground passage.

The trowel tapped against the soft, red clay. Clumps of earth fell to the tunnel floor. The indentation in the wall grew larger.

The burrowing continued, revealing folds of material embedded in the clay, discolored and shredded by dirt and time. Still, some metallic threads managed to glitter in the light of the mining lamps. Gently, the mason brushed away the clay, following the trail of golden fabric.

The other workers in the tunnel gathered to watch the digging, and when they saw it they were grateful that they were all together. No one would have wanted to find such a thing alone.

A human skull and bones, swaddled in yards of gold lamé.

FRIDAY

JULY 16

CHAPTER
1

She was the oldest one.

As Grace studied the college students positioned throughout the bustling newsroom this morning, she was keenly aware of the chasm that separated her from the other interns. At least a decade loomed between her and the best and the brightest she watched leaning against the tops of borrowed desks, scanning computer screens, and chatting it up with the so-inclined members of the morning news program staff. The interns were well educated, eager, ambitious, and rued Grace, so very young.

Their whole life's ahead of them, Grace observed as she watched one coed cross her long, tanned legs and somehow manage not to expose herself fully beneath a shamelessly short skirt. They're all on track for promising futures, poised to graduate from esteemed colleges and universities, already building their résumés in order to land that first paying television news job. Unencumbered, they're able to pursue their dreams. They have no personal baggage to tote along as they enter the workforce. They can go anywhere, do anything, accept any assignment, footloose and fancy free.

Grace Wiley Callahan well knew that was not her lot. Her slate was not as clean. She had history and responsibilities. At thirty-two years old, Grace had experienced morning sickness, marriage, motherhood, and divorce, in that order. When she was the age that these kids were, she had already tucked away the dream of a graduation ceremony, withdrawing from Fordham thirty credits short. In fact, when graduation day dawned for her friends, Grace pushed Lucy's stroller onto the college campus to watch as the diplomas were handed out. The graduates' shouts of joy were drowned out for Grace by her baby daughter's colicky cries.

Eleven years since then, and now Lucy was entering the sixth grade and Grace had already discovered fine crow's-feet at the corners of her brown eyes and the first few gray strands in her honey-colored hair. She had resolutely plucked them out the day she was notified that she had been accepted into this coveted internship program. She was getting a second chance and resolved to make it count, finally earning her degree and determined to make the most of the extraordinary opportunity at KEY News world headquarters in New York City. She was also excited about the prospect of next week's trip to Newport, Rhode Island, for *KEY to America's* weeklong location broadcasts from the seaside resort, although fully aware that none of the other interns had to worry about the child they were leaving behind.

Not for a minute, of course, would Grace regret having Lucy. No, that was the best thing she had ever done, would ever do. Marrying Frank—now that was a different story. Frank had initially wanted nothing to do with a child when Grace found herself pregnant in the spring of her junior year. But Grace had refused to terminate the pregnancy. She was determined to have her baby, with Frank or without him.

Grace gazed down at her ringless left hand and recalled how Frank had eventually, grudgingly come around. The handsome, athletic, senior business major Frank Callahan, urged by his parents to do the "right thing," ultimately proposed. With trepidation, Grace accepted, knowing they weren't starting their marriage under optimal circumstances but hoping for the best.

When Lucy was born five months after the hastily planned wedding ceremony, Grace and Frank brought the baby home to a small, basement apartment in Hoboken, New Jersey. Frank dutifully took the tube into lower Manhattan each morning to his first real job at a brokerage firm while Grace stayed home with the baby and tried to pick up some freelance reporting assignments for the local newspaper, covering town council meetings and night court sessions. But as Frank's responsibilities at the firm increased, he didn't want the added pressure of rushing home at night to be with Lucy while Grace went to work. He was making more, they could afford a bigger, better apartment, Gracie didn't have to work at that podunk newspaper.

She went along, and one year followed another. Grace spent her time raising and loving her little girl, trying not to dwell on the repercussions of her marriage to Frank. As she watched the news on television, she tried not to pine for what might have been if she had finished school and followed her plan to work in broadcast journalism. As time went on, after Lucy was tucked in bed at night, Grace found herself watching more and more of the prime-time newsmagazine shows, alone, dreading Frank's moodiness and anger and the perfumed scents that lingered on his clothing when he came home late after "business dinners."

Still, Grace stayed. For Lucy's sake, she told herself. For Lucy, she would stay in the marriage. Her child would not come from a broken home. Lucy deserved to have two parents living with her and raising her in the same place. No, Grace would stick it out. She would not leave.

Instead, Frank left her.

"Grace, would you mind faxing a copy of this tentative schedule to Professor Gordon Cox in Newport?" The producer-cameraman B. J. D'Elia held out the typed itinerary. "I know it's grunt work," he apologized, "but if I don't get out of here, I'm going to miss my train to Rhode Island."

"That's what I'm here for," she replied, taking the paper from him. She didn't relish the grunt work part especially, but she knew that trust was established bit by bit. Do the small things well now and they would trust you with the bigger things later.

"You're coming up tomorrow, right, Grace?"

"Yes."

"Can I ask you to do me another favor?" B.J. didn't wait for her answer. He was holding out a sheet of yellow lined paper. "Put together a short research package on scrimshaw and tattoos. We are doing a segment with a scrimshander and, perhaps, a tattoo artist, and we'll need to have some questions for Constance to ask during the interviews. Don't go overboard," he continued. "Just enough to cover the bases, and fax me what you come up with. The fax number at our newsroom at the Viking is on the paper."

"No problem," answered Grace as she took the information from him and noticed his strong, tanned hands.

"Thanks, Grace. Thanks a lot." He flashed a smile revealing white, even teeth and leaned closer. "I'll let you in on a secret. This is my first remote as a producer, and I'm a little nervous."

"Really? I thought you were an old hand at this."

"Nope. I've been a cameraman and editor here for six years, and at local television stations for years before that. But just a few months ago they made me a producer as well. That's the wave of the present, you know. Hyphenates. You gotta do two or three jobs for the price of one if you want to stick around a place like this."

Grace was a bit envious. She figured B.J. to be about her age, maybe a couple of years older, and yet here he was, well established in his career. She wondered if he was married and had a wife who stayed home with his child while he was carving out his place in the world. Somehow, she thought not. Not only because there was no ring, but because she just had the indefinable sense that he was available. You never knew, though. There were guys who acted unattached when out in the workforce, when in reality they had families depending on them. Frank was one of those guys. Watching B.J.'s lanky frame as he walked back to his desk, Grace found herself hoping that he was not like her former husband.

As she turned to execute her task, punching in the numbers on the fax machine phone pad, the intern with the miniskirt walked over.

"At least he gave you something to do," the dark-haired beauty whispered. "I'm going out of my mind with boredom. If I spend one more minute surfing the web, I'll slit my wrists. They don't have enough for us to do."

Grace smiled as she listened for the electronic beep signaling the fax was going through. Jocelyn Vickers was right. The interns did have a lot of free time on their hands.

"It should be better when we get to Newport, don't you think?" she offered. "There should be plenty of things they'll need us for. At the very least, we get to spend a week in a beautiful place in the summertime."

Jocelyn shrugged. "Yeah, I guess."

"I've never been to Newport before, have you?" Grace asked, wanting to extend their talk if she could. The younger interns hadn't exactly been seeking her out for conversation. They didn't seem quite able to make out what to think of her. *Grace, the old lady.* What could they possibly have in common with a divorced mom?

"Just about every summer of my life." Jocelyn sighed. "My parents have a house there."

"Really? That sounds great." As Grace took the transmitted Newport schedule out of the fax machine tray, she glanced downward and caught a glimpse of the familiar beige, black, and maroon plaid peeking from beneath Jocelyn's perfectly manicured toes. Burberry. Over a hundred bucks for a pair of plastic strapped sandals. *It must be nice.* Grace was suddenly aware that her own shoes, the black pumps she had purchased on further markdown at the DSW Shoe Warehouse, looked second-rate and hopelessly boring.

"Yeah, Newport can be fun, if you know where to go and what to do." Jocelyn swept her hand back through her long, black, expensively cut hair.

"Well, that should keep you in good stead with the folks around here, Jocelyn."

"Call me Joss." She brightened. "And, yes, I'm counting on that. In fact, I'm going up there tonight so I'll be there a little early to help out. I want to make myself invaluable to them when we're there next week. I really want to be the one who gets the full-time job when the internship is over."

You're not the only one, thought Grace, her heart sinking at the idea of Jocelyn's advantage. *You're not the only one.*

Just one was going to be selected from this summer's intern crop to get a staff position as an assistant producer. Everything depended on performance, and Grace was determined to give it her all. She really needed to get that job.

CHAPTER
2

Professor Gordon Cox pulled the document from his faculty mailbox and scanned the faxed information. He would go over the KEY News schedule in depth later. Right now he had a class to teach.

He paused before the large, ornately framed mirror and checked his appearance. A full head of silver hair complemented his dark eyes and golden tan. He may have gone totally gray a bit prematurely, but he liked the effect. A distinguished, debonair scholar, attractive to the impressionable coeds.

If only he could impress Agatha Wagstaff the way he did the coeds. With the discovery of the bones, Agatha was threatening to pull the plug on the renovations of the old slave tunnel if it turned out to be her sister's tomb. Gordon's pet project for the seventeen years he had been teaching at Salve Regina University was going to come to a screeching halt, and he was in knots about it.

Opening the Shepherd's Point tunnel to the public was a cause célèbre in history circles, and Gordon, as the driving force behind the project, had made a name for himself in the preservation community. He had heard he was up for the Stipplewood Prize, but he supposed he could kiss that and his legacy good-bye now. Agatha was as crazy as a loon, and she had always been skeptical about opening her precious tunnel for the delight of the masses. What chance was there that she'd go ahead with the plan if the tunnel turned out to have been her own sister's final resting place for the last fourteen years?

The thought that all his planning, and cajoling of Agatha, and attention to her niece, Madeleine, and her mother, Charlotte, before her—not to mention all his research, monographs, and speaking engagements—that all of it would come to naught had depressed him, deeply.

Still, Gordon knew that his was a dream job. To have the opportunity to open the eyes of others to all the cultural and historical splendor that surrounded them. To revel in his passion—and be paid for the privilege.

Of course, the pay could be better. That was why he always volunteered to teach during the summer session. He had no desire to leave Newport anyway, in this, the high season. If millionaires had chosen the historic City by the Sea as the place to build their "summer cottages," it was certainly good enough for him. Why should he go away in the most gorgeous months? No, he took his trips during the winter and spring breaks. In July and August he was content to stay right here.

Just like Charlotte Sloane.

Gordon hadn't called ahead of time to see if it was all right to bring a group of students to

Shepherd's Point. He didn't want to risk Agatha's refusal to allow entry to the grounds of the rambling Victorian mansion built atop acres of rolling farmland at the tip of Newport.

"Go ahead," he instructed as the driver slowed down at the gates. "Drive right through and over to the playhouse." As the van rocked across the dirt road worn by the excavating equipment, Gordon continued his narration for his students.

"Shepherd's Point figured prominently in the history of the African-American in Newport. The mansion was built on the site of a former shepherd's pasture. A principled man, the shepherd lent his help to the desperate, hunted slaves fleeing their southern masters. A tunnel was built up from the ocean to the small shanty that led to freedom at Shepherd's Point. Years later, when the grand home was built by the silver magnate Charles Wagstaff, Sr., the tiny farmhouse was shored up and used as a playhouse for the Wagstaff children. The Underground Railroad tunnel was left intact."

Gordon led the way out of the van, wincing at the pain in his knee. The students followed as he walked to the weathered playhouse, continuing his lecture as they moved along.

"Until now, there has been only one documented Underground Railroad tunnel open for public viewing. That one slopes toward the home of the noted abolitionist Henry Ward Beecher in Peekskill, New York. There have been rumors about the Shepherd's Point tunnel, and Newporters have talked about its existence, some even sneaking onto the estate to catch a glimpse.

"Historians have been trying for years to persuade Agatha Wagstaff to allow access to the tunnel and permit essential preservation work. At one point, she had almost acquiesced, but the work was never started. Fourteen years ago, Ms. Wagstaff's sister, her only sibling, Charlotte Wagstaff Sloane, disappeared. Agatha became a recluse, and the preservation project never happened. Shepherd's Point, as you can see, sank into decrepitude."

All eyes wandered across to the gray manor house looming at the top of the sweeping, weedy lawn.

"It was finally lack of money that persuaded Agatha to let the work begin just recently. City officials made a deal by which the back taxes on Shepherd's Point would be forgiven in exchange for the right to open the tunnel to the public."

The scholars reached the playhouse. Yellow police tape blocked the entrance, yet no one stood guard. The students watched as Gordon pulled back the tape and opened the door.

"Should we be doing this, Professor?" asked one.

"It's all right. I'll take full responsibility. I don't know what the future of this tunnel will be now, in light of what has just been discovered here, but I want you all to see this. We may be the last people to witness this historic, sacred place for a very long time."

The group passed single file through the narrow doorway and huddled in the only room. If there had once been a cot for the shepherd to sleep on or a table and little chairs for the Wagstaff girls to hold tea parties, that furniture had long since been removed. The only sign of the life that had once pulsed inside the walls was the darkened fireplace, ashes still lying on the hearth.

With the pain in his knee always present,

the professor knelt to lift a piece of the wooden floor, revealing a narrow wooden staircase. The students craned to look into the dark passage. Engrossed, none of them felt the presence behind them, blocking the doorway.

The shrill voice cut the musty air. "Out! All of you get out of here. Get off my property!"

Agatha Wagstaff, mistress of Shepherd's Point, stood before them, her blue eyes bulging from her milk-white face, her red lipstick bleeding grotesquely through the lines around her mouth.

"Agatha, please," Gordon pleaded. "I just want my students to see the tunnel. Just give us a few minutes."

"No, Gordon. You and your students, get out of here this instant or I'll call the police. Charlotte never wanted you here to begin with. She didn't want our home to become a tourist attraction. She never wanted this tunnel opened."

CHAPTER
3

After lunch, Grace gathered with the other interns in the *KTA* conference room as T-shirts were distributed. With pleasure, she inspected hers. KEY NEWS—CALLAHAN was imprinted in large black letters on the front of the white shirt. But the vain thrill was replaced by tension as the executive producer strode into the room and began to reel off what would be expected of them on the Newport remote.

"You are on call twenty-four-seven. You'll all be assigned beepers, and when you are paged you are expected to answer. Promptly." Linus Nazareth's deep voice boomed. "That's what's expected if you want to work on this broadcast. Every single person on this staff knows that this is a fact of life. And if you are thinking of a career in television news, you better get used to it. If a story breaks, there are no excuses. No hot dates or family birthday parties get in the way of your responsibilities to *KEY to America.*"

"That's okay with me, Mr. Nazareth," a young man piped up, in a soft drawl. "That's the way I expect it to be. That's what gets me psyched about working in this business. The excitement and unpredictability of it."

Nazareth looked at the lanky kid leaning against the wall and tried to take his measure. Could this saccharine enthusiasm be for real?

"Anyone might say that when they're starting out," Linus answered. "What's your name again, son?"

"Sam. Sam Watkins."

"Where do you go to school, Sam?"

"Northwestern."

"Good school. But you're not from Chicago, are you?" Linus made an educated guess, hearing the regional twang.

"No. I'm from Oklahoma. Hollis, Oklahoma, sir."

"You're a long way from home, aren't you?" Linus was constantly amazed at how willing these kids were to travel from all around the country to take a summer job that paid nothing and offered no room or board. He had heard one of them had come all the way from England this summer.

Sam nodded. "Yes, sir."

If it mattered a tinker's damn to Linus, he would have asked where the kid was staying while he worked in Manhattan, but it didn't. The interns usually camped out on the sofas or in the guest rooms of apartments in the city or homes in the suburbs of relatives or family friends. Sometimes the students availed themselves of reasonably priced campus housing at one of New York's universities. Linus wasn't interested in the details.

"Well, Sam, as I was saying, at first most young journalists are eager to drop what they're doing when a story breaks, but that can get old, real fast." Linus scanned the room. "I ain't gonna sugarcoat it. It's better if you know right up front the kind of life that's ahead of you if you decide to make your living this way."

As she listened to the executive producer rant on, Grace felt her stomach twisting. This was what she worried about when she woke up in the middle of the night. Grace knew she would hate herself if she ever had to miss her daughter's birthday. Lucy was getting older, it was true, but she still needed her mother to be there for school shows, teachers' meetings, doctors' appointments, and the myriad other events that go with raising a child. And as Lucy approached adolescence, it was as important as ever that parental involvement be strong, especially when one of those parents had chosen to move away and leave her. Still, other women did it, didn't they? Managed to be good mothers while making a living. There was a way to work things out. There had to be. As long as crucial support was available, it could all fall into place.

Please, God, let Dad stay well, she prayed. Without her father's help, Grace didn't know what she would do.

CHAPTER
4

A half hour before quitting time, Grace was finishing her Internet search. She'd found several excellent articles on the arts of scrimshawing and tattooing. There was a common thread. Both required a steady hand: one, carving designs onto bone; the other, onto human skin.

She printed out the appropriate pages, marked them to B. J. D'Elia's attention at the newsroom being set up in the Bellevue Ballroom at Newport's Hotel Viking, and fed them into the fax machine. Ten minutes later, the voice on the newsroom intercom crackled. "Grace Callahan, line two."

The only calls Grace had gotten in the few weeks she had been at KEY News had been from Lucy, making her wish she could be in two places at once, home with her daughter this summer and nailing this internship in the city.

"I'm just about to leave, sweetheart," she answered as she picked up the phone. "I should be home just after six if the trains are running with me."

The male laugh on the other end of the line startled her. "Okay, sweetheart, see you then."

"Oh, I'm sorry. I thought it was my daughter," Grace stammered. "Who's calling, please?"

"It's B.J., Grace. I got the material you just faxed. It's exactly what we need. Thanks."

"Ah, you're there already."

"Yeah. It was no problem. Took the Metro-liner right up to Kingston and a taxi from the station to the hotel. It's a nice place; you'll like it."

"I'm looking forward to it," Grace said truth-fully. She had not been away, without Lucy, since Frank took her along on a business trip to Boston four years ago, and those three days had been anything but fun.

"Grace, I know you're trying to get out of there and go home, but I was wondering if you could do a little more research for me."

"Sure. Shoot," she replied, already trying to remember the times for the later com-muter trains out of Penn Station.

"Great." B.J. launched into his request. "The local newspaper is leading with a story of a human skeleton discovered in an old tunnel on an estate up here called Shep-herd's Point. There's speculation that the bones might belong to an heiress named Charlotte Wagstaff Sloane, who disap-peared fourteen years ago. Then again, they might not. The tunnel was once part of the Underground Railroad, and God knows who could have traveled through there. But be-tween the mystery of what happened to Mrs. Sloane and the old slave saga, I think this could be something interesting for *KTA* to pursue while we're up here."

"You've got me hooked," Grace answered. "I'll get right on it, and before I leave, I'll fax you whatever I can find."

"That's terrific, Grace. I really appreciate it. And I'll see you tomorrow afternoon, right?"

"Yep. I'll be there."

Grace pushed down the button on the phone to sever the connection and was about to release it again to call her father when Jocelyn stopped at Grace's borrowed desk. "You've got to get home soon, don't you?" Joss asked.

Grace had the uneasy feeling that the other intern was checking up on her, wanting to make sure that Grace wasn't looking more devoted to the internship than Joss was. Grace didn't want to play that game.

"I was about to leave, but B.J. just called and asked me to check something for him."

"Oh yeah? What?"

What the heck? It's not a secret. "He wants some background information on an old missing-persons case up there, a woman named Charlotte Wagstaff Sloane. They found some remains on her family's estate, and they think they might be hers."

"At Shepherd's Point?" A look of recognition lit up the younger intern's face.

Grace nodded. "You know the place?"

"Yes, I know the family, too. In fact, Charlotte's daughter, Madeleine, and I have hung out together in Newport. She's a good kid, but always just a little strange, as though she's about to fade away, if you know what I mean. I guess losing her mother really freaked her out for good."

Switching gears, Joss raised her hand in a farewell salute. "Well, good luck with that, and I'll see you up there."

Grace turned back to the phone and punched in the familiar numbers. Walter Wiley answered on the third ring. "Dad, it's me. Everything going all right?"

"Fine, honey. Fine. Lucy's upstairs in her room, groaning about doing her summer reading."

"I'll get on her when I get home, Dad. Don't you get into it with her."

It was nice to have someone else doing the nagging, but she didn't want her father to aggravate himself. So far, his retirement from a career with the telephone company had been marked with a treatable prostate cancer diagnosis as well as the need to have a pacemaker implanted a few months ago. Although he claimed he felt "fit as a fiddle," Grace suspected her father didn't have the energy he'd once had. She'd already lost her mother. She couldn't stand the thought of losing Dad as well.

"I'm going to be a little late getting home, Dad. Is that all right?"

"Sure, honey. Going out with some of the people there after work, I hope."

Grace smiled to herself. Walter was forever encouraging her to socialize more.

"No, Dad. Actually, I have an assignment to work on. I'm not sure how long it will take me, though. Probably an hour or two."

"No problem, honey. I already picked up a pizza. So we're all set here."

Grace was about to hang up when she remembered. "Hey, Dad, did the check from Frank come today?" The child support payment was over a week late. Again.

There was silence on the end of the line.

"Dad?"

"No, Grace. Nothing came from Frank. But there is a letter from some Boston law firm here."

Grace tensed, an instantaneous reflex after all those legal letters that had come while she was going through her divorce. In the beginning, each one had upset her. Finally, they angered her. Should she wait until she got home? she wondered. *No, face it,* she decided.

"Open it, will you, Dad?"

"Hold on, honey."

She listened as Walter put the receiver down on the kitchen counter and imagined him walking out to the hallway and retrieving the envelope from the pile of mail on the small desk there. The seconds ticked by. It was taking too long. Eventually, she heard her father pick up the phone again.

"Grace?"

"Yes."

"It's not good, honey." His voice sounded constricted.

"What? What does it say?"

"Frank is going for full custody of Lucy. He wants her to live with him and that new wife of his in Massachusetts."

Grace tried to digest what her father was saying, neither of them aware of the young girl crouched at the top of the steps, eavesdropping on her grandfather's conversation.

CHAPTER
5

As Jocelyn pushed through the heavy re-
volving door, the blast of muggy air swept
across her face, a sharp contrast to the almost icy air-conditioning of the Broadcast
Center. From the hot sidewalk, she spotted
her parents' driver sitting in the dark green
Mercedes sedan parked at the curb across
Fifty-seventh Street. Jocelyn jaywalked across
the busy thoroughfare and got into the car,
not waiting for the chauffeur to open the door
for her.

"Okay, Carl. Let's go."

Settling back into the leather seat, Jocelyn
noticed the wicker hamper on the floor.
Good. Rosa had packed food for the trip.
Joss leaned down and flipped open the lid.
Chicken salad with raisins and walnuts, a
container of fresh melon and grapes, some
of her favorite oatmeal cookies, and bottles

of Aquafina. Perfect. As long as their kidneys held out, they wouldn't have to stop.

But as the sedan made the turn north, onto the West Side Highway, Joss groaned. The late-afternoon traffic was already slow, the cars inching their way out of Manhattan for the weekend. The three-and-a-half-hour trip to Rhode Island was going to take longer than usual.

In the ride down in the elevator, she had come up with a plan. She would talk to Tommy in person when she got up there tonight, knowing that it was a pretty good bet she could find him with the guys at the bar at Salas'. Whenever she was bored or just wanted to be sure that she could have him again if she really wanted him, Joss would stop by the place to flirt and string her old boyfriend along. Tommy was so predictable, eager as a puppy to please her, desperate to have her back, never accepting that theirs had been merely a summertime fling for Joss. Tommy was tall, great-looking, and the best marksman in his police training class, but living in Newport on a full-time basis, married to a cop, was not what Jocelyn Vickers had planned for herself. The very thought of it made her shudder.

Still, the rookie police officer could help get Joss where she did want to go. If Tommy could get her some inside information about the skeletal remains found at the old Wagstaff estate, Joss could ingratiate herself with the powers at KEY News and earn that staff position.

There was no time to waste. If she could convince Tommy to get the information now, he could have it all ready for her tonight when she met him. Searching in her Kate Spade bag for her cell phone, Joss punched in the 401 area code.

CHAPTER
6

When Grace finally got home, her father was asleep on the living room sofa. She grabbed a slice of cold pizza from the box on the kitchen table and wandered into the den, finding Lucy watching TV. Her daughter was obsessed with *Law & Order.* And since you could find it running all the time on either the networks or cable, Lucy was stationed in front of the television far too much.

"Why are you wasting your time with this, Luce?" Graced kissed the top of her daughter's head. "I don't like you watching this stuff. It's too disturbing."

"It's good, Mom. I want to see who did it." Her daughter didn't take her big brown eyes from the television set.

"But you probably already know who did it. It's a rerun."

"I know, but it's still good."

Grace sat down on the love seat, chewing the pizza and staring, unseeingly, at the screen. She had to call Frank, and she dreaded it.

"You all set for tomorrow, honey?"

"Sure, Mom."

"All packed?"

"Not yet. I'll do it after this is over."

Grace wasn't up for nagging her daughter. Not before she had to leave her for a week. Not before Lucy was going to be with Frank and that pretty, fun new stepmother who seemed to have nothing to do but get her nails done, shop, and give in to Lucy's every whim.

"All right, Luce," said Grace, getting to her feet. "I'm going upstairs to get organized."

Closing her bedroom door behind her, Grace went to the phone on the nightstand. She swallowed as she heard her former husband's voice answer on the first ring.

"Hi, Frank. It's Grace."

"Oh yes, hello. How are you?" He always sounded so formal, so devoid of emotion.

"How do you *think* I am, Frank?" She didn't wait for his response. "I got the letter from your lawyer today."

"I see. And?"

"And why are you doing this, Frank?" Grace's voice rose. "Please, I'm begging you, don't go ahead with this. Lucy doesn't need any more upset in her life."

"It's Lucy I'm thinking about, Grace." His tone was maddeningly calm. "It will be better for Lucy if she lives up here with us."

"How? How is it better, Frank? Tell me," Grace demanded. "Lucy's adjusted to her school here in Waldwick now. She's finally made some friends. It's not fair to uproot her again. She's been through enough already."

"Lucy is going into adolescence, Grace. That's a tough time. Adolescents need strong roots to hold on to and good parental role models. Parents have to be there for their kids. They have to be involved. They have to pay attention."

Grace gripped the telephone receiver, her knuckles whitening. She knew what would be coming next.

"Jan and I can give Lucy a more nurturing, stable environment than you can."

"How dare you!"

"It's true and you know it."

"I know nothing of the sort, Frank. Lucy has a very stable, loving home right here. And while we're talking about 'stable environments' and 'parental role models,' what kind of example do you think you gave Lucy? You, with all your so-called dinner meetings and business trips—fronts, and transparent ones, Frank, for your extramarital escapades. What kind of role model have *you* been?"

"If we had had a better marriage, Grace, I wouldn't have had to look elsewhere."

"Oh yeah, that's right. Poor you."

Frank ignored her sarcastic taunt.

"Look, Grace. I have no interest in getting into a rehash of our old problems. The fact of the matter is, Jan and I are very happy together, supremely happy. That will give Lucy a positive view of what a marriage can be. We have a beautiful new home here in an upscale suburb with excellent schools. Jan has given up her job and will be at home; she can be there for Lucy. As it is, Lucy is living in your father's house. You've decided to go back to school, and that's admirable. But it's taking up a lot of your time, and when you finish, I assume you'll be working full time, leaving your father to pick up the slack with Lucy's care. He's no kid, Grace. Even putting aside Lucy's welfare for a minute, how fair do you think that is to him?"

Grace had asked herself the same question. But she was certain that Dad enjoyed having them there, that he had a renewed sense of purpose since Lucy had brought youthful life into the house that had been so lonely since his wife's death.

"Dad loves Lucy, and I thank God for him, Frank. He's wonderful with her. I know for certain that he has never resented having her here. Having Lucy around keeps him energized. He adores her."

"Maybe he does, Grace. But his health isn't the greatest, and I'm her father."

"And I'm her mother, Frank. She's staying here with me," she declared firmly, holding herself back from hurling the phone across the room.

"All right, Grace. I can see we're not going to get anywhere here. Let's see what the judge says. I'll be waiting at the train station for Lucy tomorrow."

And to think that selfish bastard hadn't even wanted her to have the baby.

Grace fumed as she folded the laundry, still warm from the dryer, separating the garments into two piles. Of all the mean timing: Frank's intention of getting custody coming just before Lucy was going off to spend two weeks up there. She wouldn't put it past her former husband to have timed it so that Grace could be left alone to stew while he and his new wife worked on selling the advantages of coming to live with them to Lucy.

How quickly things could change. Just yesterday Grace had been glad that Lucy's trip was coinciding with her own assignment in Newport. Lucy had been excited at the prospect of taking the train to Rhode Island with her mother, then continuing all by herself up the tracks to Boston, where Frank would meet her. Now, Grace felt sick to her stomach at the thought of her child being separated from her and going to "them."

"Lucy," she called up the stairs from the basement. "Will you go and get our suit-cases out of the garage, please?"

"Okay, Mom."

Lucy must sense something's up, thought Grace. Usually, it would take two or three requests to get her to perform a task.

"Should I bring them down there, Mom?"

"No. Put them in our bedrooms."

Grace stacked the two laundry baskets and carried them up the cement stairs. As she entered the kitchen, she was suddenly aware that the striped wallpaper had seen better days, many better days. The path through the dining room and living room revealed that a paint job was in order, and the carpeting could really use replacing. Funny how you could walk by things, day after day, and never really see them.

She wondered what the place Lucy was going to would be like. Grace would bet Frank's new house had gleaming steel appliances and polished granite countertops in its sparkling kitchen. There would be yards and yards of ceramic-tiled and fresh wooden floors. There were probably skylights and a Jacuzzi. All the houses being built these days had skylights and Jacuzzis. She thought of the peppermint pink tub that Lucy took her baths and showers in. Like most everything else in her father's house, it was original to the 1960s construction. Scrubbed clean, but far from new and not yet old enough to be considered vintage and cool.

How could she ever compete with the surroundings that Frank could offer? Would it be better for Lucy to live in a house like that?

Stop it. Stop it right now.

This couldn't be about who had the nicer house. If that were the case, Grace would almost surely lose. She most likely would never, ever be able to offer Lucy the kind of surroundings that Frank could. Television news eventually offered a comfortable living, but except for the high-priced on-air talent, journalists didn't make the kind of money investment bankers did.

A judge would see that it wasn't about the style of the house and creature comforts it afforded, wouldn't he? A judge would know it was about stability and care and love. Those were the things a child needed.

But was Grace going to have to compete

with Frank's new wife? If Jan was willing to be a stay-at-home mother, if she was going to be there every day when Lucy came home from school, would the judge think that was a better situation for Lucy? He couldn't possibly think that being with a step-mother was preferable to being with the real mother, could he?

Grace knew that, once, it had been almost a foregone conclusion that children stayed with their mothers. But times had changed, and fathers were demanding their rights. It wasn't unheard of now for the father to get custody, as long as it was in the best interest of the child.

Surely, it was in Lucy's best interest to stay right where she was, safe with her mother. It *was* in Lucy's best interest. Wasn't it?

CHAPTER
7

Before his shift was over, the rookie police officer Thomas James made a trip to the detectives' bullpen. In case he was caught, he had his excuse prepared. He merely wanted to familiarize himself with the details of the Charlotte Wagstaff Sloane case. After all, he had been only twelve years old when the lady disappeared. If anything, his feigned conscientiousness would win him brownie points with the detectives working the newly reopened case.

It didn't take him long to find what he was looking for. Tommy had heard the detectives mention that there was a diary, a journal the woman had kept before she vanished. And here it was, or at least photocopies of the pages written in a long, flowing, feminine hand.

Tommy read the notation on the cover

page of the stack of papers: "Original returned to Agatha Wagstaff, sister."

He took the pile and nonchalantly made
his way to the copying machine. As he fed
the sheets into the tray, his heart beat faster.
In part because he knew he was doing
something wrong, very wrong. In part because he knew he would be seeing Joss in
just an hour. He had missed her so, and
she'd said she'd been thinking about him
nonstop. He was thrilled that she might be
his again.

Ever since he met her, the summer before
she started college, he had been smitten
with Joss. He knew it was a long shot. A girl
like that, from a family like hers, wasn't going
to be attracted to a basic guy like him. A guy
from a working-class background who had
to work his way through the University of
Rhode Island, a guy whose highest aspira-
tion was to become a detective on his hometown police force. Though he was six years
older than she was, a sizable gap at their
stage of the game, Joss was much more sophisticated than the local girls her age. She
had seen and been exposed to things and
places that the year-round Newport girls
didn't even know existed.

Miraculously, though, as far as Tommy as concerned, Jocelyn Vickers had been at his side all that magical summer. Lying on the beach, dancing on the wharves, holding hands on long strolls in the moonlight on the Cliff Walk. The memory of the evenings spent making out on the bench at the top of the Forty Steps as the waves crashed below them was still so vivid. Even now, he had dreams about it.

But the summer came to an end and Joss went off to college down south. For a while, she returned his lovesick letters and spent time with him on the telephone, but at Thanksgiving she told him it was better that they be only friends. She had immersed herself in her new life at Vanderbilt. Strange how that Vanderbilt family had not only made its mark in his hometown but played a role in taking away the girl he adored.

These past summers, Tommy had nevertheless waited for Joss to come back up north, hoping their paths would cross. And they did meet up, from time to time, at the bars and clubs that hopped during the vacation season. He suspected Joss was playing him when she flirted and pouted if he told her he had been dating other girls. He'd try to play it cool, but he'd quickly melt, confessing that no matter who he went out with, he always wished he was with her instead. He consoled himself with the fact that Joss never came out and told him there was absolutely no chance.

Tommy fed the last sheet into the copier and lifted the still warm pages from the side of the machine.

This would show Joss how much he loved her. He was risking his career for her.

CHAPTER
8

It didn't matter that the official results weren't back yet. The bones in the tunnel were Charlotte's. There was no question about it.

How Charlotte got there was a long-ago, yet still painfully clear, memory. Everything had gone so utterly wrong. What started out as a desire to make things right had turned into the worst possible nightmare.

Charlotte had been distraught but still breathtakingly beautiful as she'd agreed to go to the playhouse and talk away from the mansion, away from the chance that little Madeleine would overhear their conversation. As they'd talked, Charlotte accepted the handkerchief offered to wipe her tears, but there was no comforting her.

If only she'd been more receptive. If only she'd offered some small solution to the problem. Instead, she had wept as she studied the photograph taken just hours before at the country club, unable to focus on anything else. She hadn't seen the need in the eyes of her playhouse companion, hadn't considered how their conversation would determine whether the future would be worth living.

The rage at the idea of a dream shattered had been crushing. Even now, fourteen years later, it was hard to accept the blind fury that had led to grabbing the iron tool from the fireplace and smashing it against Charlotte's head.

SATURDAY

JULY 17

CHAPTER
9

The dentist had long since retired, but before he closed his practice he had sent his records on Charlotte Wagstaff Sloane to the Newport Police Department. For years the X-rays of Charlotte's molars and bicuspids had gathered dust in the "cold case" file. The dental records, filed with the State Medical Examiner's Office now, should be enough to identify the remains if they were those of her mother, but twenty-year-old Madeleine Sloane had given a blood sample in case DNA testing was necessary.

As she drove her yellow Mustang convertible along Ocean Avenue, Madeleine took one hand off the steering wheel and ripped the Band-Aid off the inside of her elbow, not wanting to be reminded of any of it. Not the loss of her mother when Madeleine was six years old, not the years of living alone with

her broken father, not the constant aware-
ness that people still whispered and gos-
siped about what had happened.

Under a clear sky and a blazing yellow
sun, the sparkling deep blue waters of
Rhode Island Sound glimmered to her left.
On the horizon, white sails billowed in the
breeze, giving their boat owners pure pleasure. On the other side of the road, kite en-
thusiasts flew their creations at Brenton
Point State Park. Along with the traditional
flat and box kites, brightly colored plastic
frogs and whales and whirligigs danced in
the ocean air, celebrating summer vacation,
freedom, life.

Envious, Madeleine wondered what it was
like to be as carefree as the kite fliers were,
as the sailors must be. What was it like to
simply enjoy the moment without always
having a sad tug of memory?

Steering the car around the bend, the
wind whipping through her short, sun-
streaked blond hair, Madeleine tried to remember a time when she hadn't felt torn.
Vaguely, she could recall going to kinder-
garten, her pretty mother holding her firmly
by the hand, both of her parents smiling and
making a fuss as their little girl went off to

school. She could remember them picking her up at the end of that first session and taking her for a banana split at La Forge, Charlotte and Oliver Sloane praising their daughter for her important accomplishment. She had felt very special, very secure, very loved.

But by the time she went to first grade, things were different. Madeleine would often hear her mother and father's fights, ending with maternal tears and paternal trips to the study and the solace of the amber liquid that filled the crystal decanters on the butler's table.

And then, just after school got out for the summer, Mommy was gone. Just like that. After another day of Mommy and Daddy fighting.

Fourteen years. Through most of grammar school, all of high school, and now her first two years at Salve Regina. Madeleine had ached for her mother, telling herself that her mother would never have left her if she could have helped it. Madeleine would never allow herself to think that her mother would have gone away willingly. Something or someone had taken her mother from her.

But, even more than not entertaining the

notion that her mother could have abandoned her, Madeleine could not for a minute let herself think that her father had anything to do with her mother's disappearance. Madeleine knew she was in a minority. Most Newporters thought Oliver Sloane had killed his wife.

In the fall, when it was time to go back to class, the second-graders in the school yard had been eager to repeat for Madeleine's benefit the conversations they had heard at family dinner tables all over town.

"Your father never really loved your mother."

"Your father drinks too much."

"Your father killed your mother."

At first she had been wounded and embarrassed, then she became defiant, finally she pushed everyone away. Except for her father and Aunt Agatha. They both needed her.

But those relationships were problematic as well. After Charlotte disappeared, neither of her closest relatives liked or trusted the other.

The convertible turned into the entrance and rode straight through the peeling gates. Massive rhododendrons and topiary bushes which had long ago lost their expertly carved animal shapes lined the long gravel road that led to Aunt Agatha's rambling, twenty-eight-room Victorian "cottage." Madeleine counted eleven cats sunning themselves on the overgrown lawn.

Parking her car beneath the porte cochere, Madeleine saw Finola standing at the front doorway.

"Who's that?" Finola called, squinting to see.

"It's me, Finola. Madeleine. What are you doing there, waiting like a spider?"

"I'm guarding your aunt. There are reporters and such trying to muscle their way in here."

Madeleine knew that the housekeeper had to be exaggerating about the "muscling," but she was relieved that Aunt Agatha had Finola to run interference for her. The local newspaper and television people had been trying to get to Madeleine and her father, too.

Finola stood aside as Madeleine climbed the steps that led to the grand entry foyer. The young woman's nostrils flared at the smell of cat urine wafting from the once plush, royal red carpeting.

"Your aunt is in the deck room."

The frayed shades were pulled down tight, forbidding any of the glorious sun to come streaming through the many glass doors and windows designed for enjoying the sweeping views of the water. The heat in the room would be stifling by the afternoon. There was no such thing as central air-conditioning at Shepherd's Point, and Aunt Agatha wouldn't have the extra money to run it even if there were.

As Madeleine's eyes adjusted to the darkness, she spotted the diminutive figure sitting on one of the two sofas beside the Italian-tile fireplace.

"Aunt Agatha, it's me." Madeleine bent to kiss the clammy cheek.

"Ah, Madeleine. My Madeleine. How are you, my dearest?" Without waiting for a response, she called, "Finola, please get Madeleine some lemonade."

"No, thanks, Auntie. I'm not thirsty."

"You're sure? All right then. Never mind, Finola." A clawlike hand patted the worn velvet. "Come. Sit here beside me, my Madeleine."

Madeleine obediently took her place.

"I want to see it again."

"See what, dear?" Agatha asked.

"You know."

"Oh, Madeleine, why do you tear yourself up this way?" the older woman implored.

"Please, Aunt Agatha, I have to see it."

Agatha rose and slowly walked across the room to the antique mahogany desk in the corner. She took the key from under the blotter and slid it into the brass lock. Pulling the bottom drawer open, Agatha lifted out the yellow leather-bound journal.

Fool. Why am I so naïve? People lie and cheat all the time. I can't let this go on one more minute. Tonight's disappointment at the country club was enough.

The handwriting was strong and clear, so unlike the more youthful scrawl in the rest of the diary. In her childhood bedroom, Charlotte had pulled out her old diary to unburden herself that last night of her life.

Madeleine read her mother's final diary entry, as she had done easily a hundred times before, but this time she ignored her aunt's outstretched hands.

"Not this time, Aunt Agatha. I want to keep it now. It's time for it to be mine."

Agatha didn't resist the demand. "All right, dear. You're probably right."

Together, they rose from the sofa, knowing where they would go next. It was always the same. They climbed the wide staircase to the second floor, to Charlotte's old room.

The large space was virtually the same as it had been when pretty, young Charlotte left for her new life at Seaview as a married woman twenty years before, but time and neglect had left their marks. The yellow spread on the curlicued wrought-iron bed was the one that Charlotte had snuggled under, but now it was faded and covered with animal hair. The flowered wallpaper was peeling at the seams, and two strips had come down altogether. The stench of cat urine was exacerbated by windows shut tight.

A red Limoges box sat on the writing desk beneath the window. Madeleine opened the porcelain lid, knowing exactly what she would find. The plain gold band that symbolized her parents' union lay alone at the bottom as it had for the past fourteen years. She turned her mother's wedding band over in her hands and then slipped it on. She could still remember watching her mother taking the ring off to put lotion on her hands that last night. Aunt Agatha had insisted on keeping the ring right where Charlotte had left it, and Madeleine's father hadn't had the heart to fight her for it.

Madeleine took the gold band off as she heard the phone ringing in the distance. And then Finola was at the door.

"The police are on the phone, Miss Agatha."

For a moment, each of them was paralyzed, knowing that this could be the definitive news they had waited to hear for so long. The ring slipped out of Madeleine's hand, and as she bent down to pick it up, she broke the silence.

"I'll get that, Aunt Agatha."

CHAPTER
10

Minutes after the next of kin were notified, the official press release was issued.

THE OFFICE OF THE STATE MEDICAL EXAMINER, IN CONJUNCTION WITH THE RHODE ISLAND STATE POLICE AND THE NEWPORT POLICE DEPARTMENT, IS RELEASING THE FOLLOWING INFORMATION:

THE SKELETONIZED REMAINS FOUND AT SHEP-

HERD'S POINT IN NEWPORT, RHODE ISLAND, LAST WEEK, HAVE BEEN POSITIVELY IDENTIFIED BY THE USE OF DENTAL COMPARISON, COMPUTER-AIDED FACIAL/SKULL SUPERIMPOSITION, ANTHROPOLOGICAL DATA, AND PERSONAL EFFECTS AS CHARLOTTE WAGSTAFF SLOANE, A WHITE FEMALE, BORN IN NEWPORT, RHODE ISLAND. MRS. SLOANE WAS 28 YEARS OLD WHEN SHE WAS REPORTED MISSING FOURTEEN YEARS AGO.

MRS. SLOANE WAS THE VICTIM OF HOMICIDAL VIOLENCE. NO FURTHER INFORMATION WILL BE RELEASED. THIS IS AN ONGOING CRIMINAL INVESTIGATION.

CHAPTER
11

The *Seawolf* was Gordon Cox's pride and joy and a great way to impress women. He'd named his sailboat in honor of the father he never knew. Soon after marrying his mother in 1944, Gordon's father had joined the navy, and a few months later, he was lost at sea with seventy-nine other men aboard the USS *Seawolf,* one of America's World War II submarines.

Gordon's white hair and the crisp, white sails of the *Seawolf* flapped in the morning breeze as it came around the curve where Narragansett Bay met Newport Harbor at Shepherd's Point. Professor Cox pointed out the run-down Victorian mansion on the hill to the woman who was both his student and his much younger companion. "There it is, Judy. Shepherd's Point from a different angle."

The pretty, red-haired coed adjusted the brim of her baseball cap to ensure protection of her fair-skinned face from the sun's strong rays. "It looks a lot better from this distance," she said, squinting. "Seeing it up close yesterday with the rest of the class was kinda sad. It must have been beautiful, but it's depressing to see what's happened to it now. I hope someone with bags of money buys it and fixes it up."

"Well, that's exactly what it would take," Gordon said. "Bags and bags of money."

"Do you think Agatha Wagstaff will sell it?" Judy asked, rifling through her canvas tote, looking for sunblock.

"I doubt it. Agatha is determined to pass it

along to her niece," Gordon answered. "But I wouldn't be surprised if Madeleine Sloane sells Shepherd's Point when she inherits it. Even if she could afford it, I don't think she'll have much interest in keeping the place, especially if the bones that were found in the tunnel turn out to be her mother's."

Judy's eyes searched the coastline. "Where is the tunnel? I don't see it."

Gordon made the adjustments necessary to steer the *Seawolf* toward the opening in the land at the water's edge, a course he had taken many times before. As the dark, boarded-up hole came into view, he was hopeful. Maybe finding Charlotte would make the preservation of the tunnel an even more important project. After all, Gordon thought, if people's interest in the Underground Railroad didn't pull them in, the American fascination with a "high society" murder would.

CHAPTER
12

They were minutes from arriving at the Kingston station, and Grace was apprehensive. This was a first for Lucy and for her.

"All right, honey. Now remember, just stay here in your seat and don't get into any conversations with anyone."

"I know, Mom. I know." Lucy sighed with exasperation. "I'm not a baby, you know."

"You're my baby, and I'm telling you again, don't talk to strangers."

"I won't, Mom."

Grace gazed with love at the freckles that sprinkled Lucy's nose and the sooty lashes that were canopies for those big, brown eyes. The braces would be coming off next year, and Lucy was beginning to develop beneath that T-shirt. Her baby was growing up.

The time had passed so quickly, yet it was hard for Grace to recall what life had been like before Lucy. Her daughter had been her focus for a third of her own life. Of course, the aim was to raise an independent adult, but it was difficult to let go, even gradually, hard to imagine what her life would be like without Lucy.

At least she had seven more years before Lucy would go off to college. Seven years was a good while yet. But if Frank won his case, if Lucy went to live with him, Grace wouldn't even have that time. Weekend visits and a couple of weeks in the summer or at Christmas vacation weren't going to cut it. With the back of her hand, Grace wiped the tears that were forming at the corners of her eyes.

"Ah, Mom, don't cry. I'll be fine."

"I know you will, sweetheart, I know you will." Grace kissed the top of her daughter's head, inhaling the sweet, familiar scent of shampoo. "I'm being ridiculous."

The train was slowing down. Grace lifted her suitcase down from the overhead storage compartment.

"Now, you have the money I gave you? And the cell phone? And you know Daddy's number, right?"

Lucy nodded, pleased. She had been begging for a cell phone. Her mother was lending her hers for this trip. It was a start, at least. "Yeah, I've got it, Mom."

"Maybe you'll get a little something to bring back for Grandpa?"

"Yep. Dad says we're going to do some sightseeing while I'm there. I'll find something nice for Grandpa."

"Good girl."

The car had stopped moving. It was time to get off.

"All right, Luce. Have a great time. Daddy will be right there waiting for you at the station."

"Don't worry, Mom. I'm fine."

"I know you are, Lucy. Bye-bye, sweetheart. I love you."

"I love you, too, Mom." Lucy stood from her seat and wrapped her arms around her mother, hugging Grace tightly.

She was still a child after all, thought Grace, as she stepped down to the platform in front of the shingled railroad station. Lucy was still her little girl, and Frank couldn't take her away.

But should she be giving Frank this ammunition? Should she be pursuing this dream of hers, traveling for her career at a time like this?

As she flagged down a taxi, Grace knew she was at one of life's crossroads. She could give up the internship, choose something to do that was less demanding, more predictable. Something with which Frank couldn't find fault. Or she could go ahead, and not allow Frank to dictate what her professional life would be.

By the time the car reached the mammoth span of the Newport Bridge, Grace knew what she had to do. She stared out at the pleasure boats dotting the deep blue Narragansett Bay, certain that she had to go forward, she had to be true to herself. In the end, that was the role model she wanted her daughter to see.

CHAPTER
13

The taxi turned into the semicircular driveway at the entrance to the Hotel Viking.
Guests sunned themselves in the white
wooden rocking chairs on the porch that
lined the front of the large, brick, colonial-
style structure. In her research, Grace had
read that the classic hotel was built in the
1920s to accommodate some of the out-of-
town guests of the mansion owners. Grace
imagined the well-heeled visitors arriving for
their stay in Newport. She smiled in appreciation at the pink and purple petunias, golden
hibiscus, and cheerful daisies waving from
the window boxes and planters.

The lobby rang of white-paneled grace,
with original chandeliers and woodwork. A
wonderful brass mail chute stood guard beside the elevators. Grace went directly to the
front desk to check in.

The uniformed reception clerk pulled a slip of white paper from the mail slot assigned to Grace's room. "You have a message waiting, Ms. Callahan."

Grace read the note, a bit disappointed that now she couldn't go to see her room and freshen up. B.J. wanted her to come directly to the news work space. "Which way to the Bellevue Ballroom?" she asked.

"To your left, around the corner." The clerk pointed.

"Thank you." Grace nodded, beginning to pull her suitcase along with her.

"Ms. Callahan, someone will be happy to take your bag up to your room if you like."

"That would be great. Thanks."

Grace caught her breath as she entered the ballroom. It had been transformed from an opulent spot for business meetings, society parties, and weddings into the base of operations for the *KEY to America* team. Long tables had been brought in for the computers, telephones, videotape editing decks, fax machines, and copiers. Along the side wall, technicians were running yards of electrical cables, setting up for transmissions to New York and then, within nanoseconds, to the rest of the United States. Grace spotted B.J. at the large buffet table set up at the rear of the room. He saw her at the same time. "Come on over," he called, gesturing to her.

Grace glanced at the platters of sandwiches, cookies, and fruit.

"I'm glad you're here. If you hadn't arrived soon, I was going to have to leave without you," B.J. said. "I thought you'd want to come with me. I'm going to see if we can get some video over at Shepherd's Point . . . and, if we're really lucky, someone will talk to us. Get yourself something to eat. You can take it with you in the car."

Grace wrapped a tuna sandwich in a napkin, grabbed a bottle of water, and hurriedly followed B.J. out through the lobby.

"We just got word that dental records confirm that the remains they found in that old slave tunnel belong to Charlotte Sloane," B.J. said over his shoulder as he led the way to the car.

"You buried the lead," Grace replied.

CHAPTER
14

Zoe Quigley watched as Grace left the ballroom with that tall, good-looking white male producer. B.J. they called him. If Zoe were the gambling sort, her money would bet that B.J. was interested in more than Grace Callahan's mind.

I didn't come three thousand miles and give up my summer holiday for this.

None of the *KTA* producers had come over to Zoe with a lick of substantive work to be done. Photocopying and answering the phones were all she had been entrusted with at the Broadcast Center in New York. So far, it didn't look like it would be any different in Newport.

Next they'll have me fetching their coffee.

Flipping back her long braided hair, Zoe was determined. She wasn't going to let it get to her. She was going to win the job with KEY News. When she went back to England, she could use the trophy as a tool in getting another job there. This accomplishment here in the States, along with the documentary she was filming entirely on her own, could land her a spot with the BBC.

This time in Rhode Island was fortuitous. Black heritage in the state ran complicated and deep. There was plenty to show the pervasive evils of the American slave trade. In her free time, Zoe planned to take her camcorder and document the struggle of blacks in the so-called land of liberty, focusing on one black in particular. A female slave named Mariah.

She knew it wasn't going to be easy to juggle both tasks, but she also knew she could do it. Zoe prided herself on facing reality, and this she also believed to be true: in America, if you were black, you usually had to try harder.

She was still struggling to wrap her mind around it. In England, skin color didn't matter much. One was judged by class, not race. When one opened one's mouth and spoke, certain assumptions were made. A proper accent, signifying social status and the right education, opened doors. Perhaps, in its own way, that was discriminatory, too. But how one spoke, with hard work, could be changed. Skin color couldn't.

CHAPTER
15

Dear God, people really lived like this? Grace was awed at the majesty of the architectural masterpieces they passed on their ride south on Bellevue Avenue. It was almost unbelievable, mansion after mansion, each one different, each one planned and executed with exacting attention to even the tiniest detail. This couldn't be the United States. This was like driving down a road flanked by European palaces. Classical Greece, imperial Rome, Renaissance Italy, and Bourbon Paris were all represented in the architectures of the mansions that sat on acres of exquisitely maintained property. Again, Grace tried to imagine what it had been like to live as one of the wealthy here during the Gilded Age, when carriages and fine livery traveled along Bellevue Avenue.

Of course, you had to have a staff of house-keepers, carpenters, gardeners, grounds-keepers, maids, butlers, cooks, laundresses, grooms, coachmen, and footmen to keep it all going. But when you made millions and millions of dollars in railroads, oil, coal, to-bacco, shipping, banking, and real estate—and didn't have to pay federal income taxes—you could afford all the help you needed. It must have been a nice life.

But times had changed and so had the cost of labor and the tax laws. Even many of the wealthiest families had decided that they could no longer afford to maintain these places. Donating their homes to the Preser-vation Society of Newport County was the way to go. Now, the Preservation Society took care of the precious landmarks, open-ing them to the public for guided tours and renting them out for social functions.

Grace knew from the reading she'd done that the year-round influx of tourists had res-cued Newport. The city's fortunes had faded away with the chaos of the two World Wars.

A military sameness drifted over the town after the U.S. Navy's Atlantic Fleet was quartered there. The downtown area became full of bars and cheap stores catering to the servicemen. With no industry finding its way to Newport, except for the manufacturing of some rather less-than-glamorous torpedoes on Goat Island, it wasn't until the sixties that Newport got some attention again with the start of the now world-famous jazz festivals and John and Jackie Kennedy's visits in the summers. The next decade, the naval fleet departed from Narragansett Bay. Then Newport began to find its future in its textured past . . . in tourism.

B.J. steered the car onto Ocean Avenue, past the cabanas of exclusive Bailey's Beach club, past the gorgeous, somewhat newer homes overlooking the Rhode Island Sound. As he slowed down in front of Shepherd's Point, it was clear that the Preservation Society had not been able to make any inroads with Agatha Wagstaff's estate. Perched on a hill, it was like something out of an old gothic film. Dark, shuttered, and overgrown with ivy and wisteria gone wild.

A figure wearing dark green pants, a long-sleeved shirt, and a wide-brimmed straw hat was whacking away with a scythe at some tall, dried-out grass near the gates.

"Buddy, give it up. You ain't makin' a dent," B.J. muttered as he turned the car into the driveway, switching off the ignition and getting out. Grace followed.

"Excuse me," B.J. called, approaching the man. "We're with KEY News."

As the man lowered his scythe, Grace saw that he was quite elderly. Or at least he looked that way. White hair peaked from beneath the tattered hat. The suntanned face had the wrinkled, weathered look of someone who had spent many years outdoors. The facial expression was far from welcoming.

"We'd like to take some pictures of the house, and we're wondering if there is anyone at home right now who would be willing to talk to us," B.J. continued.

A gnarled hand gripped the handle of the scythe, and for an instant, Grace was afraid the old coot might take a swipe at them. Instinctively, she pulled back at the alcohol on the man's breath.

"It's a free country, or at least they say it is," the old man said. "But this here is private property. Take your pictures from the road if you want, but you're not setting foot on Miss Wagstaff's land."

"Would *you* be willing to talk to us?" B.J. tried again.

"I doubt it, but 'bout what?" The old guy sneered.

He knows damned well about what, thought Grace.

"About Charlotte Wagstaff Sloane," B.J. said. "You've heard about her remains being identified this morning as those in the tunnel?"

The man's shoulders slumped. His tone changed as he murmured, "No, I hadn't heard that yet."

So much for my instincts, thought Grace. The old guy was clearly shaken. It was a horrible feeling, breaking bad news to someone while acting in a journalistic capacity. She thought fleetingly about the poor families who had figured out that their sons and daughters in the military had died from reports on television before the army chaplain came to their door to notify them.

"I'm sorry, Mr. . . . ? What is your name, sir?"

"Dugan. Terence Dugan."

"And you work for Miss Wagstaff, Mr. Dugan?" asked B.J.

"Been gardener here for forty-two years. I remember when Miss Charlotte was born. Such a lovely little baby." The rheumy eyes watered.

Grace observed B.J. as he continued with his gentle prodding.

"Well, we're very sorry, Mr. Dugan. I can tell you cared about Charlotte."

The old man put down the scythe and pulled a soiled handkerchief from his back pocket. He wiped the dampness from his eyes and the perspiration from his furrowed brow.

"Miss Agatha is going to be real torn up about this. She really raised Miss Charlotte, you know. Their mother was never right after that baby was born, and she passed on when Miss Charlotte was just a few weeks old. Everybody said she was too old to have that baby. Miss Agatha was already twenty years old when Miss Charlotte came. Can you imagine?" Terence didn't wait for an answer to his question. "Mr. Charles died just two years later. So, with no mother or father alive, Miss Agatha devoted her life to raising Miss Charlotte."

"It must have been torture for Miss Agatha, all these years, not knowing what happened to her sister," B.J. led on.

"That's not the half of it. She had to live all these years, knowing that no-good Oliver Sloane had probably murdered her sister."

"That's enough, Terence!" A female voice shouted from the other side of the gate. "If you know what's good for you, you'll stop your blabbing this instant."

Madeleine Sloane led the way as the three of them trudged through the tall grass up the hill to the playhouse. B.J. carried his video camera and equipment case, while Grace carried the tripod.

"I can't let this go on one minute longer," Madeleine said with fierce determination in her voice. "It's time to set the record straight, time to open everything up and let the chips fall where they may."

"Why don't we talk with you first, Madeleine?" B.J. suggested, thrilled at the opportunity to talk to the daughter of Charlotte Wagstaff Sloane and knowing that it was more important to get this exclusive interview than to get the B-roll of the estate grounds and the tunnel. He didn't want to give Madeleine time for any second thoughts about her spur-of-the-moment agreement to talk to them.

"Fine," said Madeleine. "Where do you want to do it?"

B.J. scanned the area for the spot that had the best lighting. The summer sun was high in the sky, and Madeleine would have to squint if they shot in this open area. A large oak at the side of the playhouse offered a shady spot. It was so bright today there would still be enough light beneath the branches for a good picture.

As B.J. set up the tripod and camera and connected the wires for the microphone, Grace stood beside Madeleine and waited.

"I'm very sorry about your mother," Grace offered.

"Thank you."

In the awkward silence that followed, Grace looked down and noticed the small, dark tattoo on Madeleine's sandaled foot. Aware that Grace was staring at the tattoo, Madeleine shifted her right foot, pointing it out in front of her in the grass.

"I doubt my mother would have liked it, but I actually had it done for her. I wanted it to remind me of her. I don't remember much, I was only six when she disappeared, but I can remember her saying, 'Always put your best foot forward, Madeleine.' So I had this angel tattooed on my right foot to remember her. She always called me her angel."

"That's a sweet story," said Grace, smiling ruefully. "My mother used to say the same thing to me."

Madeleine searched Grace's face. "Your mother is dead, too?"

"Yes. She died six years ago." *But at least I had her while I was growing up,* thought Grace. *At least she was there when I graduated from high school, she was there for my wedding, there when Lucy was born. At least I had her for all those milestones.* Though she still missed her mother every single day, still ached to talk with her mother and share what was going on in her life, wished that she could use her as a sounding board about what was going on now with Frank and the custody issue, Grace counted herself lucky to have had her mother for as long as she had. The thought of growing up motherless was too sad to contemplate for long. But that was the anguished experience of the young woman who stood beside her now.

"I'm sorry for you, too." Madeleine searched for the information. "Pardon me, but I didn't catch your name."

"Grace. Grace Callahan."

"And what do you do for KEY News again?"

"Actually, I'm an intern."

Madeleine looked at her skeptically.

"I know," Grace said. "I look too old to be an intern. It's a long story. I hope to parlay this internship into a staff position. But I have competition. All the other interns want the assistant producer job, too."

B.J. had finished setting up. He held the tiny black microphone toward Madeleine. "Now if you just stand right over here, I'll ask you questions from behind the camera. Grace, you stand behind me to the side, and Ms. Sloane, if you'll please look at Grace when you answer, that would be great. It will look better if you don't stare directly into the camera."

"You can call me Madeleine." She attached the microphone and, at B.J.'s suggestion, slid the wire under her T-shirt. Grace took her position at B.J.'s side.

"All set?" B.J. asked.

Madeleine nodded.

"Okay." B.J. focused on the miniature image of Madeleine Sloane in the tiny video monitor attached to the top of the camera. Her short blond hair ruffled in the gentle breeze that was blowing up from the bay.

She was wringing her delicate hands, which she had clasped in front of her thin body. The trunk of the oak tree stood behind her.

"First of all, Madeleine, how and when did you get the news that your mother's remains had been identified?"

Madeleine cleared her throat. "I was here, visiting with my aunt Agatha, when we got the phone call. That was just a little while before I met you down at the gate."

"What was your reaction to the news?"

Madeleine's mouth turned up at one corner, and she shook her head at the question. Grace always hated it when the reporters on television jammed microphones into victims' faces and asked how they felt about a tragedy. *How do you think they felt, for God's sake?* Miserable, awful, devastated, heartbroken. But somehow, as Madeleine was doing now, the bereaved often managed to answer.

"Honestly? Honestly, I was relieved. I've wondered what happened to my mother for the last fourteen years. I never was sure if she was dead or alive. The uncertainty was horrible. Now, at least, I know for certain she's gone. Maybe that will make things easier."

B.J. switched gears. "Did the police tell you where they are going with the investigation?"

"No. And I didn't ask them," Madeleine answered curtly.

"You seem angry."

"Wouldn't you be if your mother had been lying dead in a tunnel and the local police had never found her?" Madeleine didn't wait for an answer to her question. "Because of their incompetence, my father has been unfairly blamed all these years. His life has been a living hell, everyone whispering about him, saying he had done away with my mother."

"With all due respect, Madeleine, the fact that your mother's remains were found in the tunnel doesn't prove that your father didn't kill her."

"Well, I know he didn't. I've always known that he couldn't have hurt her. He loved my mother very much. If the police had found my mother early on, there might have been more clues for them to work with to find the real killer. But I'll tell you one thing. My father didn't kill my mother. I'm sure he didn't."

B.J. pulled his head back from the camera eyepiece and looked over, first at Grace, then at Madeleine.

"Who do you think killed your mother, Madeleine?"

The young woman hesitated. She felt as though the answer was just beyond her grasp. It was frustrating not being able to come out and name her mother's killer. But she couldn't. Not yet anyway.

"That's all I have to say, at this point," Madeleine declared adamantly. "Now take your other pictures, if you like, as quickly as you can, and then go. If Aunt Agatha sees you out here, she'll have a fit."

"We understand," said B.J., clicking off his camera. "Can we have ten or fifteen minutes?"

"All right, but no more than that," said Madeleine. "I've got to get home to be with my father."

CHAPTER
16

The radio news echoed with the medical examiner's findings. To the last person who had seen Charlotte alive, it was really no surprise that this day had come. It could have come at any time. But the hope was always that it would come later, after everyone was dead and gone. Just like Charlotte.

Digging up her bones meant digging up the sordid details that had led to her death. That couldn't be allowed to happen. It was worrisome that the handkerchief had remained in the pocket of her dress, right where Charlotte had tucked it after borrowing it to wipe her tears. But at least the photograph hadn't surfaced.

In the heat of the moment, the photo Charlotte had ranted about that night had been dropped down over her body as it lay on the slave tunnel floor. When there was time to think more clearly, the realization that the murder weapon had been left behind as well necessitated another nocturnal visit to the playhouse. The iron fireplace shovel was wiped clean, to be buried in the tunnel wall along with the body. But the photograph was gone.

Someone else had gotten to it first.

Panic had been followed with some measure of relief, as the man's billfold was discovered alongside the playhouse daybed. As long as the foolishly forgotten wallet served as blackmail, incriminating its guiltless owner, there was a degree of confi-dence that the photograph would never come to light.

Fourteen years ago, a letter had been sent, warning the trespasser that the wallet could be used to place him at the play-house that fateful night. He had been too stupid or scared to realize that the photo-graph could prove much worse to Char-lotte's killer.

They had reached a stalemate. The mur-derer possessing the wallet. The trespassing owner of the wallet holding on to the photo. Both sides had remained silent, neither wanting any trouble. It was crucial that things stay that way.

In a courtroom, that photograph could supply a direct link to Charlotte's killer.

CHAPTER
17

The landscaper could take care of it, but Elsa preferred to do it herself. She enjoyed providing the food that beckoned the songbirds and occasional ring-necked pheasant to her backyard. She was pouring seed into the feeder for her beloved birds when she heard the telephone. Hurrying across the manicured lawn to the flagstone patio, she snatched the cordless phone from the wrought-iron table next to the chaise longue.

"Hello?" she answered, a bit out of breath.

"Elsa, it's Oliver."

Her heart leapt, as it had for years, at the sound of his voice. Most of her adult life had been spent loving Oliver Sloane.

"I have news, Elsa. The remains were definitely Charlotte's. The dental records confirm it."

"Oh, I'm so sorry, Oliver dear. I know this has been an excruciating nightmare for you, and for Madeleine, for all of us really. But at least now we know, Oliver. It was the not knowing what happened to our Charlotte that was the hardest part."

"That and having this whole damned town thinking I killed her."

Elsa could hear the depression and cynicism in his polished baritone. She ached at the agony he had been forced to endure.

"I have never, not for one single moment, Oliver, thought that you had anything to do with Charlotte's disappearance. I have believed in your innocence with all my heart and soul. You know that."

"Well, you are the only one, Elsa. You and Madeleine. Charlotte's best friend and Charlotte's daughter are the only ones who have stood by me. Everyone else in Newport has treated me like a criminal."

"That might be different now, Oliver."

"Why? Why will it be any different now, Elsa? They only have a body, or what's left of one. They don't have the killer."

Elsa knew he was right. What a horrible ordeal this all had been. And it would never be over for Oliver, unless they found out who murdered Charlotte.

Elsa loved Oliver with a depth only intensified by the long years that she had watched him suffer, wanting to help him but unable to. As the time since Charlotte's disappearance lengthened, Elsa had hoped that Oliver would forget his wife, or at least move on emotionally from her and they could move forward as a couple. But he was racked with guilt over the lack of attentiveness he had shown Charlotte in the months before she disappeared and over the argument he and Charlotte had the last night he saw her. He had confided as much to Elsa over and over again in Scotch-soaked confessions these last fourteen years.

"If only I had been more discreet," he was repeating now. "What could I have been thinking of? Did I really think Charlotte wouldn't find out that I was unfaithful? What a fool I was. I would do anything to do it all over again."

Elsa tried to soothe him, tried to be patient. "That's all over now, darling. You have to move forward. Enough of your life has been consumed by this. You have to live what's left of it. There are still good years ahead—for you, for us."

"Please, Elsa. Don't start with all that now. You more than anyone know how long I have prayed that Charlotte would somehow come back to me. It was a miracle that I ever had her. If Agatha hadn't intervened, I never would have had her at all. I haven't led you on, Elsa. I may have slipped up along the way, but my heart has always really belonged to Charlotte."

"But Charlotte isn't coming back, Oliver. We can be together now. We can get married. You're officially a widower." The second the words were out of her mouth, Elsa regretted them. Oliver may have been without a wife for fourteen years, but this was not the time to pounce on him about another marriage. It was just that she wanted to be Mrs. Oliver Sloane so very much. Though none of the other middle-aged women in town would want that honor, Elsa Gravell had given up the prospect of any other husband or children of her own, believing without a doubt that her happiness was bound to Oliver Sloane's.

"I just found out for certain that my wife is

dead, Elsa. Allow me to grieve," Oliver snapped.

Elsa heard the phone line go dead and cursed herself. There was little chance now that Oliver would escort her to the Vickerses' party tonight, and Elsa knew better than to bring it up. But she was determined that he go with her, as scheduled, to the Ball Bleu at The Elms on Wednesday. Elsa was chairing the event herself this year, and she wanted Oliver at her side, in spite of Charlotte's identification. In fact, he had to attend *because* of it—in Charlotte's memory—just as he had every year since the night she'd disappeared. Charlotte and Elsa had cochaired that first fund-raising event for the Endangered Birds of Rhode Island fourteen years ago. It was gratifying to see how the fund-raiser had grown, and Oliver, to his credit, had bravely attended each and every year, making his wife's cause his own, ignoring the whispers and icy stares.

She mustn't push Oliver, though. She mustn't alienate him, especially now, when there was finally a chance that they could be together as man and wife. Yes, she had been Charlotte's best friend as they grew up and went to school together—Charlotte, popular and outgoing, Elsa, quieter and more studious. She had been the maid of honor at Charlotte's wedding, and she was the godmother of Charlotte's daughter. They had shared a special love for birds and traveled far and wide, spending hours on end together, waiting for just a glimpse of some rare specimen. But her allegiance to Charlotte had ended many years ago. It was Oliver she loved, and Elsa was determined to have him, no matter how long it took.

CHAPTER
18

Grace and B.J. returned to the Viking ballroom and reported to the assignment desk. Dominick O'Donnell, *KTA*'s senior producer, peered at them over his reading glasses as B.J. told him what they had gotten at Shepherd's Point. Dominick listened and made his judgment call.

"The interview with Charlotte Sloane's daughter may be an exclusive, but you need more than that to make a piece of national interest. This might be a big local story, but we have to flesh it out before we can hook a network audience. Hold on to the tape and see what else develops."

B.J. decided to fight for the airtime. "But, Dom, with the identification of Charlotte Sloane's remains and the video from the old slave tunnel, I think we have enough to put together a good piece."

Dominick scanned the computer screen on his desk. "Look, Beej, you've got stories scheduled for every single day this week, and I've yet to see any one of the takeouts you're responsible for. How are those coming?"

"Don't worry, Dom. They're under control."

"Well, if you can get those done and still find time to come up with something worthwhile on the Sloane case, fine. But, I'm telling you, B.J., we need more. You have to get reactions from other people who knew Charlotte Sloane. Her husband comes immediately to mind. Talk to other people in town who knew her, who remember when she disappeared. And, obviously, you'd want to talk to the police, too."

B.J. knew when to back off. "All right, Dom, we'll get back to you when we have more."

After a quick phone call to Massachusetts to confirm that Lucy had arrived safely, Grace could feel the other interns watching her as she stood with B.J. at the assignment desk. She was torn between satisfaction that B.J. was so generously including her as he worked and concern that she was estranging herself from her peers. This competition for the one assistant producer spot was a bad thing. Each of the interns was going to resent it when any of the others got to do something that furthered their experience, believing that it worked against their own chances of winning the staff job.

But Grace's concern about the feelings of at least one intern dissipated as Joss Vickers approached the assignment desk and made her announcement.

"My parents are having a clambake tonight, and everyone from the *KTA* staff is invited."

"Really? That sounds like fun," said Dominick. "I've never been to a clambake."

"Me neither," said B.J. "Count me in."

No, Grace decided as she watched the

producers scribble down the Vickerses' address. It was not Joss Vickers's feelings that Grace should worry about. Joss knew how to compete just fine.

CHAPTER
19

After the day he'd had, going to the Vickerses' party was the last thing he wanted to do. With Charlotte Sloane's case suddenly white hot again, Detective Al Manzorella was both excited and enervated.

Al sighed as he changed his shirt. Now, they had a body. For fourteen years, Al had been certain that Charlotte was dead, but it was only today that the fact had been proven. Still, there wasn't enough to pin Charlotte's murder on that miserable husband of hers, or on anyone else for that matter. Other than the fireplace shovel, the only evidence was Charlotte's diary, the earring, and the remarkably preserved silk handkerchief that had been balled up in the pocket of her evening gown. How, or why, Charlotte had gone to Shepherd's Point, instead of to her marital home at Seaview, after leaving the country club on the night she disappeared was anyone's guess.

"Are you ready, honey?" Seanna's eyes sparkled as she stood in the bedroom doorway, wearing her new outfit. His wife was thrilled about being invited to the clambake hosted by those rich "summer people." Seanna had met Vanessa Vickers when she came into the antiques shop where Seanna worked part time. They had struck up a conversation, and Vanessa, after dropping a wad of dough, had magnanimously invited Seanna and her husband to the party.

"Be right there," he called.

Al couldn't bring himself to let his wife down. Seanna didn't have much glamour in her life, and he was sorry about that. She deserved more than he was able to give her. She never complained about his long hours or the paycheck that never went quite far enough to allow them to go on a grand vacation or buy a bigger house.

"Want to take your car or mine?" she asked.

"Let's take yours," he said, running a comb through his thick, black hair. Maybe the clambake would be fun, though he doubted it. But perhaps it wouldn't be a total loss. You never knew what kind of information you could pick up at a gathering like this.

CHAPTER
20

The process had begun early in the day, when Mickey sent his crew out to pick fresh rockweed, a dark green seaweed oozing with bubbles filled with salt water. The bubbles were essential to the traditional clambake process, providing the steam for cooking.

The bonfire was built with care, alternating layers of wood and rock. The blazing fire would heat the rocks to very high temperatures, and once the fire settled down, a bed of hot coals and scalding rocks would be left behind. The coals and stones were covered with the mounds of damp rockweed, the salt-water bubbles bursting when heated, emitting the seawater that would steam and season the food.

All of this was done hours before the first guest arrived. Mickey Hager was fastidious in his preparations and took enormous pride in his job as bakemaster. Presiding over the clambake, he took care that the traditional cooking process passed down from the Native Americans to the early New England colonists and on through three centuries was executed to perfection. Mickey was so good at his job that Seasons Clambakes was booked for parties, weddings, class reunions, and corporate functions right through the autumn and already had plenty of commitments for next spring and summer. On the beach, at a private home, or at one of Newport's many scenic locations, Seasons Clambakes guaranteed a distinctive good time, and customers were willing to pay well for it.

The Vickerses were repeat customers, and Mickey knew their property well. A restored carriage house that had once sheltered the carts and coaches of one of the wealthy Newport summer families had been converted into a home with every possible convenience. While the Vickerses' house did not have the grand scale of the Bellevue Avenue mansions, it did have many features that the "cottages" did not. Central air-conditioning, satellite television, and a Sub-Zero refrigerator with ice that came on demand from the opening in the door made living in the twenty-first century a lot more comfortable than it was in the Gilded Age.

Mickey worked quickly, nestling layers of lobsters, steamers, mussels, and corn in metal baskets into the rockweed, arranging the racks to guarantee perfect cooking and flavoring. He and his assistant covered the area with canvas, trying to capture as much heat as possible.

Mickey stood back and surveyed his work with satisfaction. Yes, business was real good right now, but Mickey knew he had to stay on top of things. He had busted his hump to get here, and there was no way he was going back to taking orders from other people, working waitstaff at the country club.

"Hiya, Mickey."

He turned in the direction of the voice. It was that hard body, Joss Vickers. She was wearing a tight-fitting black T-shirt and a pair of white shorts that certainly couldn't pass the country club dress code. Those tanned legs of hers didn't quit. *Man, she was a looker.*

She was also a flirt, and Mickey had watched her work her spell on teenage boys as well as the older male friends of her parents. She was an equal-opportunity tease. Joss had the power, and she reveled in seeing what it could do.

Whenever Mickey saw Joss, memories of the first time he had viewed her flashed through his mind. It was Madeleine Sloane's sixth birthday, and the party was held at the country club pool. Even then, shockingly, Joss had oozed sexuality. The six-year-old had worn a leopard-print, one-piece bathing suit, her little legs already shapely and firm, her expression somehow knowing. As he served her lemonade and chocolate cake, he'd been ashamed of himself, an eighteen-year-old guy having thoughts like that about a little girl. Now, he felt his cheeks grow warm at the memory.

"Hi," he answered, careful not to address her by name. By extension, she was his employer. He didn't feel comfortable calling her Joss, yet he wasn't going to call her Miss Vickers either. Mickey wiped his brow, grate-

ful that the heat from the clambake fire provided an excuse for his blushing face.

"Looks like everything is all set," said Joss,
surveying the clambake bed.

"Yep. We've got everything under control.
It's going to be a good party."

Joss flashed a smile, her eyes narrowing.
"That's great, Mickey, because it's important
to me that everyone here has a really good
time tonight. In addition to our Newport
friends, there will be a lot of people from
KEY News here, and I want to make a fabulous impression."

CHAPTER
21

The suitcase lay open on the double bed in
the hotel room. Grace hunted through the
contents, already sickeningly sure that she
hadn't packed correctly. Or more to the point,
she hadn't had the right things to pack.

She had to start paying more attention to

her wardrobe now that she was going into the working world. She'd observed that the attire at the KEY News Broadcast Center in New York City wasn't necessarily business formal, but most people did dress stylishly. Here in Newport, the producers, writers, and directorial types seemed to be favoring the Ralph Lauren look, lots of khaki pants, white blouses or T-shirts, and sweaters tied around the waist or neck. Grace had also spotted quite a few jean jackets draped over the back of the chairs in the ballroom workstation.

Grace had packed several pairs of linen slacks that she pulled from her suitcase. They were hopelessly wrinkled. She checked the closet. Great, there was an ironing board inside but no iron.

She wasn't sure if linen slacks were appropriate for a clambake, and she wished she had time to find a Gap and pick up some khakis, but B.J. had offered her a lift and she was supposed to meet him in the lobby in twenty minutes. Grace walked over to the bedside table and picked up the phone to ask if she could get an iron sent up to the room.

"Izzie, before you leave, can you bring an iron up to two-oh-one?"

What choice did she have? This wasn't a request, this was an order from the head housekeeper, and Izzie knew that the woman was watching her for any signs of slacking off.

"Of course, Eileen, I'll do it right away."

As she waited for the service elevator, Izzie raised her right arm out to her side, using the steam iron as a barbell. She repeated the movement, up and down, up and down. Izzie was still trying to get her strength back. Since the operation, it was so much harder to do her physically demanding job. Making beds, emptying trash, cleaning toilets, and scrubbing bathtubs was not a lot of fun under the best of circumstances. But after breast cancer surgery and treatment it was next to impossible. Izzie wasn't sure how much longer she could do it. She went home exhausted every day, collapsing in bed as soon as she got into the house.

As she got off the elevator on the second floor, Izzie began to feel light-headed. She talked to herself as she had so often since Padraic passed away. *You can do it, Izzie girl. You can do it.*

She made it to the hotel room door and knocked.

"Just a minute" came the call from inside.

But by the time the door opened, Izzie had slid to the floor.

"Oh my God, are you all right?" Grace crouched toward the chambermaid. "Hang on. I'll call for help."

"No. Don't." The woman was surprisingly adamant.

"Well, what can I do to help you? A glass of water?"

Holding on to the doorjamb, the frail woman struggled to get to her feet while looking from side to side down the hallway. "I don't want anyone to see me like this. I don't suppose I could come inside for a minute?"

Grace was not in the habit of having people she had never met come into her hotel room, but there was something in the expression on the woman's careworn face that prompted her to escort the stranger in and steer her to the love seat at the side of the room. As the chambermaid sat down, Grace went into the bathroom, coming out again with a glass of water. "Here, take a sip of this."

As the woman obeyed, Grace noticed the

boyishly short, feathery, gray hair. She recognized the new growth. That was just the way her mother's hair had looked when it grew in again after chemotherapy.

"I'm Grace Callahan."

"Izzie O'Malley," the woman said softly.

"Please, Izzie. Let me call down to the front desk. They can send someone up to check on you."

"No, thank you, Miss. That isn't a good idea. I don't want them thinking I can't do my job."

Grace nodded with understanding. "All right, but maybe I could call a friend or relative to come pick you up."

Izzie shook her head. "No, I'll be fine, if I can just sit here a minute longer." She glanced at the linen slacks lying on top of the bed. "Go ahead and do what you were going to do, please. I'll leave in just a little bit."

Grace glanced at the digital clock on the nightstand. B.J. was probably already downstairs waiting for her. She plugged in the iron.

"You're here with the KEY people from New York?" Izzie asked, spotting the logo on the canvas tote bag parked on the chair by the desk.

"Yes."

"That must be exciting."

"We'll see. This is my first assignment out on the road and I'm trying to prove myself to them. So I'm a little nervous." Grace didn't feel it necessary to explain the whole internship situation, but she did think that Izzie could identify with needing to please one's employer. "I have a lot riding on this. I want to impress my bosses."

As Grace slid the iron back and forth across the linen, Izzie rose from the love seat.

"I'm all right now."

"You're sure? Maybe my friend and I can drop you at home?"

"No, Miss. You've been too kind already. Thank you very much."

Walking slowly back down the hallway to the elevator, Izzie felt better. There were nice people out there, and Grace Callahan was one of them. She hoped the young woman did well with that job of hers.

By the time Izzie let herself into her small, shingled bungalow, she had come up with a tentative plan. If she decided to go public with what she knew, Grace Callahan was going to be the one she told.

One good turn deserved another.

It was still light, the summer sun a good two hours from setting. Long trestle tables covered with red-and-white checkered cloths and festooned with clusters of red and blue balloons signaled that the Vickerses were prepared to serve over one hundred guests. The tables were clustered in the center of the spacious yard. A billowing white tent sheltered the portable dance floor laid down in front of the five-piece band tuning up beyond the clambake pit. At the corners of the property, stations were set up for entertainment. A face painter, a juggler, a palm reader, and even a booth offering henna tattoos.

"Whoa," exclaimed B.J. as he and Grace took in the scene. "This is something, all right."

"Well, you haven't seen anything till you come to a party at my house," Grace responded. "I'll have to invite you next time.

My father grills one mean hot dog on his little hibachi."

B.J. grinned, his brown eyes twinkling with amusement. "Come on. Let's get a drink."

Grace didn't recognize most of the faces they passed on their way to the bar. "All these people aren't from KEY, are they?" she asked.

B.J. shook his head. "Nope. I've never seen most of these people before. Joss told me that her parents were having the party for their friends anyway and suggested that she just go ahead and invite the *KTA* staff."

Must be nice, thought Grace, as she took a sip of ice-cold beer and surveyed the scene. It *was* nice to have the kind of money that allowed you to breezily add another forty or fifty people to your guest list with no regard for the cost.

"Grace, I don't want you to think that I'm all work and no play, but I was thinking that we could schmooze around here tonight and see if we can find anyone who could help us with our Charlotte Sloane story. You know, what Dominick said we needed. People who were in Newport at the time, people who knew her?"

"Did you bring your camera?"

"Yeah, it's in the trunk. But I wasn't thinking so much about getting video. I was only thinking about getting background stuff and maybe getting them to talk for the camera later if we need them."

Grace nodded, wanting to seem game for B.J.'s benefit. The fact was, she would have been just as glad to relax tonight. It had been a long day, starting very early to catch the morning train, followed by the emotion of letting Lucy go off to her father and new stepmother. Grace hadn't had a moment to breathe since she had arrived in Newport and the prospect of kicking back tonight had been an attractive one. But she wasn't about to say that to B.J.

"Sure. Great."

"Want to split up?" B.J. suggested. "We can talk to more people that way."

Grace took another drink of beer. What was she going to say to that? *No? I want to stick with you? I don't really feel confident going out on my own? I was hoping that you and I could hang out together tonight?*

"Fine," she said, without enthusiasm.

Grace moved around the perimeter of the yard, stopping to view the juggler work his balancing act with his multicolored spheres. As she watched, a balding, aristocratic-looking man walked up and stopped beside her. Though attired casually, he had dressed with care. White slacks, finely creased, an open-necked blue oxford shirt with the sleeves precisely rolled up over his tan forearms, and brown leather boat shoes, no socks.

"Are you a friend of the Vickerses or one of these TV people?" The distinguished-looking man seemed to sniff at the second choice.

"Well, maybe both," Grace answered. "I am with KEY News. I'm interning this summer with Joss Vickers."

Grace felt the man appraising her, sensed he was thinking she looked too old to be an intern. She decided to volunteer the information before he asked.

"I've gotten a late start. I'm just finishing college now."

"I see."

Grace chose to ignore the condescension in his tone. She wasn't going to get anywhere if her skin was too thin.

"My name is Grace Callahan." She switched her drink to her left hand and extended the other one to the man.

"Kyle Seaton."

Grace was familiar with the name she had seen on the shooting notes for the week.

"Oh, yes. You're the scrimshander, aren't you?"

Kyle nodded, pleased at the recognition. He immediately pulled a business card from his shirt pocket and held it toward her. "Scrimshander, scrimshaw dealer, and collector."

"I can truthfully say I have never met anyone in your line of work before," said Grace, taking the card. "It's very interesting. I've done a little research on it for the broadcast this week."

"Ah, yes. *KEY to America* comes to Newport and interviews the local color," Kyle said with a trace of sarcasm. "I'm already wondering if I'll live to regret my decision to have you people come to my shop."

"Why?"

"Because I have been the dealer of record to discerning scrimshaw collectors for the past two decades, and I don't want to tarnish my reputation by appealing to the masses now."

"Then why did you agree?" asked Grace, genuinely interested.

Kyle shrugged. "Foolish vanity, I suppose. What is it about being on television that makes otherwise sane people expose themselves like that?"

Grace wasn't sure of the answer, but she had often asked herself the same thing as she watched people reveal the most personal information, and do the most embarrassing things, for a television audience. Tummy tucks and liposuctions and face-lifts in cosmetic makeovers for the public to gawk at. Proclamations of undying love and devotion followed by the humiliation of rejection in dating contests for home viewers to cluck at. Swallowing insects and worms in survival challenges designed to make the audience gasp and groan. But the television producers didn't seem to be hurting for subjects willing to do anything for their fifteen minutes of fame.

Grace decided to steer clear of the uncomfortable topic lest she somehow influence Kyle Seaton away from his commitment to *KTA*. "So you've been a Newporter for a long time?"

"A true Newporter has been here all his life," Kyle declared. "I am a *true* Newporter."

"I see," said Grace. "Then you were here when Charlotte Sloane disappeared."

Kyle's solemn face darkened further. "Yes. I was. In fact, I knew Charlotte since we were young children. Our families had adjoining cabanas at Bailey's Beach."

Pay dirt.

"Do you have any theories, then, on what happened to Charlotte?" Grace asked.

"No, I don't. Though you've heard, of course, the whole town thinks her husband had something to do with it. Sad sort, Oliver. But I'll say this for him: he has quite a marvelous scrimshaw collection. He had been a wonderful customer over the years. Charlotte was, too, before she disappeared. Always buying some special piece for his birthdays and their anniversaries. But with Charlotte gone, and all the talk, I thought it best to discourage Oliver from coming to my shop."

"I understand it was on their wedding anniversary that Charlotte disappeared," Grace led.

"Yes, I think you're right, though the party that night wasn't an anniversary party but a fund-raiser for the endangered birds that Charlotte and Elsa Gravell were so worried about. I was there. I heard that Charlotte left the club by herself, in tears, that evening, but I didn't see that myself."

"What do you think that was all about?"

Kyle looked down at her sharply. "That's really none of my business." Left unsaid but clearly implied was *It's none of yours either, Ms. Callahan.*

"Hey, Grace, come on over here," the voice slurred, with a pronounced twang.

Sam Watkins, the intern from Oklahoma, waved at Grace, beckoning her to join the other interns who were clustered around the tattoo artist's entertainment station. Joss and Zoe Quigley, the student who had come all the way from England to intern at KEY News, were watching as an eagle was drawn on Sam's hairless chest.

"It's patriotic, don't you think, Gracie?" asked Sam, his head bent downward trying to view the handiwork. "Rusty here is doing a right fine job."

"We're losing the light. I want to get this done before sundown. Hold still," commanded the tattoo artist, squeezing a bit more brown color from a toothpaste-like tube and giving a final dab to the eagle with his brush. "Now wait till it dries and pick it off somewhere safe. Outside or over the sink." The artist sat back to admire his creation.

"How long will it last?" asked Zoe, mesmerized.

"Just a few days to a week," said Rusty. "It depends on how much you rub it or how much you use soap and water on it."

Fun, painless, temporary henna tattoos. No lifetime commitment to a design carved into the skin. Grace thought of Madeleine's angel tattoo and the pain that must have been associated with its engraving, the real desire to commemorate her lost mother with a symbol she would see every day for the rest of her life. The idea was growing on Grace, but she didn't quite have the guts to get one of her own. But here was a chance to try it out without reaching a point of no return.

"Do you have time to do a small one on me?" she asked.

Rusty looked at his watch and glanced at the darkening sky. *Why not?* He was getting paid by the hour.

"Okay, if we hurry. What'll it be?"

"Can you do an ivy leaf?"

"Sure, that's no big deal. Where do you want it?"

"On my foot."

Rusty shrugged. It wasn't, by a long shot,

the worst place he had ever been asked to do a tattoo.

Grace began to slip off her sandal.

"Leave it on," said Rusty. "I'll do it right above the strap line, so you can still wear your shoes while it dries."

Grace watched as the swirling lines of henna swept across the top of her right foot. But the fascination was over for Sam, Joss, and Zoe, who moved on toward the bar.

"Actually, this tattoo might last a little longer than your friend's," volunteered Rusty as he worked. "The skin on the hands and feet is more porous, and the henna sets in better."

"I've just begun thinking about getting a permanent tattoo," Grace mused.

"I can do that for you," said Rusty. "That's my main business. This is just a sideline, to make some extra money. Come down to my place on Broadway and I can give you whatever you want. But let me warn you. It will hurt like hell if you have a real tattoo done on your foot. The needle will be pushing right against the bones."

Grace bent over to inspect the finished product.

"Why'd ya pick an ivy leaf?" asked Rusty, capping the henna tube.

"Ivy was my mother's name."

"That's funny. I had another girl come in recently and have a tattoo on her foot for her mother."

"Was it Madeleine Sloane?" asked Grace.

"As a matter of fact, it was." Rusty looked at Grace quizzically. "You know Madeleine?"

"I just met her today. I saw her tattoo. That's what gave me the idea," Grace said.

"Sad about her mother, huh?" Rusty tossed the henna tube into his paint box.

"Yes. Very sad."

"I was kinda surprised to see her here tonight, after the news I heard on the radio today," said Rusty.

Grace looked around. "Madeleine's here?"

"Yeah, I saw her before with some older lady with birds all over her blouse. I was thinking those birds could sure make great tattoo designs."

After Grace left, Rusty packed up his tattoo supplies, relieved to be getting away from all these highfalutin folk. This wasn't a world that he was comfortable in. All the posturing and putting on airs weren't for him. They never had been.

Even back when he was a twenty-one-year-old sailor stationed at the naval base, he was always nervous with his assignment as the admiral's driver. He'd have preferred to be just one of the other enlisted guys instead of chauffeuring the brass around in his dress whites.

Seaman Alberto S. Texiera, nicknamed Rusty for his head of thick, russet hair, saw grand ballrooms and elegant parlors as he escorted the admiral to the many functions and meetings around Newport, but he never grew to feel any ease in the upper-crust environments. To this day, he was more at home in the dimness of a local bar throwing back a few beers than at a shindig like this, even though he supposed the Vickerses would consider this an informal party.

These people all have agendas, thought Rusty. He had only a few ambitions and just wanted to stay to himself. *Live and let live.*

So far he had been able to do just that. When he'd finished his stint in the navy, he'd gone to work for the guy who ran the place where he and his pals had gotten their tattoos. The owner had catered to the base personnel, and the tattoo parlor was a no-frills affair. But Rusty had noticed that every so often, a curious civilian would wander in and ask about getting a small tattoo in a discreet spot. On the shoulder, at the top of the thigh, low on the back. Sometimes they were kids, clearly lying about being over the age of consent, but more and more the customers who came through the door were middle-class women wanting to spice things up a bit.

Rusty worked on his designs, and word of mouth spread. He became the artist customers asked for. When the owner decided to pack it in and move to Florida, Rusty applied for a small business loan and bought Broadway Tattoos from him. All had gone well for a while. But as the appetite for tattoos increased, so had the competition. Where Rusty's parlor had once been the only game in town, now there were three other places that offered tattoos. "Body art salons" they billed themselves, offering facials, treatments, and massages as well— and in an atmosphere far more posh than Rusty's. Those soccer moms in their SUVs were walking their pedicured feet through his competitors' doors now.

That was one of the reasons Rusty had been so glad when Madeleine Sloane came in last month. Though he hadn't recognized her until he saw the name she signed on her credit card receipt, he could tell when she entered the shop that she was from the right side of the tracks.

He did his very best work on her angel, explaining in advance that it would hurt like the dickens and apologizing profusely for it. As he concentrated on his artwork, his head over her foot, she told him why she was having it done. To honor her mother. Rusty had presumed that her mother had simply died, if dying was ever simple. It wasn't until he saw Madeleine's name when she pulled out her credit card that he'd put it all together.

Sloane.

This was Charlotte Sloane's daughter, the little girl, now grown up, whom Charlotte had spoken about the night Rusty had given Charlotte a lift, the night Rusty had been waiting outside the country club for the admiral, the night Charlotte had run out crying, the night Charlotte had disappeared.

Rusty had been tempted to tell Madeleine that day she came into the shop, but he couldn't speak of it, even now. Just as he had never told the police that he had given Charlotte a ride to Shepherd's Point that night. Just as he had kept it from his boss, returning to the country club before the admiral ever knew he had gone.

It was better to stay to himself.

CHAPTER
23

The several hours of cooking finally complete, Mickey reached for his bell. The clanging signaled the opening of the bake. Grace joined the other guests gathered around for the unveiling while Mickey gave them a brief explanation of the cooking process. Then the layers of canvas were peeled away to enthusiastic oohs and aahs from the audience. Billows of steam rose from the bake along with a surge of delicious aromas.

The banquet table was laden with steam trays of lobster, cod, clams, mussels, corn on the cob, sausage, onions, red bliss potatoes, and hot brown bread. Grace waited in the buffet line until it was her turn to fill her plate. Then she searched for an empty spot at the tables in the middle of the yard.

There were some open seats where a cluster of *KTA* staffers was sitting, and Grace headed in that direction. On her way, she heard someone call her name. Turning, Grace recognized Madeleine Sloane.

"Grace, hi. Come over here."

Grace was aware of her still-drying tattoo and suddenly felt self-conscious. She hoped Madeleine wouldn't notice the henna ivy leaf and think that Grace was copying or cheapening her idea. But it was fairly dark now, the tables lit with votive candles, and Madeleine didn't look down as Grace approached.

"Hi, Madeleine. I didn't think I'd be seeing you here tonight."

Madeleine shrugged. "I didn't see the point in sitting at home. I tried to get my father to come, too, but that was useless."

Madeleine introduced Grace to the woman sitting at her side.

"Elsa, this is Grace Callahan, the news intern from KEY I was telling you about. Grace, this is my godmother, Elsa Gravell."

Balancing her plate in her left palm, Grace bent forward to shake the woman's hand. In the candlelight, Grace could see the tropical birds that Rusty had raved about on Elsa's blouse.

"Madeleine was very impressed with you today, Grace," Elsa said, shaking Grace's hand but with little firmness to the grip. "She said you were very polite and sensitive."

"Not like those other sharks that have been circling our waters for years," Madeleine piped up.

Grace smiled. "Give me time. I'm new at this."

"I hope you never get like them," Madeleine said. "But television is the happening place, isn't it? Look at our Professor Cox here." Madeleine gestured toward the man who sat across the table from her. "Even my esteemed history professor wants to get on TV."

Grace looked at the man. From what she could tell in this light, his was a handsome face, with a strong nose and dark eyes. In a strange way, silver hair made him look a bit younger, but he was probably somewhere in his fifties.

"Professor *Gordon* Cox?" asked Grace.

"Yes. I am he." The man began to rise from his seat.

"Please. Don't get up," said Grace. "It's just that I recognize your name. I faxed you some material yesterday from New York."

"Oh, yes. I got it. Thank you very much."

"You're very welcome."

"Professor Cox is the best teacher at Salve Regina," Madeleine declared. "Even though he's already nagging me about getting my aunt Agatha to let the work start up again on the tunnel at Shepherd's Point."

"Thank you, dear, but I wouldn't go that far about the 'best teacher' part," said the professor, clearly pleased.

"Well, I would. He really makes history come alive, not like those other teachers who drone on and on until you want to scream. You're lucky to have him consulting on the show for the week, Grace."

"I'm sure we are," said Grace.

There was a seat open on the other side of Madeleine, but no one had actually invited her to sit down. So Grace excused herself and went to join the KEY News group.

The lobster was delicious, and the corn on the cob was fresh and sweet, but Grace didn't appreciate it as much as she normally would.

Could Joss be flirting any more openly with B.J.?

Grace tried to look like she was not paying any attention, but it was hard to miss the batting eyelashes, the hanging on every word, and the manicured hands that periodically touched B.J.'s arm. Grace was a bit disappointed in B.J. He appeared to be lapping it up.

She was wiping her hands with the hot moist towelette supplied to everyone at the table when Linus Nazareth approached the group. "Everyone having a good time?" he asked.

There was a chorus of affirmatives.

"I think we should all give our hostess, Joss, a round of applause, don't you?"

The staffers obliged with cheering and clapping made more intense by all the alcohol consumed.

"It's my and my family's pleasure, Mr. Nazareth." Joss beamed, rising from her chair and impulsively giving Linus a kiss on the cheek. Every other female at the table watched in revulsion as he put his arm around the intern and squeezed her closer to him. The executive producer was legendary for his philandering, but no one wanted, even for a moment, to contemplate the image of this portly male well into his fifties involved with a kid more than thirty years his junior.

Grace glanced over at Beth Terry, the unit manager. She looked especially stricken. Grace had heard office gossip about Beth's devotion to her boss. It was sad, really, to see the hurt look on Beth's round face, and Grace resolved to make sure no such hang-dog expression appeared on her own if she were to observe Joss and B.J. falling all over each other again.

She would act as if it didn't bother her. Even if it killed her.

Grace excused herself, stopped to compliment the bakemaster on the sumptuous feast, and headed toward the house. She waited her turn to use the powder room. The henna was dry now, and Grace patted at the top of her foot with some tissue. Rusty had done a nice job with the ivy leaf. When she came out of the bathroom, Grace bumped into Madeleine in the hallway.

"We meet again. Are you following me or something?"

Grace could smell the alcohol on Madeleine's breath.

"I doubt it, since I was here first," said Grace.

Madeleine chuckled. "Oh yeah, you're right." She cast her eyes downward, spying the ivy leaf on Grace's foot. "You got a tattoo." There was no accusation in her voice, only observation.

"Kinda. It's only henna. I hope you don't mind."

"Why would I mind?"

Grace grimaced in discomfort. "I thought you might think I was copying you or something. I was, I guess."

"Imitation is the sincerest form of flattery," Madeleine shot back, unperturbed. "Wait while I use the bathroom and you can tell me all about it."

When they went back outside again, the band was blaring and the portable dance floor was crowded with guests gyrating to one of the Rolling Stones' biggest hits. Grace and Madeleine watched in amazement as Sam Watkins grabbed the microphone from the lead singer and began to belt out his own rendition of "Brown Sugar." He might have been slurring the words, but there was no denying he was a Stones fan through and through. The musicians didn't skip a beat as their new soloist did his best Mick Jagger imitation:

Gold coast slave ship bound for cotton fields,
Sold in a market down in New Orleans.
Scarred old slaver knows he's doin' alright.
Hear him whip the women just around midnight.

"Wow. Is he loaded!" Grace observed as she looked around and noticed Zoe wincing at the lyrics.

"That makes two of us," said Madeleine, running her tapering fingers through her short hair, attempting to clear her mind. "Let's try to find a quiet place."

"Nowhere out here," said Grace, looking around the yard. "Should we go back inside the house?"

"Sure."

There was no one in the living room. They sat down on the plush sofa, and Grace stuck out her foot.

"What do you think?"

"I think it looks good," said Madeleine as she inspected the tattoo. "Why the ivy leaf?"

"My mother's name was Ivy."

"Cool." Madeleine sat on the sofa, resting her blond head on its back cushion, and stared up at the ceiling. "Sister, I've had way too much to drink."

"That's understandable," Grace offered. "With the day you've just had."

"Days, weeks, months, years, actually. They've all been pretty sad." Madeleine exhaled deeply. "But maybe they'll get better now. One can hope anyway."

"It takes a long time to get over losing your mother. I don't know if you ever fully do." There was a wistfulness in Grace's voice.

Madeleine lifted her head and looked at Grace. "Do you still think about yours?"

"All the time."

"How long has she been gone? I think you told me before, but I've forgotten."

"Six years. But I was lucky, I had her while I was growing up. When I look at my own daughter, I can't imagine her not having a mother."

Madeleine nodded, understanding that Grace was acknowledging the loss that had permeated Madeleine's childhood. "My father has done the best he could all these years, raising me with love and tenderness while all the gossips in this town sniped about him. And my aunt Agatha has showered me with all the affection she could, considering her fragile state. I love them both so much for what they've endured.

"But I've dreamt about my mother all these years, you know."

"Happy dreams?" Grace asked.

"Sometimes happy, mostly troubled." Madeleine hiccuped.

Grace didn't want to push. She waited for Madeleine to continue if she chose.

"There's one that I have over and over. It's always the same. And I don't know which part is real and which part is the dream. It's about the last night I was with her, the night Aunt Agatha was babysitting for me while my parents were at the party. I know that part of it is real, because I remember waking up at Shepherd's Point that night and seeing my mother writing in her diary. I watched her take off her wedding ring and rub her favorite lotion on her hands. In the dream it's the same. I go in and find my mother writing at the desk in her old room at Aunt Agatha's.

She looks like a fairy princess, with her hair all piled up on the top of her head and wearing a beautiful golden gown. When she sees me, she stops writing and brings me back to bed and tucks me in. I look up at her face and notice one of her earrings is missing, and I tell her so. She takes the other earring off and slips it in the pocket of her gown. Then the phone rings and she goes to answer it."

"Who is on the phone?"

"I don't know. But I get up out of bed and follow her back to her room. She sees me and puts her finger up to her lips, wordlessly instructing me to keep quiet. And I hear her say into the phone, 'I'll meet you at the gate.' Then she hangs up the telephone and tells me to get back into bed."

"And do you?"

"In the dream, I always have. And that's what I told the police at the time. That my mother must have driven off with whoever she met at the gate. But since the bones were found in the tunnel, the dreams I've been having are different. Last night's dream was so vivid, I woke up in a cold sweat."

"Because?" Grace couldn't help but prod now.

"Because I dreamt that I followed my mother down to the gate."

"And?"

"And, I don't know." Madeleine shook her head, trying to recall. "There were headlights in the dream, and my mother stood in front of them and waited for someone to get out of the car."

"Who was it? Could you tell who got out of the car?"

"No. That's when I woke up."

They sat quietly for a few moments until Grace broke the silence. "I don't know all that much about it, but you were a very little girl when your mother disappeared. Maybe things that you saw back then have been buried deep inside all this time. Maybe your subconscious is ready to let them come out."

"Do you think I could know who my mother's killer is?"

"Anything is possible."

"I know anything is possible. But do you think I do?"

"I don't know, Madeleine. I have no idea."

"What should I do, Grace?" She looked insistently into the intern's eyes. "What would *you* do?"

Grace saw the anguish in the young woman's face and struggled to think of the right thing to say. "Well, I guess I would wait and see if more came back to me in my dreams, or maybe I would try hypnosis and see if anything came out that way. I can't really tell you what to do, Madeleine. I'm not a trained professional."

"Oh, yeah, that's right. You're Grace Callahan, a TV news person." Madeleine groaned, her demeanor changing in an instant. "How could I have forgotten? How stupid of me, spilling my guts to you."

"Madeleine, please, don't feel like that."

"You'll go back now and tell your news friends what I've told you, won't you?"

Grace was torn between wanting to do just that—or at least telling B.J. what Madeleine had spoken of—and wanting to honor the confidence shared by a young woman with whom she was united in a painful bond. It would be an act of betrayal to broadcast what Madeleine, in great vulnerability, had confided. Technically, Grace had never indicated that their conversation would be off the record, but morally, she felt bound to honor the intimacy.

"No, Madeleine. I'm not going to tell anyone. I promise."

"I would really appreciate that, Grace."
Madeleine seemed to relax a bit.

The silence that followed was awkward.

"Want to go back outside?" asked Grace.
"The fireworks will probably be starting soon."

They rose from the sofa as the eavesdrop-
per in the hallway just outside the living
room retreated.

CHAPTER
24

Dessert was strawberry shortcake and an
ice-cream sundae bar, but the grand finale
of the clambake was to be the fireworks, gra-
ciously provided by the city of Newport. Rain
on the Fourth of July, followed by a soggy
weekend, had postponed the pyrotechnic
display until tonight.

The guests, given flashlights by their
thoughtful hosts, paraded down Narra-

gansett Avenue for two long blocks to the Cliff Walk. Some enthusiastically sang "Yankee Doodle Dandy" in their alcohol-induced patriotic fervor. They gathered at the top of the cliff on the ocean's edge and waited for the fireworks to be shot off from the water off Easton's Beach down to their left. A long, steep staircase led ominously from the Cliff Walk to the rocks pounded by the surf below.

Grace found herself standing next to Professor Cox. "Those are the Forty Steps," he volunteered, noticing her peering downward. "The servants in all the mansions here had nowhere to gather on their one night off a week. This was where they came to socialize. Of course, the steps were wooden back then. Now they're stone."

"Interesting," said Grace, picturing the hardworking domestics dancing in the moonlight on the cliffs or resting on the steps with their bottles of ale. Maybe they had even skinny-dipped in the cold Atlantic water. But somehow Grace doubted it. Not the females at least. That was a pretty straitlaced era, and a young girl's reputation would be irreparably ruined by a stunt like that.

The first boom reverberated through the summer night air, and the crowd roared.

Rockets whizzed into the sky, bursting into giant blossoms of gold and silver, followed by sprays of red, white, and blue. Over and over, the brilliant explosions rocked the sky, holding the mortals below spellbound.

Grace looked over to where Professor Cox had been standing to share an appreciative glance. But the professor wasn't there.

Instead, several feet away, Grace saw Madeleine Sloane, wiping a tear from her eye. Grace wasn't sure if she should go over to her, and before she could make up her mind, she watched Madeleine turn her back on the dark ocean and the glowing fireworks and disappear into the crowd.

CHAPTER
25

Madeleine could figure it out. If she remembered any more, if any more came back to her, she might be able to piece together what happened.

It was a chance that couldn't be taken.

No matter how unfortunate, there was no getting around it. There was really no other way. It had to be taken care of now, before she ranted on to anyone else. Madeleine had already said too much to that Grace Callahan.

The fireworks were over. People were sauntering back to the Vickerses' for one last drink before calling it a night. In the hubbub, it wasn't hard to separate from one's companions.

Where was Madeleine?

Eyes searched the crowd, watching as the

guests headed back on Narragansett Avenue. The last stragglers finally passed and still there was no sign of Madeleine. Had she gone back to the house ahead of everyone else?

A last glance toward the Cliff Walk revealed the solitary figure sitting on the iron bench at the top of the Forty Steps. The low roar of the ocean blocked out any sound of the murderer's approach.

CHAPTER
26

Sam Watkins knelt beneath the giant elm tree, retching violently. He had definitely had too much to drink. Too many beers and all that seafood were a killer combination.

Sam looked around furtively, hoping that no one had witnessed his pathetic display. That definitely wouldn't be a plus in his quest to win the full-time spot at KEY News. They'd think that he was just another boozing frat boy—that he wasn't serious about his career. He uttered a low groan as a second wave of nausea hit.

Finally, he was able to get to his feet. Sam staggered at first, then became a bit more sure-footed, coming out from behind the tree and taking a few steps toward the road. In the distance, he could see the backs of the last party guests returning to the house. Good. No one had seen him.

Sam turned his head in the direction of the ocean, just to make sure that there was no one behind him. He didn't want any surprises.

It was then he saw what he prayed was a drunken man's mirage. On shaky legs, Sam tried to move forward, on instinct, wanting to help. But the vision at the cliff's edge and the alcohol overwhelmed him. He staggered backward, falling down again beneath the elm, as a woman's scream was muffled by the roar of the crashing surf.

SUNDAY

JULY 18

CHAPTER
27

Grace slept fitfully, periodically peeking at the digital clock as it marked the passing of the night. She got up again and again, to get a glass of water, to fiddle with the thermostat on the air conditioner, to play back the message.

"Hi, Mom. It's Lucy. Guess what? Daddy and Jan and I are coming to Newport! Daddy knew about your hotel and he got a room for us there. Isn't that cool? We can hang out. Well, call me back at Daddy's. Love you."

It had been too late to return the call when she had gotten back to the Viking, and that was probably just as well. Grace didn't want to get Frank on the phone and get into an argument about how utterly inappropriate his intentions were. He would just feign ignorance and innocence.

Grace's intuition told her that her former husband had a plan, though she wasn't sure yet what it was. Maybe he was trying to psyche her out, make her more nervous than she already was on her first out-of-town assignment. He probably wanted her to fail. Or maybe Frank would be looking for things to use against her in his court case. He'd be watching her, taking mental, if not written, notes on the long hours she worked here in order to have evidence when the time came.

Was she being paranoid? Grace wondered as she punched at the pillow. No. That was how Frank Callahan worked. When he wanted something, Frank used all his considerable energies and resources to get it.

But Lucy wasn't something. She was everything.

CHAPTER
28

The loose-fitting cotton slacks and long-sleeved blouse she took from the hook on the back of her closet door were the same clothes she had worn the previous morning and the one before that, but Elsa couldn't have cared less. She was not out to impress anyone this early. In fact, experience told her that there wouldn't be many people out there to impress. She would be home again, showered, and dressed in more socially acceptable attire before most of the residents and vacationers in this town were even out of bed.

Elsa grunted a bit as she bent over to tie her rubber-soled walking shoes. She was feeling more than her age this morning. At forty-two, one shouldn't be stiff when getting out of bed. She wrote it off to the balled-up position she had found herself in when she awakened. Her sleep had not been a relaxed one, and her muscles were tense.

She walked down the wide, elaborately carved staircase and picked up the binoculars and her cell phone from the large marble-topped table in the expansive foyer. Glancing out the long, leaded-glass window, Elsa decided not to stop to brew her usual cup of breakfast tea. It was getting lighter outside and she had to hurry. She could have her tea later. Maybe she would bake some nice raisin scones and bring them over to Oliver and they could have tea together.

Elsa listened to the driveway's crushed stones crunching beneath her shoes as she began her walk. As she'd expected, when she reached the road, it was deserted. Only the low roar of the ocean and the occasional call of one of her feathered friends filled the air.

At the end of Ruggles Avenue, she reached one of the several entrances to the Cliff Walk. Elsa didn't need her binoculars to identify the familiar black-legged kittiwakes gliding above the water. She knew they nested in colonies on the cliff edge. The seagulls were joined by sandpipers and plovers, none of them rare to the Rhode Island coast. Of course, she was always on the lookout for one of the native species in imminent danger. The pied-billed grebe, the northern harrier, the barn owl, the American bittern, and the upland sandpiper. These five birds were threatened with extinction in Rhode Island. That fact greatly disturbed Elsa, and she had made it her crusade to save them. Chairing the annual fund-raiser— this year at The Elms—was her contribution to the cause.

Heading north on the walkway, Elsa looked for the orchard oriole she had spotted yesterday in the hedgerow at the edge of The Breakers' sweeping lawn. It had been a male with a distinctive, dark chestnut color and a short, pointed bill. The orchard oriole was uncommon, though not endangered, but as far as Elsa could determine now as she searched the hedgerows, he had chosen to make himself scarce this morning.

Was it only yesterday that she saw the bird? So much had happened. Charlotte's identification, Oliver's grief intensified again. Elsa had wanted Oliver to come to the Vickerses' party with her, wanted them to be seen as a couple. But maybe it was just as well Oliver hadn't come. It would have appeared unseemly for him to be out partying last night. He would have been criticized for going.

People were more understanding, though, of Madeleine's attendance. The poor child had been through so much. Everyone agreed that Madeleine had done nothing wrong, and people were supportive of the idea that the young woman accepted the invitation to be in a festive atmosphere, celebrating life.

The sun's bottom rim had risen over the horizon now. Elsa continued up the Cliff Walk, past The Breakers. She saw nothing unusual but appreciated the familiar winged creatures that glided across the sky above her.

She went as far as the bench at the end of Narragansett Avenue, her customary spot to sit, rest, and meditate for a while before heading back. She seated herself, feeling the coolness of the metal through her thin slacks. She noticed the cigarette butts and empty beer cans carelessly left behind by the fireworks-watching revelers the night before. An early-morning jogger saluted her as he sailed by.

Elsa got up from the bench and stretched,

taking in a deep breath of the fresh morning air. The sea was especially glorious today, she thought, as she took a few paces closer to it. The Forty Steps lay beneath her now, with Madeleine's twisted body at their base.

CHAPTER
29

Officer Tommy James came out of the Dunkin' Donuts with two crullers and a disposable cup full of steaming coffee. He was settled into the squad car, looking forward to his breakfast, when the call came in on the radio. He shoved the coffee into the holder and slammed the car into gear. Pulling out onto Broadway, he didn't bother turning on the siren. There was no traffic on an early Sunday morning.

As he sped onto Narragansett Avenue, Tommy passed the Vickerses' house and felt a twinge. He was hurt that Joss hadn't invited him to her party. He'd had to hear about it from one of the guys at the station house. Seemed they all had a good time. Police had responded several times after neighbors called to complain about the noise.

Joss should have invited him. Especially since he had gone out on a limb and copied that diary for her. What was she thinking? Was she only using him?

In his heart, he knew she was. Yet he still couldn't give up on her.

Tommy drove up the curb at the end of the street and stopped, getting out quickly. The scent from a giant honeysuckle at the side of the road filled his nostrils. Funny how you could notice something like that at a time like this.

The small group of joggers who had gathered at the top of the Forty Steps moved aside as Officer James approached. A middle-aged woman with binoculars around her neck grabbed him by the arm. She was sobbing as she pointed downward. "I'm the one who called. I'm Elsa Gravell, and that is my godchild, Madeleine Sloane."

Tommy ran down the steep stone steps, stopping at the battered body that lay on the landing near the ocean's edge. The head was twisted at a grotesque angle. Unblinking brown eyes stared from the motionless face. He went through the motions, feeling the young woman's neck for a pulse. As he expected, there was none.

Madeleine Sloane. Tommy considered the name.

Joss will want to know about this.

CHAPTER
30

Sam was awakened by the sensation of something crawling over his face. He swatted at the bug and opened his eyes, squinting against the morning light, grimacing at the horrible taste in his mouth. On his back, he looked up to see the thick canopy of leaves above him and reached out to feel the dewy grass that had been his mattress.

Dear Jesus, he had slept out here all night. Or rather passed out.

He sat up, his head throbbing as he began

to recall what had happened. The party. The beer. The fireworks. The vomiting. The horrific sight at the cliff's edge.

Maybe that last had been only something he imagined in his drunken stupor. If he was hallucinating now, he was really going to have to swear off the alcohol, tough as that would be. But if what he had seen had really happened, that would be a lot tougher to deal with.

Getting to his feet, Sam brushed the stray blades of grass from his pants and smoothed out his rumpled shirt. He braced himself as he came from behind the giant elm and looked toward the ocean.

The police car. The crowd. The ambulance driving up.

No. He hadn't imagined it. It had really happened.

CHAPTER
31

The angry ring of the phone cut through the quiet hotel room.

"Hello?"

"Hi, Grace. It's B.J. Did I wake you?"

"I wish you had," said Grace. "I've been lying here for hours, wide awake."

"Well, throw on some clothes and meet me out front right away. Madeleine Sloane's been found dead."

Grace bolted upright in the bed.

"Oh my God, no." Her voice cracked.

"We can talk about it in the car. Now get going."

Grace pulled on a pair of jeans and a maroon Fordham T-shirt. As she ran a toothbrush around her mouth, her heart beat faster. How could this be? She had just seen Madeleine at the fireworks. Grace thought she'd been weeping for her mother. Grace had identified with that. They both had lost their mothers, their touchstones.

Grace brushed back her hair in a ponytail, wound a covered elastic around it, stuffed her feet into her sneakers, and sped out the door. Even the seconds it took to wait for the elevator were too much. She found the stairwell. As her legs hammered down the steps, she realized she was getting her first taste. This was what it was like to be covering a breaking story.

But this wasn't a story involving anonymous people, or a situation where it would be easy to maintain an emotional distance. Grace had known Madeleine, if only for a little while, and she had liked her. The fact that Madeleine was dead left Grace feeling sick.

B.J. was in the driver's seat waiting. As she got into the car, Grace noticed that he had his camera lying on the backseat, ready to grab when they arrived at the scene.

"What do you know?" she asked as she snapped her seat belt into place.

"Just that Madeleine's body was found this

morning, right where we watched the fire-works last night."

"My God, I was just talking to her at the party." Grace swallowed.

It was a short ride from the Viking down Bellevue Avenue to Narragansett. B.J. had a heavy foot, and the whole trip took less than three minutes. As B.J. parked behind the ambulance and police cars, Grace asked, "How did you find out about this?"

B.J. turned off the ignition. "The assignment desk got two calls. One from Joss and another from Sam. The interns are really paying off this year."

CHAPTER
32

The morning sun sparkled outside, but Agatha wailed in the shuttered dimness of her cluttered bedroom. Piles of old newspapers and magazines, boxes of outdated clothing, and empty cookie tins were scattered across the floor. Three cats lay curled on the worn carpet, watching disdainfully as their mistress sobbed on her unmade bed.

She'd brought this on herself. She should never have listened to Gordon Cox. She should never have let them into the tunnel. It should have been treated like the sacred burial place it had turned out to be. It should have been left alone.

With every fiber of her being she knew that, if they had never found Charlotte, Madeleine would still be alive.

Now, her beloved Madeleine was gone.

Agatha wiped her face against the frayed satin pillowcase, her troubled mind suddenly lucid. She should have sold this place years ago, just as Charlotte had encouraged her to do. If she had only done that, the next owner could have dealt with the damned preservationists and their obsession with the slave tunnel. If she had sold it as Charlotte had wanted, they would have been long gone from this place and Charlotte wouldn't have been entombed all these interminable years, just a few acres away from where Agatha lay now. If Agatha had sold Shepherd's Point then Madeleine would be alive.

None of this unbearable heartache would have happened.

It was all her fault.

Agatha didn't respond to the tapping at the door.

"It's Finola, Miss Agatha."

Still no answer.

The housekeeper entered the room, wincing at the mess that Agatha wouldn't allow her to clean up. It was hard to watch, even with her failing eyesight. Finola had been at Shepherd's Point in its glory days, when the mahogany shone, the silver was mirror-polished, and the crystal gleamed. The large staff had worked long days making sure that the Oriental carpets were beaten and the lush draperies cleaned. The brass fittings in the bathrooms sparkled, as did the ceramic fixtures. The glass-fronted cabinets in the kitchen and pantry showcased glowing copper pots and fine porcelain dinner services. Shepherd's Point had been a magnificent estate, frequently opening its doors for lavish parties and entertainment.

All that had changed, long ago, when the last silver mine was fully tapped. The staff now consisted of just herself and Terence—

and the house and grounds looked it. They were both getting on in years, and there was no way they could do the work that a dozen people had once done. Finola did the shopping and the cooking, and did her best to keep things picked up. But even that was difficult with Miss Agatha not wanting things moved around in any way.

Out of loyalty, she stayed, because the Good Lord knew that the money wasn't the draw. Finola's pay had been the same since Miss Charlotte had disappeared, and even that amount wasn't dependable every two weeks. Still, Finola had a room to sleep in and food to eat, and truth be told, she didn't feel up to looking for work with another family. As eccentric as Miss Agatha was, she was familiar, and Finola knew she could handle her job at Shepherd's Point.

"I brought you a nice hot cup of tea, Miss Agatha."

The frail figure on the bed didn't move.

"Come now, it will make you feel better."

"Nothing is going to make me feel better, Finola. Nothing. Madeleine is gone."

Finola had no response. She knew her mistress was right.

CHAPTER
33

The satellite trucks lined Narragansett Avenue. WJAR, WPRI, and WLNE, the NBC, CBS, and ABC Providence affiliates had sent news personnel to cover the sensational story. This story was going to lead the local broadcasts that evening. It had all the elements. A young woman found dead the day after the identification of her missing mother's remains. A body found off the cliffs that shouldered the mansions of Newport high society. A present-day murder wrapped in the mystery of a fourteen-year-old disappearance.

Grace scanned the satellite trucks. So far, KEY News was the only network presence. "Why aren't any of the other networks here?" she asked B.J.

"We lucked out," replied B.J., switching off his camera. "We just happened to be nearby.

The other nets will get their video from their affiliates. Which reminds me, we have to see if we can contact someone from a local station and get file tape of whatever they did on the Charlotte Sloane story back then."

"Fine. I'll ask around," said Grace as she remembered her conversation the night before. "And I wanted to tell you, B.J., I met someone at the clambake who knew Charlotte Sloane since they were kids together. It's our scrimshander, Kyle Seaton. I don't know if we're going to be able to get him to talk about Charlotte for the camera, though."

"Why not?"

Grace grimaced. "Just a feeling I got. I don't know how to describe him, really. I guess you would say he's an uptight sort. Very proper."

"Snobby?" asked B.J.

"I guess you could say that."

"Well, let's turn on the charm when we shoot the scrimshaw takeout on him and see if we can get him to cooperate on the Sloane stories."

Grace noticed that there was only one black person in the sea of whites milling around the Cliff Walk. It was Zoe Quigley, who was taking pictures of the Atlantic Ocean with her camcorder.

If Grace felt that her age made her stick out among the younger interns, what must it be like to be the only black person in a situation like this? In any situation, for that matter?

Zoe had come all the way from England to do her internship, so the young woman certainly had gumption. Maybe she was so self-assured that she didn't even think about being in a minority. But Grace somehow doubted that. Zoe had to be conscious of it.

As if she had felt Grace's eyes upon her, Zoe turned and waved. Grace walked toward her. "I was going to go over to the affiliates and see if we can find file tape of old stories they've done on Charlotte Sloane's disappearance. Want to come with me?"

Zoe seemed to weigh her response. "Thanks ever so much, but actually, I have something else I'm working on." Zoe didn't elaborate on what that might be, and Grace instinctively didn't ask. She didn't want to get into a competitive thing.

"Oh, okay. I guess I'll see you later, back at the Viking?"

"Brilliant," said Zoe. "See you later, then, Grace."

CHAPTER
34

Walking past the fabulous estates, Zoe was glad she'd worn her trainers. It was quite a distance on foot from the Cliff Walk back to the hotel. But from there, the Touro Synagogue was just around the corner. She joined the group gathered in front of the beautifully proportioned building and waited for the Sunday afternoon tour to begin. The docent came out to welcome the sightseers. Noticing Zoe's camera, he made an announcement. "We ask that you refrain from taking pictures on this tour." Zoe slid the camera into her knapsack.

"Good afternoon, ladies and gentlemen. On this quiet street in Newport, a principle has triumphed. For over two hundred years, the small synagogue standing here has testified that men may seek eternal truths in their own particular way without hindrance from the civil government. George Washington visited this synagogue twice, and every year, we observe the anniversary of his letter guaranteeing Jews the same religious freedom that all other Americans enjoyed. Allow me to read to you a portion of Washington's famous letter to the synagogue's founding congregation."

Zoe listened as the docent read the first president's words with all the solemnity the young man could muster.

"All possess alike liberty of conscience and immunities of citizenship. It is now no more that toleration is spoken of, as if it was by the indulgence of one class of people, that another enjoyed the exercise of their inherent natural right." The docent looked up for a moment, to make sure he had everyone's full attention for Washington's now famous words. "For happily, the Government of the United States gives to bigotry no sanction, to persecution no assistance."

The group followed the guide into the coolness of the synagogue interior.

"This is the longest surviving Jewish house of worship in the United States," the docent announced. "As you'll notice, the magnificent chamber contains a gallery supported by twelve Ionic columns, representing the twelve tribes of Israel. The five massive brass candelabra hanging from the ceiling are gifts from congregation members."

The docent pointed to the east end of the sanctuary. "The Holy Ark contains the Torah scrolls. Ours is the oldest Torah in the United States. And above the Ark is a representation of the Ten Commandments in Hebrew."

The group looked upward as the guide continued on.

"The raised ceremonial platform in the middle of the room is the central bimah. From here the Torah is read or a cantor stands to chant. Take note of the mysterious trapdoor under the bimah, which leads to an earthen-floored basement room. The room below is said to have been used as a stop on the Underground Railroad to hide escaped slaves."

As the tour group moved on, Zoe held back. She took her forbidden camera from her knapsack and trained it on the trapdoor.

CHAPTER
35

Even with a summer weekend head count of over 125,000, Newport was still, in many ways, a small town. Before the news could make the local television stations or *The Newport Daily News,* word of Madeleine Sloane's death was spreading through the city's full-time population.

At the kitchen of Seasons Clambakes, one of the lobster suppliers had heard it from one of the other fishermen down at the dock, who'd heard it from a friend on the ambulance corps. The ambulance had acted as a hearse, taking Madeleine's body directly to the medical examiner's office.

Mickey tried to keep his mind off Madeleine's death along with his aching back and focus on the job at hand. There was still much to do in preparation for the big wedding reception he was doing this afternoon at Eisenhower House out at Fort Adams. The stately mansion, once the summer White House to President Dwight Eisenhower, sat on sweeping lawns and offered colossal views of Newport Harbor and Narragansett Bay. The tents on the lawn had been erected yesterday, but the linen hadn't been delivered as scheduled. China, glassware, and silver service couldn't be set until that linen arrived.

There was the familiar ache in his stomach again. The one that was his companion whenever he worried, which meant he had the stomachache pretty much all the time. He wrote it off as one of the hazards of having one's own business. It went with the territory. But in his heart of hearts, he knew that it went back to something else.

The stomachaches had started when he was just eighteen and Charlotte Sloane caught him stealing that money at the country club.

CHAPTER
36

"New York wants a piece on Madeleine Sloane for the *Sunday Evening Headlines.* Since you have the interview with her, I thought I'd give you first crack. You want to produce?"

B.J. held the cell phone to his ear and made the mental calculations necessary to answer the senior producer's question. Sure, it would be a coup to produce his first piece for *Evening Headlines,* but he still had some editing to do on his piece on the history of the Vanderbilt family, already scheduled for tomorrow morning's broadcast. Still, blowing off the opportunity to produce for *Evening Headlines* was not a smart career move.

"Count me in, Dom," B.J. answered, knowing that this would be a late night. He'd do the package for *Evening Headlines* and finish his piece for *KTA* afterward.

"Constance won't be arriving until about four o'clock," Dominick O'Donnell said. "You'll have to plan on writing the piece for her, and you can shoot her stand-up after she gets here."

Jesus, thought B.J. *Anything else?*

"Am I editing, too?" he asked, dreading an affirmative answer.

"I hope not, but we'll have to see how things shake out."

B.J. flipped his cell phone closed and looked for Grace in the thinning crowd. He spotted her talking to a dark-haired woman near the WPRI satellite truck. *God, Grace is a stunner,* he thought, looking at the first woman who had truly interested him since Meryl. That budding romance had ended so painfully that he'd protected himself from getting really involved with anyone else. Maybe it was finally time to break the drought.

He headed toward Grace, his mind speeding ahead to his more immediate concern, reviewing his elements for the piece. All right, he had the interview with Madeleine Sloane—that was exclusive material and should be the highlight of the package. He had the video of the shroud-covered body being carried up the steps and loaded into the back of the ambulance. And he had gotten some sound bites with onlookers at the cliff. But he'd have to give some background on the strange twist of Madeleine's mother's disappearance and the identification of her remains just the day before. He could use the video of Shepherd's Point and the slave tunnel to cover some of that narration, but he still needed pictures from fourteen years ago. He uttered a silent prayer that Grace was having some success with that.

"Oh, B.J. Hi," Grace said as he reached her. "This is Pam Watts. Pam is an anchor at WPRI in Providence."

B.J. extended his hand to the anchor-woman, noticing immediately her kind, dark eyes and winning smile.

"Pam covered the story of Charlotte Sloane's disappearance fourteen years ago. She has video of the fund-raiser at the country club the night Charlotte Sloane disappeared, along with some of the search that was done afterward," Grace continued. "And she thinks her station will let us buy the file tape."

"There *is* a God," B.J. whispered. He could have kissed both Pam Watts and Grace. But it wasn't the first time he'd wanted to kiss his new intern.

CHAPTER
37

Zoe collapsed on her bed, exhausted by the heat of an American summer. Not bothering to unlace them, she pried the trainers off her feet, disgusted. If her documentary was going to be any good at all, she was going to need much more than thirty seconds of video of a trapdoor at a Jewish synagogue.

She knew what she wanted to capture, but Zoe was beginning to think that it was going to be harder than she had anticipated. She wanted to re-create, more or less, a female slave's voyage to freedom. Her research had located a worthy subject in a slave named Mariah, who had stolen away in the cargo hold next to the boiler of a passenger ship sailing from Norfolk, Virginia, to Newport. The trip was nearly unbearable because of the heat and dust in the airless room, but somehow Mariah and ten other fugitives had survived. Assisted by a bold sea captain, Mariah and the others had been dropped off at the ocean entrance to the tunnel at Shepherd's Point. From there, Mariah had been smuggled to the Touro Synagogue and then to the Bethel A.M.E. Church in Providence on her way to freedom in Canada.

Don't you dare get discouraged, Zoe told herself as she played back the video of the synagogue's trapdoor on the tiny video screen. *You have no right to be disheartened. Think of what Mariah went through.*

Producing a documentary or winning a job at KEY News should be nothing compared with that.

CHAPTER
38

Grace was mesmerized as she watched Constance Young stand on the Cliff Walk, the bright blue of the Atlantic Ocean framing the anchorwoman's blond hair. Constance was dressed in a pair of white slacks and a navy-and-white-striped nautical-style top, oozing presence from every immaculate inch. Did she have star power, or did her position automatically make her a star? Grace suspected the former. There were other morning anchors who, while good at their jobs, did not have Constance Young's telegenic appeal.

B.J. handed Constance a copy of the script he had roughed out, having highlighted the part where Constance would be on camera. She was to appear in the middle of the piece, after the explanation of the events known so far regarding Madeleine's death and the sound bites from her interview, bridging to the story of her mother's disappearance. The newswoman read it over a few times, signaled she was ready to begin, and disappeared down the Forty Steps.

Hoisting the video camera to his shoulder, B.J. stood at the top of the stone staircase and called out, "Go."

Constance began her slow walk up the steps toward the camera. "Was Madeleine Sloane's death an accident, a suicide, or a murder? Police are trying to figure that out, but this is not the first time that the Sloane name has been associated with mystery in this city by the sea."

"Got it," said B.J. "Got it right on the first take."

"I think we should shoot another one," said Constance. "The wind was blowing my hair in my face."

B.J. hadn't noticed it, but he wasn't about to contradict Constance. Whatever the anchorwoman wanted was, by definition, fine with him. Constance went back down the steps and retraced her steps up, recording another perfect bridge.

He liked to imagine what it must have been like to be the lord of one of these manors. He never grew tired of the game, though lately, with his bum knee, Gordon didn't enjoy his customary Sunday-afternoon constitutional along the Cliff Walk as much as he once did. Today, in fact, he'd had to force himself to get out. Sitting at home and brooding wasn't going to get him anywhere.

As the professor stopped to watch the KEY News people doing their work, he knew he had to clear his head. Not only did he have papers that needed grading and an important lecture to give tomorrow afternoon but he was expected to report to the *KEY to America* broadcast location at 6:00 A.M., with lots of fascinating historical anecdotes to offer the television audience from 7:00 till 9:00. He had to get to bed early tonight. The exercise and salt air might help him sleep.

Gordon doubted that combination would be enough.

Just as he'd had many sleepless nights after Charlotte's disappearance, he knew he would have many sleepless nights after her daughter's death as well. Though Madeleine had helped him persuade Agatha to open the tunnel, she wasn't enthusiastic about seeing the project continue. After her mother's remains had been identified as having lain there for fourteen years, Madeleine didn't like the idea of tourists traipsing through the tunnel. Gordon had gotten the feeling at the clambake that Madeleine would have been a big problem in his quest to get the tunnel restored.

A big problem. If she had lived.

Grace noticed him first.

"B.J.," she hissed, "there's Professor Cox. He was sitting with Madeleine at the clambake last night. Want to see if he'll say something?"

The producer looked in the direction Grace indicated and then glanced at his watch.

"Good catch, Gracie. But we don't have time now. We have to get back to the hotel and have this piece edited. We can get the professor tomorrow, if we need him."

CHAPTER
39

Tommy hung up the receiver and stared glumly at the phone as Detective Manzorella came into the squad room. Noticing the expression on the rookie's face, Manzorella was pretty sure he could predict what the matter was. Tommy James's obsession with Joss Vickers was no secret.

"Don't tell me," the detective said. "The Vickers girl shot you down again."

"I don't understand it," Tommy sputtered, slamming his fist on the desk. "I do everything I can to please her, but she's always making excuses about being too busy to see me."

Manzorella put his hand on Tommy's shoulder, feeling sorry for him. The kid just didn't get it. Joss Vickers was never going to end up with a Newport cop. It didn't work that way. With rare exceptions, the rich married their own.

"Stop wasting your time, Tommy," Manzorella said. "There are lots of other fish in the sea. There are plenty of local girls who would be thrilled to go out with you, man."

"But I don't want them. I want Joss. I can't forget the summer we had." The patrolman's eyes welled up, and Manzorella looked away.

"Most of us have had beautiful summers with girls we'll never forget, Tommy. But that doesn't mean we end up going off into the sunset with them and living happily ever after. Guys like us don't get the debutantes. They'll have flings with us, but they don't marry us."

Tommy looked with interest at the detective. "You had someone in your life like Joss?"

"Yeah. A long time ago. I was a lifeguard at Bailey's Beach, where her family had a membership. That time was magic. Lots of music and moonlight."

"So you understand," said Tommy.

"Yeah, I understand, kid. But when the summer was over, so was the relationship. That's just the way things go. Take my advice, Tommy. You've got to get over Joss Vickers. You're going nowhere with a girl like her."

CHAPTER
40

Grace was certain that Joss shot her dagger eyes when she entered the ballroom work space with B.J. and Constance Young. Sam, though, was in no condition to be jealous of Grace's proximity to power. He looked hungover, his eyes red-rimmed, as he guzzled a large bottled water. Zoe was nowhere to be seen.

B.J. sat down with the editor Dominick had scheduled for him, so Grace went over to join her peers. "Hi, you guys."

The lack of enthusiasm in their responses was deafening.

"Nice catch this morning, calling in with the word on Madeleine Sloane," Grace offered, trying to be upbeat and cordial. "How did you two know about it?"

"I have a friend on the Newport Police Department. He told me about it," said Joss, her expression sullen. "But what good did it do me? B.J. has the hots for you, and you're his fair-haired girl. You're getting to do more than any of us, and I'm sick of it." She turned her back on Grace and stalked away.

After a stunned pause, Grace looked at Sam.

"I was out there early this morning, and I saw her." Sam groaned. "What a mess."

"Oh," said Grace, surprised at the happenstance and trying hard to act as if Joss's cutting remarks hadn't bothered her. "Were you jogging or something? Is that why you were on the Cliff Walk, Sam?"

"No. I wasn't jogging. I was just out there."

Sam would have almost felt sorry for Grace if she hadn't been such competition. Joss was really dissing her, even though Grace hadn't actually done anything wrong. It wasn't Grace's fault that B.J. liked her.

Watching Grace cross the newsroom and pull a chair up next to the producer at the portable editing bay, Sam wished there was a female producer who would take a liking to him. He wouldn't be averse to playing up to her if it would help reach his goal. But Sam hadn't observed anyone who seemed open to that possibility. He was going to have to do something else to set himself apart from the other interns.

Once he had made the call to the assignment desk, he'd taken off from the scene of Madeleine's fall, before the police had time to spot him and ask him any questions. But Sam had seen what he had seen the night before. That knowledge made him an eyewitness to murder.

He cracked open another bottle of water, knowing he could parlay his knowledge into an advantage. That knowledge would get him the assistant producer job he craved. Sam could distinguish himself from all the other interns.

CHAPTER
41

Like mother, like daughter. First, Charlotte; now, Madeleine.

One murder had followed another, the second predicated on the first.

Everyone would be looking for the link. It was just as crucial now as it had been fourteen years ago that the photo didn't show up.

Another letter was in order. It was time to write it now and get it into Monday morning's mail. The pen, held in the left hand to disguise the handwriting, glided over the plain white paper, adding two lines at the end to make the threat real.

I still have the wallet left behind in the play-house the night Charlotte Sloane died. If you go to the police with the photo, I'll produce the wallet. Who do you think the police will believe? You or me?

CHAPTER
42

Was that Lucy standing in the doorway?

Grace squinted, her heart beating faster. Yes. It *was* Lucy, and there were Frank and Jan standing behind her, searching the ballroom.

Grace wanted to slide beneath the table and hide, but she knew that wouldn't work. She had to be a grown-up and face this head on.

"Excuse me, B.J. I'll be right back."

Lucy spotted her mother and called out. Heads around the ballroom turned in the direction of the young voice and watched as the child hugged her mother. Grace felt her face reddening.

"Hello, Frank. Hello, Jan," she said over Lucy's head, suddenly conscious of her unmade-up face and the tired T-shirt she was wearing. Frank looked better than ever, lean and fit, his muscular forearms tanned beneath the sleeves of his golf shirt. Even though he repelled her at this point, Grace had to admit that Frank was a remarkable physical specimen. Though Lucy hadn't inherited his piercing blue eyes, Grace was glad her daughter had her father's straight nose and dazzling smile.

"How's my Lucy?" she whispered as she hugged her daughter's thin shoulders again.

Frank's wife looked like she had just stepped out of a Talbots window, in her perfectly pressed khakis and kelly green cotton sweater tied just so over her shoulders. Jan's smooth, bleached-blond hair was tied back with a black grosgrain ribbon, chosen to coordinate with the black band of her Movado watch and her soft Italian-leather sandals. Grace spotted the French pedicure on the new wife's toes. It matched the manicured fingers that sported that honey of a diamond solitaire. Very prosperous, very put together, very pampered, very different from Grace.

"We checked in a little while ago and wanted to see if we could take you out to dinner," Frank said. Lucy beamed.

Good going, Frank, thought Grace. *Make it look like you're Mr. Nice Guy in front of*

Lucy. You're aiming to rip my heart out, but you'll play the gracious dinner host.

"Gee, thanks very much, but I don't know when I'll be finished here. I don't want to hold you up."

"We can wait." Grace felt the smugness in Frank's voice.

"Yeah, Mom. We can wait."

She was damned if she did, damned if she didn't. Though Grace wanted to spend time with Lucy and hated to disappoint her daughter, the last thing she wanted was to spend the evening in a restaurant sitting across the table from Frank and his wife making polite small talk. She wanted to strangle Frank, not break bread with him. Yet if she used work as her excuse, it could just give Frank fuel for his argument that her career was going to make her inaccessible to Lucy.

"All right. I think I should be finished here around seven."

"Great. The concierge told me there's a good Italian restaurant not too far away from here. Let's say seven-thirty at Sardella's?"

"We'll probably need a reservation," Grace said, hoping that he wouldn't be able to get one.

"I'll talk to the concierge and make it happen." Frank winked as he rubbed his thumb and forefinger together. Obnoxious to the last.

CHAPTER
43

B.J. was pleased as he fed the edited package on Madeleine Sloane's death on the satellite to New York with a half hour to spare before the *Evening Headlines* began. He was thinking about how good he would look to the higher-ups when Sam approached him.

"I need to talk with you," the intern said.

"All right. Give me two minutes. I'm almost done here."

B.J. held on to the telephone line until he got an all clear from the record room at the Broadcast Center in New York. Disconnecting, he turned to Sam. "What's up?"

"I think I have something that could help the show tomorrow morning."

The producer looked at Sam inquisitively.

"I was out there on the Cliff Walk last night. I saw what happened to Madeleine Sloane."

"Jesus, man." B.J. took hold of Sam's arm. "What did you see?"

Sam looked uncomfortable. "I don't think I should say yet."

"What do you mean?"

"Well, I was thinking I could go on air tomorrow morning and tell what I saw then."

The suggestion immediately raised B.J.'s suspicions. What was this kid pulling? Yet it would be a helluva coup to have an eyewitness as an exclusive interview on their first day in Newport.

"You know what, Sam? I think we need to talk to Nazareth about this."

As they went to find *KTA*'s executive producer, the intern had to keep himself from smiling in satisfaction. This was exactly what he had wanted.

"Did you tell the police anything?" Linus asked.

"No."

The executive producer was not perturbed. In fact, he was pleased.

"Well tell me, then. What did you see?"

"With all due respect, sir, I'd insist on saying it for the first time on the air tomorrow."

Linus had to give this kid credit. He was manipulating the situation to his absolute best advantage. Just by this act of bravado and cunning, when the internship was completed, Sam had gotten Linus's vote for the a.p. job. And his vote was the only vote that mattered.

The executive producer wished that he knew in advance what the kid was going to say, but not knowing wasn't a deal breaker. After all, how did one ever know for certain what a person was going to say on live TV? In more than three decades in the business, Linus could remember more than one occasion where he'd been surprised with what a subject had said on air. Pre-interviews, done in advance of the on-air segments, usually gave an idea of what was going to be discussed. But there was absolutely no guarantee that an interviewee wouldn't just have off and talk about something entirely different. That was what made live TV exciting.

If Sam had seen what happened to Madeleine Sloane, Linus wanted him to talk about it exclusively on *KTA*. Sam wanted the assistant producer job. Linus couldn't imagine that the kid would screw them on the broadcast.

His decision made, Linus picked up the phone and called New York.

"Change the promo after the *Evening Headlines* tonight, pronto," he commanded. "It should read, 'Live and exclusive on tomorrow morning's *KEY to America*. . . . The eyewitness to the death of a daughter of Newport society tells what he saw.'"

"What video should we cover with?" the promotion producer frantically yelled back from New York.

"Take some of the video from Constance's package of the body bag being carried up the steps and we'll feed you video of the eyewitness right away," Linus barked as he turned to B.J. "Grab your camera, get a shot of Sam, and feed the video to New York. *Now.*"

CHAPTER
44

After watching the reports of Madeleine's death on the local news, it was time to turn to KEY. Constance Young's report covered the bases. It was tough watching video of Madeleine's body bag. It was even worse watching scenes from all those years ago— seeing just a glimpse of a younger version of the face of Charlotte's killer. The same face, not terribly changed by time, that stared back from the mirror each morning. The old file tape showed the country club, the men in their tuxedos and the women in their sum- mer gowns. Flowing blue, red, white, yellow, and green designer frocks were worn by the society ladies, but Charlotte, in her strapless gold lamé, stood out. There were pictures of the police canvassing the wealthy neighbor- hoods surrounding Oliver's home and Shep- herd's Point, and flyers with Charlotte's smiling face being tacked to telephone poles and taped in store windows around Newport.

That had been a terrifying time, and the memory of the constant worry about being found out came flooding back. After the news piece ended, Charlotte's and Madeleine's killer stared at the television set, not really taking in any of the other featured reports.

Forensic science was better than it had ever been. If that old photograph was turned in, it wouldn't be too hard to figure everything out.

Maybe it was time to move out of town, to hide away.

But where? There was too much history here, a life established. Starting over somewhere else couldn't be the answer. Once things started to unravel, there would, realistically, be nowhere to hide. All that could be done was to wait. Try to act as if nothing was amiss, and hope that there would be no more success in tracking the killer now than there had been fourteen years ago. Crimes still went unsolved all the time.

Feeling a little better, the killer reached for the remote control and was about to snap off the television when the deep voice boomed.

"Live and exclusive on tomorrow morning's *KEY to America*. The eyewitness to the death of a daughter of Newport society tells what he saw."

The body bag on the Cliff Walk. A young man's face.

The drunken kid from the clambake had seen the whole thing?

CHAPTER
45

Grace shouldn't have been surprised. A table was waiting for them at precisely 7:30 at Sardella's. The party of four was escorted to a cozy room at the side of the restaurant. As they took their seats, Grace was already thinking about the drink she wanted to order.

"How do you like the hotel?" she asked, casting for small talk. "It's nice, isn't it?"

"You should see our rooms, Mom," Lucy answered with enthusiasm. "We have a suite. And there's a Jacuzzi in the bathroom."

"Great, honey." Grace forced a smile, cursing Jacuzzis. Her own room was okay, but the bathroom was minuscule and she could barely turn around in the tiny shower stall. Oh well, what did it matter? She was hardly in the room. In fact, she couldn't have cared less about having a Jacuzzi for herself. It was the whole idea that everything Frank offered Lucy was so much more glamorous and lush than what Grace could that bothered her.

The waitress arrived and reeled off the specials for the evening.

"What will you have, Grace?" Frank asked as the waitress went to fetch their drink orders.

"The eggplant parm sounds good to me."

"Lucy?"

"Penne with vodka sauce."

Frank frowned.

"The alcohol burns off when it's heated, Frank. It's absolutely fine for Lucy to have vodka sauce."

"Yeah, Dad. Mom makes it at home for Grandpa and me sometimes."

Watching the pinched expression on Frank's face, Grace briefly wondered if this, too, was going to be used against her. Then she dismissed the thought as ludicrous. She couldn't let herself become paranoid about how Frank would interpret every little thing.

Grace turned to Jan. "What are you going to have?"

The blonde smiled sweetly. "I'm going to let Frank order for me."

So that was how it was between them, thought Grace. Better Jan than her.

CHAPTER
46

Eight-foot-high wrought-iron panels mounted between dressed limestone piers set atop a four-foot limestone wall made The Breakers a veritable fortress. The satellite truck pulled through the massive, ornate black iron gates. Scott Huffman didn't have to be concerned with the top of the truck clearing the entry façade. Thirty feet high, the gate was topped by elaborate scrollwork incorporating the Vanderbilt symbols of acorns and oak leaves.

The gatekeeper's cottage, immediately to the left once inside the gates, had been left open by agreement with the Preservation Society, to provide a place for the driver to relieve himself, if need be, overnight. With its ultra-expensive equipment, the satellite truck could not be left unguarded until the early-morning hours when the *KEY to America* staff would arrive to broadcast from The Breakers.

It was going to be a long night. Scott had prepared himself, filling a cooler with sandwiches and cans of soda and smuggling out a pillow and blanket from the hotel. He went down his checklist, making sure he had everything he needed inside the truck so that there would be no problems in the morning.

"Damn it," Scott cursed as he realized some cable was missing.

CHAPTER
47

Sam wasn't having any second thoughts. In fact, he was positive he was doing the right thing, the smart thing. He was excited about the coup he was scoring for *KEY to America* and for himself. Linus Nazareth had stopped by the newsroom on his way out to dinner to pat him on the shoulder. The guy loved him, thought Sam with satisfaction. The assistant producer job at the end of the internship would surely be his.

Sam knew he should get to bed. He wanted to be fresh for his first appearance on national television. He was just about to call it a night when one of the phones rang.

"It's Scott Huffman over at The Breakers. I think we're going to need some more yellow-jacketed cable. Can someone bring some over?"

"Where can I find it?" asked Sam, thinking that it never hurt to score more brownie points.

"In one of the crates against the wall at the back of the ballroom."

"All right. I'll bring it over right away."

Sam hung up the phone, found the cable, and inquired at the assignment desk about borrowing a car to drive to The Breakers.

CHAPTER
48

The wooden chair rocked silently in the shadows on the hotel porch; time was growing short. But young people liked to go out and party when they were in a town like Newport, and it made sense to wait here and see if the bigmouthed kid came out.

And if he did come out? What then? How would he be eliminated?

There was no time to plan, just as there

had been no time with Madeleine last night or with Charlotte all those years ago. It had to be done on instinct with something at hand.

CHAPTER
49

Grace had no desire to linger over coffee. Dinner had already been interminable.

"We were thinking of heading down to Bowen's Wharf for a while, do a little browsing in the shops, look at the boats," Frank said, setting his espresso cup back in its saucer.

"That sounds like fun," Grace answered politely.

"Want to come with us, Mom?"

Grace smiled at her daughter and reached out to stroke the top of her head. "Thanks, Luce, but I have to get back. I have to be up early in the morning," Grace said, thanking

God she had an excuse to get away from Frank and his wife. She had watched Frank intermittently put his arm around Jan and hold her hand all through the meal. Enough was enough. Grace couldn't help wondering whether Frank was always like this with Jan or whether he being so loving just to show Grace how "supremely happy" they were. Perfect parents to raise Lucy.

It was only a few blocks back to the hotel, and Grace welcomed the chance to walk in the night air and clear her head. She had to get her mind off the upcoming custody battle. There was little or nothing she could do about it while she was in Newport. When she got back home, she would make an appointment with her lawyer. This week she had to concentrate on the only thing she could control right now—her performance with *KTA*, with the goal of winning the staff job.

Everything was relative, though, wasn't it? Sure, Grace was sick at the thought of losing Lucy, and of course, she wanted the job; but in light of what had happened to Madeleine, Grace felt guilty about obsessing over her own concerns. Her problems seemed minor in comparison.

Two days ago, Grace had never even heard of Madeleine Sloane. Yet Madeleine's death, coming on the heels of their talk in the Vickerses' living room, had left Grace shaken. Madeleine had been trying to make sense of her dreams, had been searching her memory for something that would reveal her mother's killer. Had Madeleine figured something out in the time between their conversation and the time she died? Had that led to her death?

As she reached the hotel porch, Grace was contemplating going to the police with the details of her conversation with Madeleine. But bumping into Sam on his way out the front entrance distracted her for the moment.

"Where are you off to?" she asked, squinting in the light that streamed from the hotel.

"I have to bring this cable over to the satellite truck at The Breakers," Sam said, holding up the coil of yellow electrical cord.

CHAPTER
50

Waiting had paid off.

There he was, talking to that Grace Callahan. As she left to go inside the hotel, Sam gave a ticket to the parking valet.

Up from the rocking chair, passing right behind the kid as he waited unknowingly on the porch, going straight to the vehicle that had been parked across the street. Gripping the steering wheel, watching through the driver's-side window as he got into the car that was brought around for him. He pulled out onto Bellevue Avenue heading in the direction of the mansions. A quick U-turn enabled the tail.

Where was this blabbermouth kid going?

Past Redwood Library and the Tennis Hall of Fame, past the shopping center, past The Elms. No matter where he was going, it could be dealt with. Every place was familiar. As long as he could be gotten alone.

His car slowed down as if he was searching the street signs. He made the left on Narragansett, then a right on Ochre Point, pulling into the parking lot across the street from The Breakers.

The vehicle that followed kept right on driving, passing the lot and making a turn onto the next side street. The headlights were switched off as it slid to the curb.

There was a tire iron in the trunk.

Sam held out the cable to the truck driver. "Is this what you wanted?"

"Yeah. That's it. Thanks, kid."

Sam turned to leave.

"I should have asked you, but I didn't think of it," said Scott. "I've got a whopper of a headache. You don't happen to have any aspirin on you, do you, kid?"

"Nope. Sorry." Sam shook his head. "But you want me to go out and get you some?"

The driver thought of the long night looming ahead. It would be nice to have a little break. The kid looked like he could be trusted. It wasn't like there was anything important to do. It was only babysitting the truck.

"Actually, I have a few other things I could

pick up. How would you feel about waiting here and keeping an eye on things for me?"

"I guess that would be okay," said Sam with hesitation, wanting to go back to the hotel and get to bed. "You won't be too long, will you? I have to take a leak."

"There's always the bushes, kid. Or the gatehouse is open. You can go in there."

CHAPTER
51

The night-duty police officers arrived at the Hotel Viking, went to the ballroom, and demanded to talk with the executive producer of *KEY to America*. Beth Terry was covering the assignment desk.

"May I ask what this is in reference to?" she inquired.

"Your scheduled interview with the alleged witness to Madeleine Sloane's death," said the officer. "We want to know more about it."

"I see. Well, Mr. Nazareth is out at dinner," said Beth. "But I can try to reach him on his cell phone." It wasn't smart to alienate the police, she thought. There was no telling how KEY News might need Newport law enforcement in the days to come. She made the call as the officers stood by.

"Linus, it's Beth. I'm sorry to interrupt your dinner," she lied. Actually, she was glad to distract Linus from Lauren Adams, the *KTA* lifestyle correspondent with whom he was surely nuzzling.

"What is it?"

"The Newport Police are here. They want to talk with you about the interview we're doing tomorrow morning on the Madeleine Sloane murder."

"They don't know who the interview is with, do they?" Linus asked from his candlelit table at the Clarke Cooke House.

Beth looked at the policemen. "I don't think so," she answered.

"Is Sam around?" asked Linus, taking his companion's hand and winking at her.

"Just left," Beth answered, smiling at the policemen.

"Good. I'm not about to be bullied by some

rinky-dink cops. I've stood up to the feds; I can certainly stand up to the Newport Police. They can talk to Sam all they want *after* the show tomorrow."

CHAPTER
52

He pulled up the toilet seat and did what he had to do. As he pushed down the flush lever, Sam thought he heard something outside the closed door, but when he came out of the bathroom there was no one to be seen.

He stood in the doorway of the gate-keeper's cottage, looking out at the satellite truck, hoping the driver wouldn't be gone too long. He needed to plan what he was going to say in the morning. It would be best to be nat-ural and conversational and tell it just as he'd seen and heard it, omitting the part about be-ing loaded and barfing under the tree.

The violent struggle and the piercing scream. *Poor Madeleine Sloane.*

Sam let out a deep sigh and closed his eyes as he pictured it again. He hadn't actually seen the attacker's face, but at least he could give a general description of body size and what the killer had been wearing. That was something to go on. Maybe not as much as Linus Nazareth was hoping for, but Sam hadn't wanted to reveal that in advance. Let Linus think he had something huge to tell. Something that warranted being interviewed on national television. It was still news, wasn't it, that he had witnessed a murder?

Sensing a movement behind him, Sam turned and finally did see the face of Madeleine's killer in the split second before the tire iron came down directly on his head.

CHAPTER
53

She'd dressed in white shorts and her white KEY News T-shirt so she'd be more visible in the darkness. With her long, black braids flapping against her neck, Zoe jogged along Bellevue Avenue, retracing the path she had taken this afternoon when she left the media frenzy at the Forty Steps to get to her self-imposed assignment at Touro Synagogue. She felt at ease as she ran past the mansions on the boulevard, which was well lit by electrified gaslights.

Zoe marveled as she passed the conspicuous examples of wealth. Wealth built on the backs of cheap labor, both black and white. But the whites had been, for the most part, immigrants who had chosen to come to America in search of a better life. The blacks, by contrast, had been captured like animals, shackled, and forced to leave their homelands. Once they were here, their skin color determined their dismal fates. Rhode Island may have been the first state to pass an antislavery law, and the American Civil War may have technically freed the slaves, but when these mansions were built, people of color were still second-class citizens.

Zoe trotted right past the intersection with Narragansett Avenue, having no desire to head to the Forty Steps, the scene of Madeleine Sloane's demise, at the end of the block. Four intersections later, she saw the sign for Victoria Avenue. On impulse, she turned left, to explore the street whose name reminded her of England.

Her trainers pounded against the macadam on the quiet street. There wasn't much to see. The lighting was much poorer than it had been on Bellevue. Halfway down the long block, Zoe was about to turn back when she heard the noise. It sounded like someone was closing the bonnet of a car.

The headlights flashed on, blinding her. The car screeched from the curb, headed right at her. Zoe ran off the road into the grass and strained to see the driver who was in such a hurry. The automobile passed by so quickly, it was impossible to get a good look inside. But the license plate was illuminated, and Zoe managed to make out the first three letters before the car swerved to the left and out of sight.

S-E-A.

The driver had been much luckier. In the glare of the headlights, the killer had clearly seen all the letters of the last name emblazoned above the KEY News logo on Zoe's shirt.

CHAPTER
54

Inside the brown paper bag were a bottle of aspirin and three cans of cold beer. That should be enough to get him through the night.

Scott opened the door of the satellite truck and was surprised not to find the kid inside. The surprise turned to anger when he checked the gatehouse. It was empty.

"That little s.o.b.," Scott muttered. The kid had taken off and left the truck unattended. If anything happened to that truck, that irresponsible jerk's ass would be grass. He went back out again and checked the truck over.

Thank God, everything seemed to be in order.

MONDAY

JULY 19

CHAPTER
55

A large, white tent had been set up on The Breakers' lawn to shelter the *KTA* hosts and their guests, but there was no need for it. As the first light peeked over the ocean's horizon, it was clear that there would be no rain. The weather for *KEY to America*'s first broadcast from the City by the Sea was going to be picture perfect. Constance Young and Harry Granger would be able to conduct the show under the open sky.

Constance and Harry arrived early, just as they did at the Broadcast Center in New York, giving them time to scan the major morning newspapers and look over last-minute notes and prepared questions for the upcoming interviews. They joined scores of KEY News employees milling around the grounds of the estate, each executing the editorial and production tasks that needed to be done to get the broadcast on the air. When the opening theme music was played over the network and Constance and Harry welcomed America to Newport, it would all appear seamless, the hundreds of staff hours that went into producing two hours of television unbeknownst to the viewers at home.

Grace observed the bustling activity with excitement. These were the preparations for *live* television. Professional, well-thought-out, well-executed plans. Yet the *KTA* staffers were always aware that the unexpected could happen at any time while millions of people watched.

That was one of the primary reasons Constance and Harry were paid the big bucks. If something went awry on the air, the cohosts were the ones who had to handle it with grace, aplomb, and lightning-quick wit. It wasn't easy to do, but they made it look as if it were. Most times, the audience never even knew that something had gone wrong.

With the start of the broadcast a scant forty-five minutes away, the exclusive interview subject had not shown up. Repeated phone calls to Sam's room at the hotel had gone unanswered.

The executive producer was yelling across the lawn to anyone who would listen. "Where the hell is he? Where in the hell is the kid? The intern. Sam Watkins."

Feeling she might have something to offer, with trepidation Grace walked over to Linus. "Sam left the newsroom last night to bring some cable to the satellite truck, and he told me he was coming right back to go to bed," she said.

"Well then, check with the truck operator, will you?" Linus's face was reddening. "See if he knows anything."

Grace followed the yards of electrical cable out to the gravel driveway where the truck was parked. The operator's recollection didn't paint Sam in a flattering light.

"Yeah, the kid brought the cable and that's the last I saw of him. I'm not surprised he hasn't shown up like he was supposed to this morning. If you ask me, he's not reliable. Sam said he would watch this truck for me last night, but when I came back from running an errand, he was nowhere to be found."

*   *   *

"For God's sake, will somebody go back to the hotel and try to find him?" Linus barked as he paced the lawn. "I'm gonna kill that goddamn kid."

The executive producer looked around frantically. Who wasn't needed to do a particular job as the minutes ticked away until the start of the broadcast? His eyes fell on Grace again. "You. He's your buddy. Go see if you can find him."

There was no answer.

Grace banged on the door and called Sam's name, knowing that she was making enough noise to wake up the guests who still tried to sleep in other rooms up and down the hallway. Sam couldn't possibly be sleeping through this racket, could he?

She was about to look for the hotel service phone to ask if someone could come up to open the room when she noticed the maid's cart turn into the hall. Izzie O'Malley was pushing it.

"Oh, Izzie. Do you remember me? Room two-oh-one?" Grace barely waited for Izzie to nod in recognition. "I have an emergency. I have to see if one of our interns is in his room. He's supposed to be on the show in just a little while. Can you possibly open the door for me?"

The chambermaid hesitated for a moment before taking the master key card from her pocket. *What the hell?* She wouldn't be working here much longer. And who would even know? Yes, Grace had helped her; now she would help Grace.

Izzie inserted the card in the lock, watching for the blink of the green light. Together, the two women entered the quiet room.

The bed had not been slept in.

CHAPTER
56

Someone noticed that the car Sam had borrowed occupied a space in The Breakers' tourist parking lot. The news staffers buzzed with speculation. Maybe Sam really had nothing to say, maybe he really hadn't seen anything and the whole thing was an act of fraternity-house bravado. Maybe Sam had gotten scared that he would be caught in a lie, or maybe the intern was afraid that telling what he did see would put him in jeopardy.

Grace arrived back at The Breakers just in time to hear Linus yelling.

"I don't give a good goddamn what the kid's problem is. Sam Watkins is off this show." Linus slammed his clenched fist into his open palm. "Nobody makes an ass out of me," he bellowed. "We promised an exclusive, and we damn well better give them something that can make good on that promo. Think, everybody. Think fast."

Grace braced herself.

"Excuse me, Mr. Nazareth."

The executive producer turned to look at her, his eyes bulging with anger. Grace noticed a vein throbbing beneath the skin on his right temple.

"What is it?" he barked.

She took a deep breath and blurted it out, praying that Linus wouldn't dismiss her suggestion as ridiculous. "Professor Cox, our consultant, knew Madeleine Sloane and her mother. In fact, he was sitting with Madeleine at the clambake. He may not be a witness to her death, but he was with her on the night she died."

Grace could almost see the wheels spinning in the executive producer's head as he considered her suggestion.

"The eyewitness to the death of a daughter of Newport society tells what he saw," Linus muttered to himself. "It's not an exact fit, is it?"

Rebuked, Grace bit her lower lip.

"But it's the only thing we've got," Linus continued. "And it's better than anything anyone else around here has come up with. Let's go with it."

Grace felt a rush of satisfaction. Emboldened, she asked, "Don't you first have to see if Professor Cox is willing to talk about Madeleine?"

A sly smile spread over Linus's face. "Oh, he'll talk, all right. Gordon Cox is on our payroll for the week."

CHAPTER
57

The shot from the helicopter provided the first video for the broadcast, a sweeping aerial view of the mansions that dotted the Cliff Walk.

"Good morning," Constance Young's energized voice welcomed the television audience. "It's Monday, July nineteenth, and this is *KEY to America,* coming to you this morning from Newport, Rhode Island."

The *KTA* theme music began, the graphics ran on the screen, and the director switched to the primary camera shot, showing Constance and Harry standing on The Breakers' lawn with the Atlantic Ocean gleaming in the morning sun behind them.

"All this week, we'll be broadcasting from this glorious city by the sea, sharing with you the beauty and history of this remarkable town." Constance seemed to ignore the fact that the breeze blowing off the water was pushing her carefully styled hair into her face. "This morning we start off here at The Breakers, the seventy-room *cottage* that Cornelius Vanderbilt II had built for his family's summer vacations."

The camera panned over the Renaissance Revival–style structure's oceanside façade. Four stories of Indiana limestone, hand-carved columns, open balconies, and multiple chimneys glistened.

"But, first, here's Harry with the morning's news."

CHAPTER
58

It was early. None of the other guests had left their rooms yet, so Izzie could take her sweet time in this one. It was a checkout and had to be cleaned from top to bottom.

She switched on the television in the armoire, keeping the volume just high enough to hear as she stripped the sheets from the double bed. Izzie groaned as she tugged at the clean fitted sheet, securing it over the mattress. Her arm was really paining her this morning. She had to take a little rest.

How much longer could she keep this up? As it was, she had barely made it to Mass yesterday morning and had spent most of the day sleeping, not bothering to turn on the TV or open the newspaper. After all that rest, she was still exhausted.

Taking a seat on the chair at the desk, Izzie happily watched the aerial shot of the Cliff Walk, thinking of all the times that she and Padraic had strolled there, hand in hand. It was one of their favorite things to do, especially in the last months, when he was so sick. Such a soothing and cleansing pastime, costing absolutely nothing. The right price for their eternally tight budget.

She sat on the edge of the bed and watched a bit more, but when the panoramic views of Newport stopped and they started with the news, Izzie forced herself to get up. She didn't want to hear about fighting in Iraq or suicide bombings in Israel. She felt sorry for those people over there, but she had plenty of problems of her own right here.

Izzie didn't want to bring herself down. Her doctor was always telling her it was important to have positive thoughts. He claimed that it would help her immune system.

As she pulled back the shower curtain to scour the tub, Izzie caught a snippet of conversation that drew her back to the bedroom.

"These are what are known as the Forty Steps, and this is where Madeleine Sloane's body was found Sunday morning."

As she focused on the screen, Izzie's hand went to her chest, covering the spot where her heart beat beneath, the spot where her left breast had once been. The picture of the steep stone steps and the crashing waves was taken from high above, and the video was shaking a bit. Izzie watched intently as the shot changed and that pretty Constance Young reappeared on the screen.

"Professor Gordon Cox, our KEY News historical consultant for the week, was among the last people who saw Madeleine Sloane alive Saturday night. Thank you for being with us, Professor Cox."

The teacher nodded, a solemn expression on his face. Solemn or sour, Izzie couldn't decide which.

CHAPTER
59

The professor was painfully aware of the television camera trained upon him, uncomfortable with the questions he was being asked, resentful of being called in as a last-minute replacement to fulfill Linus Nazareth's sensational promise.

This was not what he had signed on for, thought Gordon as he stood talking with Constance Young at the top of the Forty Steps. He was supposed to discuss Newport's history, one of his areas of professional expertise—not rehash Charlotte Sloane's disappearance or describe his time with Madeleine the night she died.

Gordon cleared his throat. "Well, Madeleine had seemed to be doing pretty well, to me, considering the fact that she had just learned that her mother's remains had been identified as those found in the old slave tunnel at Shepherd's Point."

"There have been reports that Madeleine had been drinking that night," Constance led.

Gordon glowered at the cohost. "Just about everyone at the clambake had been drinking. Madeleine didn't seem to be overly affected to me."

"If you had to speculate, Professor, would you say that it was more likely that Madeleine fell down these steps or that she was pushed?"

"I wouldn't care to speculate one way or the other. All I can say is that Madeleine Sloane was quite a fine young woman, and her death is a very great tragedy."

As he pulled off his microphone at the end of the segment, Gordon fumed inside. Yet his anger was assuaged almost immediately as he remembered a very important fact. Shepherd's Point might become the Preservation Society's property sooner rather than later.

Agatha Wagstaff now had no heirs.

CHAPTER
60

Monday was usually Mickey's day off, a welcome respite following the hectic weekends. After the Vickerses' clambake Saturday night and the wedding at the Eisenhower House yesterday, he wished he could sleep until noon. But he had set his alarm for 7:00, determined to catch up with his bookkeeping.

Though the business was doing amazingly well and he could easily afford an accountant to do the work for him, Mickey didn't trust anyone with his financials. He knew how easy it was to lie and cheat.

Mickey rolled over in bed, pleased with how far he had come. The boy raised by middle-class parents in Newport's Fifth Ward had made it much further, on the economic scale at least, than his parents ever had. When his mother had wrung her hands in despair over his grades at Rogers High

School, Mickey had ignored her pleas. He didn't want to go to college anyway. Those were four wasted years as far as Mickey was concerned. He wanted to get out in the world and make money.

It hadn't turned out to be as easy as he had thought it would be, though. The world hadn't exactly welcomed him with open arms. Mickey quickly discovered how hard it was to make a buck, especially with no college degree. But he was stubborn and full of pride. He wouldn't admit that his parents had been right. He was going to show them and everyone else that Mickey Hager was somebody to be reckoned with.

And he had. His house was bigger, his cars were newer, his bank accounts were fatter than his parents' had ever been. Seasons Clambakes was making money hand over fist, and the deluxe catering business that had spun off was thriving as well. Mickey thought with satisfaction of the job that was coming up on Wednesday, the formal charity affair at The Elms. Everyone who was anyone in Newport would be there to see what his company could do. After that shindig, Mickey was certain the sky would be the limit for his catering business.

His hand fumbled for the remote control on the nightstand. Mickey pointed and clicked at the plasma TV built into the wall across from his bed. The tape of Madeleine Sloane's face appeared, large and clear, and spoke from the big screen. "If the police had found my mother early on, there might have been more clues for them to work with to find the real killer. But I'll tell you one thing. My father didn't kill my mother. I'm sure he didn't."

Mickey listened as the *KTA* cohosts speculated on possible connections between the deaths of the society mother and daughter. What did it matter, all this time later, who killed Charlotte Sloane? All Mickey knew was that it was a blessing Charlotte had disappeared right after she caught him ripping off the country club, before she had a chance to blow the whistle on his scheme. The money that he had embezzled from those pompous snobs had been the seed money for Seasons Clambakes.

CHAPTER
61

Grace watched on a monitor as Caridad Vega delivered the national weather report from the studio in New York. In the downtime in Newport, Constance's hair and makeup were retouched and Harry played a quick makeshift stickball game with crew members. Batting a rubber ball with a truncated boom mike pole relieved some of the tension. The first hour of the summer vacation show had been anything but light and carefree.

"We've had enough blood and guts in the last hour," Linus called across the lawn. "Now we'll leave 'em on a happier note."

The cohosts got into position again, taking off the sunglasses they had donned during the break. The floor manager signaled to begin, and Harry did the honors, teasing to the segment that would appear after the commercial break.

"Coming up, a tour of The Breakers. We'll show you the opulence and the glory of Newport's most famous Gilded Age mansion."

The camera followed Constance and Professor Cox as they strolled through the lofty arches of the Great Hall. The Vanderbilts' oak leaf and acorn motif appeared again and again on the plaques of rare Italian marble. A freestanding bronze candelabra hung from the breathtakingly high ceiling, a ceiling painted to represent the view an open courtyard would have afforded—a blue sky. At the back of the room, glass walls opened out to a mosaic-roofed loggia pulling the eye onward to the ocean.

They and the audience at home toured the Music Room, the Morning Room, the Billiard Room, the Breakfast Room, and spent extra time in the Dining Room, the most imposing and richly embellished room in the house. Two stories high, with a dozen enormous red-and-cream-rose alabaster columns. The vaulted ceiling was carved, painted, and gilded, rising in stages to an elaborately framed oil-on-canvas painting of Aurora, goddess of dawn, on the ceiling. Two towering Baccarat chandeliers, each composed of thousands of crystal balls and beads, hung above the sixteenth-century-style oak and lemonwood table.

"This table could be extended to seat thirty-four guests," Gordon said.

"My goodness," said Constance, looking up and around. "What a domestic staff they needed to run this place. I can't imagine having to clean those chandeliers alone."

"Shall we go upstairs and see the bedrooms?" Gordon offered.

"Yes. Let's."

A broad grand staircase with an ornately detailed bronze and wrought-iron railing swept up to the second floor. As cohost and professor climbed the red-carpeted marble steps, Constance asked, "How did they heat this place? It must have cost a fortune."

The professor smiled, pleased to display his knowledge. "Well, since the Vanderbilts were primarily here during the summer season, that helped. But an enormous heating plant beneath the caretaker's cottage was joined to the basement of the house by a tunnel. Several hundred tons of coal could be stored at once in the underground boiler room."

CHAPTER
62

His head throbbed with a pain worse than any he had ever felt. Sam used every bit of strength he had to open his eyelids. But after all the effort, there was only blackness. Was he blind?

The floor beneath his body was cool and damp, and the smell was musty. His reeling brain tried, in vain, to bring order to the chaotic input from his senses. Where was he? What had happened?

No answers came to him as he slipped back into unconsciousness.

CHAPTER
63

Elsa switched off the television set and pulled her silk robe closer around her body. Watching the news had been a mistake. It just made her feel worse.

Skipping her morning walk had also been a mistake. She should have gotten out and walked along the seaside, looking for her glorious birds. The combination of ocean air, exercise, and her feathered darlings always made her feel better.

But there was no way she was going to leave this house this morning, not when Oliver had finally come to her bed.

He slept upstairs now, finally, after a night of thrashing and sighing and choked weeping over his daughter's death. It was not the way she would have wanted things, but Elsa would take Oliver any way she could get him. If he had to come to her for comfort in his anguish, it was still better than not having him come to her at all.

She went to the kitchen, sliced an orange in half, twisted it over the juicer, and poured the nectar into a small glass. While the oatmeal cooked on the stovetop, Elsa washed some fat blueberries and chopped some walnuts to sprinkle on top. A good nutritious breakfast would make her broken lover feel better.

That was her job now. To help Oliver through this horrible loss. To make him whole again. To make Oliver see that life was still worth living.

With her.

Balancing the breakfast tray on her hip, Elsa opened the door to her bedroom, trying not to make any noise. But inside, there was no one to rouse. Her bed was empty, a mess of crumbled sheets.

She could hear water running in the bathroom. Elsa knocked softly on the closed door. "Oliver, dear, I've made you some breakfast."

He emerged, eyes bloodshot, hair disheveled. Her tortured prince, embattled by his raging demons.

"I couldn't eat a thing."

"You must, dearest," Elsa urged. "The days ahead won't be easy. You have to keep up your strength."

"What strength, Elsa?" Oliver sighed. "I have no strength left, no reason to go on now."

Elsa winced within, stung by the slight to her. But eventually and ever so slowly, time would heal this wound.

"Parents lose children and carry on, Oliver," she said softly.

He turned on her and fairly spat with contempt. "Spoken as only someone who has never had children could."

CHAPTER
64

All in all, Linus was pleased with their first broadcast. They had survived Sam's no-show, and thanks to that other intern's quick thinking, they'd been able to sub in Professor Cox to talk about Madeleine's last night.

He prayed the audience wasn't any the wiser.

Linus still seethed at the thought of Sam, though. That damn kid, if he showed up, could kiss his career with KEY News goodbye. To think that, just last night, he had been ready to give Sam the staff job.

Feeling the sun's rays strengthening, the executive producer twisted the cap on the bottled water and took a long swig. He wiped the beads of perspiration from his brow with his forearm and looked around the lawn.

There she was, gathering the cohosts' completed scripts. Grace Callahan.

She was older than the others, more mature. That was a good thing. Grace thought on her feet. She didn't crumble in a crisis. He should give her more to do and see if Grace had what it took to become a permanent part of the *KTA* staff.

CHAPTER
65

If that was what KEY News considered an eyewitness, then they were pretty hard up, thought Tommy. *We've waited for an eyewitness who hasn't shown up.*

Officer James and Detective Manzorella had stood, out of camera range, through the entire broadcast, waiting to see if Professor Cox was the only guest to talk about seeing Madeleine Sloane on the night she died. As far as Tommy was concerned, the only redeeming feature of the two hours spent at The Breakers this morning was the chance to catch glimpses of Joss as she glided around doing errands.

"I can't believe they can get away with that," he said as they walked out through the iron gates. "They made it sound like they had somebody who had seen her murdered."

"That's the way they do it, Tommy. They make it sound like they have something bigger, more sensational than they actually do. They tease the audience to get 'em to watch." Detective Manzorella slapped Tommy on the shoulder. "Don't worry, kid. We'll get our man, one way or another."

CHAPTER
66

Rusty slept until noon, a deep, exhausted sleep. There wasn't any reason to get up earlier. No one came in for tattoos in the morning anymore. Rusty had taken to opening the store on the floor below in the late afternoon and staying until midnight, accommodating the customers who came in after being emboldened by a few cocktails.

He pulled back the curtain, squinting at the bright sunlight that streamed into the small bedroom. It was going to be a scorcher.

His stomach rumbled, reminding him that he hadn't bothered having any supper the night before. Rusty pulled on a pair of shorts and slipped on his moccasins, not bothering with a fresh T-shirt. He would just go out, pick up a coffee and a newspaper, and come right back. He'd shower and dress for the day later.

The sidewalk was already growing hot. He could feel the warmth penetrating the soles of his moccasins as he walked up Broadway and ducked inside the deli. Rusty grabbed a copy of *The Newport Daily News* and waited his turn on line to order.

The front page of the paper blazed with the news of Madeleine Sloane's death. The police still weren't sure if it was a murder, a suicide, or an accident. As Rusty turned the pages, he caught his breath at a picture of Madeleine's mother, Charlotte, dressed in an evening gown on the night she had last been seen alive.

Yes, Charlotte had been gorgeous that night, even in her distraught state. A damsel in distress, needing a knight to rescue her. The admiral's car had acted as Rusty's shining steed.

"What'll it be, Rusty?"

"Coffee, with two sugars, Joey, and a buttered roll. You got any with poppy seeds left?" Rusty looked up from the paper and smiled at the familiar face behind the deli counter. But Joey wasn't smiling back. He was staring at Rusty's shirt.

Rusty looked down and saw the dried blood spattered against the white cotton.

"Occupational hazard." He shrugged.

CHAPTER
67

After treating themselves to a lunch of juicy cheeseburgers and crispy fries at the Brick Alley Pub, Grace and B.J. crossed Thames Street and headed for their scheduled visit to Kyle Seaton's scrimshaw shop on Bowen's Wharf. The engraved sign over the shop indicated that Kyle had been doing business at this location for twenty-five years.

Inside the store, glass display cabinets contained pieces of scrimshaw in a wide array of shapes and functions. Walking stick and umbrella handles, letter openers, and cutlery joined cuff links, earrings, hair clips, and bracelets, all engraved and resting on folds of black velvet. Grace picked up a carved paperweight on the counter, thinking it might make a nice souvenir gift for her father. Turning it over, she whistled softly as she saw the price.

"That's whale's tooth, of course," said the scrimshander, walking over to them. "And, as I'm sure you must know, the Endangered Species Act of 1973 makes it illegal to obtain the material now. So these antique pieces are quite valuable."

"It's beautiful," said Grace, gently putting the paperweight down. "So all these pieces are made of whale's teeth?"

"Whale and elephant ivory mostly here. I do carry some walrus ivory as well, fashioned by the Eskimos. Nineteenth-century American whalers in the arctic took thousands of pounds of walrus ivory, and much of it made its way into the commercial trade in the form of the walking sticks and knife handles you see in the display case."

Grace and B.J. looked in direction that Kyle indicated.

"It's okay if I shoot all this stuff, right?" B.J. asked.

"Shoot away," the proprietor agreed. "There are some cane handles and corkscrews made of boar tusks over there." Kyle nodded at a case at the rear of the store. "I even have a couple of pieces of engraved hippo tusk. Hippo ivory is the hardest of all the ivories and the rarest. Because the tusk is so hard, it was used rarely for scrimshaw, except by the most determined artisans."

"This is great," said B.J., hoisting his camera up and looking through the eyepiece. "We'll have plenty of video material for our taped piece tomorrow. It'll lead to the live on-air segment with you and Constance and Harry, where you'll give a demonstration of how the scrimshaw engraving is actually done."

"And how long, exactly, do you allow for that, sir?" Kyle asked, looking over his reading glasses at B.J. "I forgot to ask you that when we spoke on the phone."

"Two minutes, give or take a few seconds."

Kyle looked at B.J. with disdain. "Out of the question. You understand that we will be able to do almost nothing in such a ridiculous time frame. Scrimshanding is an exacting, painstaking art."

"Maybe I can get them to stretch it to three minutes. Will that help?" B.J. asked.

"Hardly." Kyle sniffed.

"I have an idea," Grace offered. The two men turned to her and waited.

"In the research I did, I read that there was a large market for fake scrimshaw," she paused. "Fakeshaw, I think they called it. It's really plastic scrimshaw. Plastic that looks like ivory."

"I'm familiar with it." Kyle frowned. "Worthless trash."

"Well, like it or not, that's the scrimshaw most people buy. The kind that they can pick up for ten or twenty dollars or so at a gift or souvenir shop."

"And your point is?" Kyle looked at Grace as if she were a bug.

"How about if, in the live segment tomorrow, you demonstrated how to tell fakeshaw from the real thing? That could be really interesting to our viewers. Everybody dreams about coming across a treasure at a garage sale or an auction. Show them how to check if that piece of scrimshaw they find in a box at a tag sale is the real thing."

B.J. nodded with enthusiasm. "I like that idea. Let's go with that."

Kyle paled beneath his tan.

Before they left the shop, B.J. broached the subject. "Grace says you told her that you were at the party the night Charlotte Sloane disappeared."

"Yes. I was." Kyle looked almost defiant.

"And you were at the clambake the other night when Madeleine Sloane was killed," B.J. led.

"What's that supposed to mean?" snapped Kyle.

"Just an observation," said B.J. "Do you have any thoughts about what happened to either, or both, women?"

"No, I don't," Kyle answered shortly. "But I am wondering what I'm going to do with the scrimshaw piece Madeleine had ordered for her father's birthday."

CHAPTER
68

Detective Manzorella tossed the lab report onto his desk.

The crack in Charlotte Sloane's skull signaled that blunt-force trauma was the likely cause of death. Microscopic bits of her blood had been found on the iron fireplace shovel that had been buried in the tunnel along with Charlotte's body. But no fingerprints had been found.

That wasn't unexpected. On a hard, nonporous surface like iron, a fingerprint might not last fourteen days, let alone fourteen years. But on absorbent surfaces, like paper, decades-old fingerprints could be detected now.

The shovel was not going to lead to Charlotte's killer. They may have the murder weapon, but there was still no conclusive evidence pointing to the murderer.

CHAPTER
69

When Grace and B.J. got back to the Viking, the newsroom was almost empty.

"I bet everybody's out, at the beach or something, catching rays," B.J. grumbled. "But damn it, I've got to write this script, get Constance or Harry to track it, and get it edited."

"Life in the fast lane, Beej," Grace joked.

The producer nodded, smiling. "You should go out and do something fun, Grace. After all, you're not getting paid for this."

Grace shrugged. "The allure of lying in the sun is long gone for me, and the other interns don't exactly seek me out, or haven't you noticed?"

"Speaking of interns, I wonder if Sam has had the guts to show his face." B.J. looked around the ballroom.

No Sam. No Joss. No Zoe, either.

As B.J. opened up his laptop to begin writing the scrimshaw script, Grace wandered over to the assignment desk. Again, Beth Terry was at the helm, this time eating chocolate fudge from a box.

"I was wondering, Beth, any sign of Sam?"

"None."

"Do you think that maybe the police should be called?"

"Yes, Grace. I do. But Linus thinks we should wait awhile. And he's the boss."

CHAPTER
70

Joss Vickers was not at the beach. Though, as she came through the heavy door of the Newport Police Department headquarters and was hit by the blast of hot late-afternoon air, she was proud of herself. She had foregone the immediate pleasure of a dip in the refreshing Atlantic for her more important goal.

Crossing the street, Joss patted the pocket of her shorts, satisfied with the contents. She'd had to promise to have dinner tonight with Tommy to get what she wanted, but it was worth it. Though Tommy had said he would take a picture of them for her, Joss had insisted on seeing them herself. The pieces of evidence the police were not revealing to the public. A silk handkerchief and a single earring that had been entombed with Charlotte Sloane's bones. Both were in good condition, protected all these years, buried in the pocket of Charlotte's dress.

Tommy hadn't had the courage to smuggle the earring or the handkerchief out of the police station, but he had taken them from the evidence room and showed them to Joss in the officers' lounge area. He guarded the door, just in case, but they really had plenty of time. No one was stopping in for coffee on a scorching day like this one.

Joss got into the green Mercedes, switched on the ignition, and turned up the air-conditioning. She rummaged though her Kate Spade bag, found a barrette, and clipped her long hair up off her neck. As the cool air began to circulate through the sedan, Joss pulled the folded sheet of paper from her pocket, opened it, and began to study the sketches she had hurriedly drawn.

A golden disc, slightly smaller than a quarter, set with diamonds in the design of the face of a clock. Engraved in tiny letters around the rim were the words TIME FLIES. LOVE STAYS. The handkerchief was silk, the color of a lemon peel. She'd be sure to remember that particular shade.

Now Joss knew what the police knew, Tommy had reassured her. She'd read Charlotte's diary and had seen the earring and the handkerchief. She wasn't quite sure yet how she would use the clues, but she felt empowered having the insider knowledge. At the very least, she could toss the information to Linus and impress him. But that would come only later, if she couldn't figure out more herself. If she could track down the Sloane women's murderer or murderers, Joss could write her own ticket with any news organization she wanted. Maybe she'd give KEY News first crack, maybe she wouldn't.

Backing the car out onto Broadway, Joss smiled, thinking about how cool it would be to be an investigative reporter. But her expression turned sullen when she spotted Grace walking along the sidewalk. Joss didn't honk the horn or wave. Instead, she felt a wave of suspicion and jealousy as she watched Grace disappear into police headquarters.

Joss pulled out her cell phone and called Tommy. He would keep tabs on Grace for her.

CHAPTER
71

Detective Al Manzorella adjusted his brightly striped tie as he escorted Grace into a small conference room. The space was barren save for a table, four chairs, and a large mirror on the wall.

"Take a seat," he said, indicating the office chair on the other side of the metal table. "What can I do for you?"

"I have something that I thought could be important to your investigation of the deaths of Charlotte and Madeleine Sloane." Grace clasped her hands on the table in front of her.

"And what would that be?" Detective Manzorella asked, taking a seat across from her.

"I had a conversation with Madeleine Sloane on the night she died."

"Were you a friend of hers?" The detective's eyes searched Grace's face.

"No. Well, yes, I suppose I was, or I could have been." Grace fumbled with the words. This detective was going to think she was a crackpot.

"Let me start again," Grace requested, taking a deep breath. "I only met Madeleine for the first time Saturday, the day that her mother's remains were identified. I'm here with KEY News, doing an internship on *KEY to America.* We went to Shepherd's Point to see what we could get on the Charlotte Sloane story, and that's when I met Madeleine."

"Who is *we*?" The detective wrote in his notepad.

"A KEY producer named B. J. D'Elia and me," Grace answered, hoping that she wasn't bringing B.J. into this. She hadn't even told him she was going to the police, much less what her conversation with Madeleine the night of the clambake had been like. Grace had promised to keep the talk with Madeleine confidential, but it was different now. Now, everything that Grace had ever been taught had led her here, to the authorities. It was her civic duty. She had to tell the police what she knew. With Madeleine dead, there was no longer any confidence to keep, especially if Grace's knowledge could help find out what had happened to the young woman.

"Go on," urged Detective Manzorella.

"Well, we talked a bit at Shepherd's Point, and I guess you could say we hit it off. We had something in common. Both of us had lost our mothers."

"I'm sorry."

"Thank you." *Yes,* thought Grace, *my mother would approve of my coming to the police. It's the right thing to do.* She took a deep breath and continued. "Anyway, Madeleine did a short interview with us. She was adamant that her father didn't kill her mother."

Detective Manzorella's face remained expressionless as he listened. Oliver Sloane had been the prime suspect all these years, though there was never enough to bring him in. The fact that, on the night she disappeared, Charlotte went back to Shepherd's Point instead of going to Seaview, the marital home she shared with Oliver, made everyone think that she had been running away from her husband.

Since Madeleine's death, many of the other guys in the station house were beginning to be less sure of Oliver's guilt. If Charlotte's and Madeleine's deaths were connected, it was hard to swallow the idea of a man killing his own daughter.

Still, Oliver couldn't be counted out, and Al wanted the focus to remain on him. Though he wasn't at the clambake, it would have been easy enough for Oliver to approach Madeleine at the Forty Steps.

"The reason I really came here is to tell you about the conversation I had with Madeleine at the party that night." Grace paused as she twisted her hands on the table. "Madeleine had been drinking a bit, and she spoke quite freely to me."

"What did she say?"

"She said she felt that, deep down, she might know who her mother's killer was."

Detective Manzorella peered sharply at Grace. "What do you mean, 'deep down'?"

"Madeleine said she had been having dreams about when she was a little girl on the night her mother disappeared."

"And?"

"And the dreams had been becoming more vivid."

Grace recounted what she could remember of Madeleine's conversation. The little girl awakening to find her mother writing in a diary. The single earring slipped inside the pocket of Charlotte's evening gown. Madeleine being tucked back in bed only to get up again and listen to a one-sided telephone conversation. Following her mother down to the gate to meet the caller, the headlights of the car hiding the driver, at first, from view.

"But Madeleine felt like more was coming back to her," Grace finished. "That the memory of the driver was right within her grasp. Could it be possible that Madeleine had figured out who had killed her mother and that the killer had to get rid of her because of that?"

Grace sat back in her chair, spent, her story told. On the other side of the wall, Officer Tommy James watched through the glass. He had listened to her entire tale.

CHAPTER
72

Kyle decided to close the shop a little early. That was his prerogative as owner. He enjoyed the fact that he could do as he pleased. Now that Cloris had left him, he was freer than ever.

He enjoyed being a bachelor again, and surely didn't miss his wife's constant nagging. She wanted things from him that he just couldn't or wouldn't give her. She was always complaining about his lack of responsiveness, in bed, in conversation, in emotion, in everything. Cloris was forever asking what he was up to, insinuating that he was hiding things from her. Kyle didn't miss her badgering one bit.

Turning the bolt on the front door, he surveyed the shop with satisfaction. Business was good, even more lucrative since he had established his website, expanding his customer base worldwide. Clients were finding him; he didn't need to search for them anymore. And that was a damned good thing, since Cloris was bleeding him dry in alimony payments. Thank God, she hadn't had a clue about the other money he had stashed away.

Yes, life had been pretty good the last few years, but that was changing now. The discovery of Charlotte's bones and Madeleine's death were panicking the local population and intriguing the media. The visit from those two from KEY News this afternoon had unnerved him. He was especially crazed that Grace Callahan had come up with the smart-ass suggestion that he demonstrate how to test for fakeshaw. Hoisting himself by his own petard didn't set well with him. But now, what was he going to do? Refusing the request could cast suspicion on him. He'd have to go ahead and do what they asked tomorrow morning and pray for the best.

The pressure was on the police to solve the cases, and Kyle was worried about that as well. If the cops came to his door, he didn't want to be caught with any incriminating evidence.

It was time to separate the wheat from the chaff. Kyle went from display case to display case, selecting the perfectly executed plastic pieces and removing them, rearranging the real scrimshaw objects to cover the spaces on the black velvet.

It was time to clean house.

CHAPTER
73

Her head was throbbing. When Grace got back to the hotel from the police station, she went directly to her room, not even stopping at the ballroom to see what was going on. She wanted to take a shower and lie down.

Opening the door to her room, she groaned as she noticed the red light blinking on the telephone next to the bed. Whoever it was, she didn't feel like talking. Not even to Lucy and certainly not to anyone who wanted her to do any work or run an errand for KEY News. She needed some downtime.

She undressed, peeling away her perspiration-dampened T-shirt and stepping out of the jean skirt she had thrown into her suitcase at the last minute. She wished she had brought another one. Maybe, after a little nap, she'd take a walk up the block to the Talbots she had noticed, or down to the Gap she had heard was on America's Cup Avenue and see what they were selling. She definitely needed a pair of khakis to get through this week.

Grace went into the small bathroom and searched her cosmetics kit for the travel-size bottle of Advil. Shaking out three tablets, she swallowed them down with a mouthful of water from the spigot at the sink. She pulled back the shower curtain and adjusted the water temperature to a soothing lukewarm. She stood beneath the spray, letting the water pound against her scalp. After a good ten minutes, she began to feel some relief.

Wrapping a bath towel around her body and twisting another, smaller one around her head, she went to the bed and pulled back the spread. Grace sighed with gratitude as she slipped beneath the cool, white sheets.

But the light on the phone still blinked, insisting that it be answered. She reached for the receiver, jabbed at the keypad, and smiled as she listened to B.J.'s voice. He sounded a bit nervous.

"Hey, Grace. It's me. Bartolomeo Joseph. I'm finished editing our piece on the scrimshander and I've decided that we've worked far too hard today. We need to have some fun. So, I was wondering, if you don't have other plans, if you'd like to go out for a nice, relaxed dinner. How does a little summer sushi at the Candy Store sound? Afterwards, I thought we could go out and listen to some music on Bannister's Wharf, maybe do a little dancing. I know I'd really like that. I hope you would, too. Call me on my cell."

It sounded like an actual date. She wasn't big on raw fish, but the thought of spending an evening alone with B.J. made Grace forget about her headache.

The Candy Store had been the hangout of choice for generations of the Newport sailing crowd. The dining room was wide open to the harbor and Narragansett Bay, with a long bar running the length of the room. An over-scaled antique "pond yacht" hung on the wall behind the bar, dominating the room.

The maître d' showed them to a table at

the side against the rear wall. Grace noticed that all the other tables were occupied.

"This place must be good," she said as she spread her napkin on her lap.

"Yep. I've heard it's one of the 'musts' in Newport," said B.J. "I hope it lives up to its billing."

As they waited for their wine to arrive, Grace wanted to get it out of the way. It would either relieve her or ruin the evening, but she was certain she had to tell B.J. about her visit to the police. Not only had she brought his name into things, but she wanted to confide her concerns. Yet she told herself to be careful not to make him feel that she was leaning too heavily on him.

"Here's to you, Grace," he said, holding his glass toward her. "You've been making work a lot more enjoyable for me."

Trying to decipher the meaning of the toast, Grace smiled as their glasses touched. Maybe this wasn't a date after all. Maybe this was just one colleague dining with another. She hoped not. She was feeling more and more attracted to the man who sat across from her. It wasn't just physical, though with his high cheekbones and angular jaw, B.J.'s face was certainly appealing.

But he was also smart and sophisticated, yet down to earth. He didn't take himself too seriously. Not like Frank at all.

"Should we look at the menu?"

"Yes." Grace nodded. "But you'll have to guide me. I don't know much about sushi." Oh God, she sounded like Jan fawning over Frank. Inwardly, Grace cringed, and she pinched herself under the table.

"How about we try some of almost everything then?" B.J. suggested.

Grace looked up from the menu. "I'm game, but I'll have to pass on that Dancing Eel Roll."

"Done." B.J. laughed as the waiter came to take their orders. "We'll have some pan-seared tuna with ponzu sauce and that salad of crab, octopus, conch, and shrimp in kimchi sauce to start, and a double combination platter with the California rolls, sashimi, and sushi."

Halfway through her second glass of wine, Grace made her announcement. "I went to talk to the police today, B.J."

His brown eyes widened a bit. "'Bout what? Did you tell them that Sam is missing?"

"No, I didn't think it was my place to go into that, though if Sam doesn't show up soon, somebody's got to tell them." She shook her head. "No, I wanted to tell them something that might help in the investigation of Madeleine Sloane's death."

"I don't understand. What?"

B.J. listened intently as Grace described her conversation with Madeleine at the clambake.

"Whoa," he sighed as she finished. "If Linus knew that you were sitting on this and that you went to the cops with it instead of telling him, he'd go ballistic. This is just the sort of thing he'd kill to have on the show."

"I'm not going to tell Linus, B.J. I have no desire to be interviewed on *KEY to America* about what Madeleine confided in me. It was a private conversation, and I don't want to exploit it. I only told the police because I thought they should know. It could help in the investigation."

He smiled appreciatively, reached across the table, and covered her hand with his. "You're a good girl, Grace Callahan. I don't know if that kind of thinking is going to score you points in this business, but I admire you for it."

Grace was taken aback by the thrill she felt at B.J.'s touch, a vaguely familiar feeling, now, here again, vital and exciting. The last years with Frank had been passionless. It had been a long time since she'd been touched by a man—you couldn't count the hugs she routinely got from her father. Grace didn't want to kill the mood, but before things went any further, she had to tell B.J. that she'd mentioned his name. It shouldn't be a big deal, but you never knew how somebody would react when the police were involved. Grace would dread talking to Frank about something like this. He never wanted to get involved in anything that had any chance of causing him problems or complications.

"The police asked who was with me when I met Madeleine at Shepherd's Point," she said softly. "I told them you were."

"No problema. Let them come talk to me if they want to, Grace. I have nothing to hide." He wrapped his hand tighter around hers.

The steel band was playing on the wharf when Grace and B.J. came out of the restaurant. Caught up in the heady feeling caused by a combination of the tropical beat, the warm night air, and her companion for the evening, Grace took B.J. up on his offer of another drink.

"Do you think they make piña coladas?" she asked.

"Your wish is my command," said B.J., bowing mockingly. "I'll make it myself if the bartender won't."

As he went to the bar on the dock to retrieve their drinks, Grace leaned against the railing at the water's edge and people-watched. The crowd was a festive one, dancing and laughing under the stars. Others strolled along the wharf, stopping to look in the windows of the shops that flanked the cobblestones. Everywhere she turned there was a sense of well-being and seeming ease, and Grace felt lucky to be part of it all. Tonight, she was part of a couple enjoying a summer holiday.

She saw a man and woman stepping from a sailboat onto the dock. Grace could make out the word SEAWOLF painted on the stern. As the pair drew closer, she recognized Gordon Cox with a pretty strawberry blonde a good thirty-five years his junior. The couple was almost upon her before the professor noticed Grace and quickly dropped his companion's hand. Grace pretended she hadn't seen it.

She raised her own hand in a wave. "Hi, Professor. Nice to see you again."

"Well, hello there," the professor said. Grace was fairly certain that he didn't remember her name, and she decided to let him off the hook.

"Hi, I'm Grace Callahan," she said turning to the redhead.

"Nice to meet you. I'm Judy Hazel."

"Judy is one of my history students," the professor offered a bit too hurriedly.

"I see," said Grace. "I just wanted to tell you, Professor, you did a great job on the broadcast this morning."

"Thank you, Grace. But I must say I didn't appreciate being put on the spot like that. I didn't like speculating on what might have happened to Madeleine just to provide fodder for that executive producer of yours."

Grace didn't offer the fact that she was the one who had suggested Gordon Cox to Linus. Instead, she steered the conversation in a different direction. "What do you think will happen with the tunnel now?"

"I really don't know." Gordon shook his head. "Madeleine was Agatha Wagstaff's only heir, so I suppose, in time, there is a chance that Agatha will turn over Shepherd's Point to the Preservation Society. For now, Agatha has forbidden any more work to be done on the slave tunnel. But I haven't given up on convincing her."

By the time B.J. returned with her piña colada and his Rolling Rock, the professor and his friend had moved along. Sipping her pineapple-flavored drink, Grace felt some of the magic of the evening diminish as she thought of Madeleine and the loved ones the young woman had left behind. Her father and that reclusive aunt of hers must feel devastated.

Grace knew she was one of the last people to have talked with Madeleine before she died. She felt somehow that she should pay her respects and tell Oliver Sloane and Agatha Wagstaff that, on the night she died, Madeleine had talked about how much she loved them.

Grace and B.J. walked hand in hand across Thames Street and then up the hill on Touro Street toward the Viking. As they drew closer to the hotel, Grace felt her heart beating faster, unsure of where the night was going to end up.

They were on the porch when B.J.'s beeper went off. He unclipped it from his belt and squinted to read the message.

"Crap." B.J. angrily snapped off the beeper.

"What is it?"

"Linus wants me to edit forty-five seconds out of the scrimshaw piece."

"Now?" asked Grace aware of the disappointment in her voice.

"Now."

TUESDAY

JULY 20

CHAPTER
74

Graced watched as the second *KTA* broadcast from Newport opened. Constance and Harry stood atop a stone bastion affording them and the viewers at home an exquisite, sweeping view of Narragansett Bay. Harry delivered the introduction.

"Newport's Fort Adams is the largest coastal fortification in the United States. An engineering and architectural masterpiece, from 1824 until 1950 Fort Adams housed generations of American soldiers, but now it's the centerpiece of a state park, open for the public's enjoyment."

Constance took her turn. "This eighty-acre park is one of the great open spaces of Newport. Every summer the world's best jazz musicians perform at the Newport Jazz Festival, held on the broad field in front of the fort. We'll have some of those musicians with us today. We'll also take you on a tour of where our soldiers lived and the casements where the big guns once roared. Enter with us, if you dare, one of the listening tunnels beneath the walls of the fort. Harry and I are also going to take a little sailing lesson, and we'll have a primer on the art of scrimshaw. All that and more, this morning, on *KEY to America*."

CHAPTER
75

Last night's combination of wine and rum had left Grace feeling groggy, and the blinding sunlight hurt her eyes. The jazz musicians were no draw for her this morning. The drummer seemed to be banging extra hard just for her benefit.

She went through the motions, appearing to be interested in each segment, dreading the tour she was expected to take with Professor Cox after the broadcast. All she wanted to do was escape to her room for a little nap and, maybe, see if she could catch Lucy for a quick visit.

If she got the job with *KTA,* getting up extra early would be a way of life and she could kiss late-night socializing during the week good-bye. Not that that would be a problem, since she didn't exactly have a ripping social life. But if she got a night or early-morning shift, and B.J. continued to work during the day, their time together would be limited.

Look at yourself. Already imagining a rosy future with B.J. Take it easy, girl. One night did not a relationship make.

Grace pulled it together to focus on the piece that she had worked on with B.J., the piece that had ended up cutting their night too short. Watching one of the monitors set up on the parade field, she recognized the various scrimshaw items in Kyle Seaton's shop. As requested, the scrimshander had brought along several pieces executed on whalebone along with some synthetic pieces for the live segment following the taped package. Grace glanced over at Kyle as he waited at Constance's side, ready to go on. While watching the monitor, Kyle wiped the perspiration from his forehead, adjusted the collar of his open-necked oxford shirt, and brushed at the lapels of his navy blazer. Grace smiled wryly, remembering his haughtiness at the clambake, his dismissive attitude toward television and television people. *This guy wants to look good on TV,* she thought, *just like everyone else.*

Constance's face smiled from the monitor now as the camera came back to her. "Newport native Kyle Seaton is with us today. He is one of the premier antique scrimshaw dealers in the United States. Thank you for being here."

"My pleasure." Kyle smiled, but Grace thought she noticed his upper lip quiver.

Constance picked up a whale's tooth engraved with a multimasted sailing vessel and held it for the cameraman to get a close-up.

"How do we know if a piece of scrimshaw is authentic?" she asked. "I've seen lots of pieces of scrimshaw in the shops around town, but their price tags are so low I assume they're reproductions. What if I came across a piece at an auction or a tag sale? How would I know if I was buying the real thing?"

"Well, Constance, the existence of fakes

in today's antiques market is all too common. Many owners of fake scrimshaw think that if they put a hot needle to their piece and it doesn't melt, the piece must be real. Unfortunately, this test renders mixed results at best. The hot needle test can't always distinguish between ivory, bone, or plastics made with bonemeal. Bonemeal is a main ingredient in many fakes on the market today. It gives the product an authentic look."

"So if it's not the hot needle, what is it?" Constance asked.

"A far more effective tool is the common emery board." Kyle held up a small, round, cream-colored box and removed the lid. Holding the lid in one hand, he pulled a nail file from his pocket with his other hand and stroked it across the surface. "A simple emery board, Constance, not the metal kind. You should do this on an inconspicuous spot on the piece you are testing. See the tiny deposit of dust particles collecting on the emery board?"

Constance bent to look closer and nodded. "Uh-huh."

"Now smell it," Kyle instructed.

Constance obeyed. "It smells like plastic."

"That's right. But if you did this test on

bone, the powder would smell like just that. Burnt bone. The smell you get when you are having your teeth drilled. That smell indicates the material is organic and genuine. But the fact of the matter is, Constance—and I know this might sound self-serving—your best bet for getting authentic scrimshaw is to buy from a reputable dealer."

Kyle let out a deep sigh when the segment was over. He was relieved that it was finished, but he was angry as well. That damned idea of Grace Callahan's had set him up in a situation that could lead to his own incrimination.

CHAPTER
76

After another interminable night with barely any sleep, Oliver lay in his bed, staring at the ceiling, unwilling to get up. The house was quiet, the silence an excruciating reminder that Madeleine was gone.

He must, somehow, get on with it. But how could he? He couldn't even have her funeral since the medical examiner hadn't released Madeleine's body yet. The police didn't bother to appear sympathetic, snarling at Oliver when he called, telling him that he would get the body when they were good and ready. Oliver presumed they were angry over looking so inept in not having found Charlotte's body sooner. And he also presumed that he was still their prime suspect in that old case. He supposed the police were considering him as a suspect in Madeleine's death as well.

He didn't really care anymore what the police thought, what anyone thought. Somehow he had survived losing his wife. He couldn't possibly survive losing his daughter, too.

The grandfather clock that had been in Oliver's family for five generations chimed from the downstairs hallway, a reminder that time was passing. Other people were getting up, having breakfast, dressing for work or packing a cooler to take to the beach. Life was going on for them.

He lay there, for how long he wasn't sure. Lying in the silence until he couldn't take it anymore. Oliver picked up the remote control, pointed it at the television in the armoire, and clicked on some noise.

There was Kyle Seaton talking about authenticating scrimshaw, Oliver observed with no particular enthusiasm. He watched the man's demonstration with a surreal feeling. Once, in that other life, Oliver had spent many hours in Kyle's shop. Kyle had been endlessly patient and solicitous, helping plan the acquisitions for Oliver's scrimshaw collection. But Kyle had dropped Oliver, just like everyone else had, after Charlotte disappeared.

Oliver had tried to maintain the relationship, making it a point to drop into Kyle's shop a few months after Charlotte's disappearance and tell him how much he treasured the paperweight Kyle had helped Charlotte select as a gift for what turned out to be their last Christmas together. But the scrimshander had been cool and aloof. Oliver had taken the none-too-subtle hint and had never gone to the store again.

He switched off the set, not wanting to think any more about that painful time. He had lived all these years snubbed and reviled, trying to keep his head up. For Madeleine's sake, he had managed to go on. He had no other choice. At first, his little daughter needed him. Later, he depended more and more on her for emotional support. The spitting image of her mother, Madeleine was the only person he truly loved.

Though Elsa adored him and tried to fill in the gaps in his adult life, Oliver knew that it could never work out between them. He felt too guilty about the way he had treated Charlotte. He didn't deserve another wife and anything resembling a normal married life. All these years, Oliver had used the excuse that Charlotte had not been pronounced dead and he was still a married man, but that was just an excuse. Oliver didn't want to marry Elsa.

No, it had been just Madeleine and him. Daughter and father. And that had been enough.

He ached to have his child with him again. Oliver threw back the coverlet and pulled himself into an upright position, swiveling his legs over the side of the bed. As he stood, he felt shaky. He grabbed the bedpost to steady himself. After a few moments, the light-headedness passed and he shuffled out into the hallway and down to Madeleine's room.

It smelled like her. The fragrance of her

cologne and shampoo invaded his nostrils, striking heavily with each breath he took. Oliver sat down on Madeleine's bed and lifted the pillow from it. Holding the down cushion against his face, he wept, for how long he couldn't be certain.

Finally, he heard the mellow chimes again in the distance. He had to stop crying and call the police again. Before he did anything else, he had to see about laying his little girl to rest. Once he fulfilled that duty, he didn't care what happened.

Oliver got up from the bed, walked to Madeleine's bathroom, and splashed cold water on his face. He pulled his hand back as it instinctively reached for a towel on the rod on the wall. He couldn't use a towel that Madeleine had used just days before. That would only start him weeping again. Instead, he opened the linen closet door and pulled a freshly laundered one from the shelf.

A yellow leather volume fell to the floor. Oliver picked it up but didn't open the book. If it was Madeleine's journal, it would be impossible to read now. It would be just too painful. Should he turn it over to the police, though? If Madeleine had been murdered, perhaps there would be some clue to the killer buried in the pages of her diary.

They said there was satisfaction and a closure of sorts when a killer was brought to justice. But Oliver doubted that. Nothing was going to bring his little girl back to him. What did it matter who killed Madeleine? All Oliver knew with dead-hearted certainty was his daughter was never coming home again.

CHAPTER
77

During the last quarter hour of the broadcast, the camera followed Gordon Cox as he escorted Constance and the audience beneath the walls of the fort. The professor explained as they walked.

"Over the years the designers tried to plan for every contingency, making certain that a land attack on Fort Adams would be extremely difficult. Not only would attackers have to charge up the mounded slopes protecting the fort but they'd also face cannon and musket fire from the exterior ditches. But all that wasn't enough for the American military here. They also worried about a tunneling attack."

"You mean the enemy actually digging under the walls?" asked Constance.

Gordon nodded. "Yes. The fort's builders weren't about to let that happen. So they constructed listening tunnels, like the one we're in now. If the sounds of burrowing were ever heard, the Americans would dig their own tunnel in the direction of the noise. When they got close, they would set charges and destroy the enemy's tunnel."

"Fascinating," observed Constance. "You know, Professor, I'm struck by all the tunnels in Newport we've learned of this week. These underground listening galleries here at Fort Adams, the heating tunnel at The Breakers you spoke of yesterday, and of course, the Underground Railroad tunnel at Shepherd's Point, where sadly, the remains of Charlotte Wagstaff Sloane had been buried for years. Are there any other tunnels in Newport?"

"Yes, and I think we'll be able to show you another one while you're here, Constance."

"Good, we'll look forward to that. Thank

you, Dr. Cox, professor of history at Salve Regina University here in Newport." Constance turned to look directly into the camera lens. "Professor Cox will be with us again tomorrow morning when *KEY to America* will be coming to you from historic Bowen's Wharf on Newport Harbor."

Gordon waited impatiently as a stagehand disconnected him from the microphone paraphernalia. He limped from the darkened listening tunnel out into the sunshine.

"Did you hurt yourself?" Constance asked politely.

"No, the cartilage is shot in my knee," Gordon replied. "There's nothing left at this point. It's just bone rubbing against bone."

Constance winced. "Sounds awful."

"It is," Gordon said. "One of these days I'm going to have to get a total knee replacement, but I'm not looking forward to it."

"I don't blame you."

Zoe watched Constance and Gordon in conversation and waited for her opportunity. When the cohost shook hands with the professor and walked away, Zoe approached him.

"Professor Cox?"

"Yes?" His expression was stern.

"I'm Zoe Quigley, an intern on the show."

"Oh, yes. What can I do for you, Zoe?"

"I'm working on a project, a documentary actually, on a female slave who escaped to freedom via the maritime Underground Railroad."

"Sounds interesting."

"You're familiar with the maritime Underground Railroad then?"

Gordon was insulted. "Of course I'm familiar with it. The sea provided a major escape route for slaves seeking their freedom. What most people don't realize is that slaves who escaped often did so on their own, without the aid of abolitionist organizations. Thousands of black sailors and dockworkers created their own network to freedom, helping other slaves to escape."

Zoe was relieved. The professor knew exactly what she was referring to. She was encouraged that he might be agreeable to her request. "In fairness," said Zoe, "I've read that some white sailors and captains did their part to help, too."

Gordon nodded, warming to the intern a bit, enjoying her British accent. "Yes, that's true. The sea was the primary means of transportation in the United States before the Civil War. If a slave didn't hitch a ride on a boat, he most likely would have traveled by foot, sometimes for months. The chances of being caught and taken back to a vengeful master were much greater on land."

An image of a black woman thrashing through a swamp, listening to the angry yelps of bloodhounds relentlessly tracking her flashed through Zoe's mind. How much better to hide yourself away in the boiler room or cargo hold of a ship. The accommodations may have been sweltering and suffocating, but the trip was quicker, freedom that much nearer. Mariah had been wise to choose this route.

"In my research, I've come across the paper you wrote on the slave tunnel at Shepherd's Point, Professor Cox. And I've read about your plans to work with the Preservation Society and the National Park Service to open the tunnel to the public and make it part of the National Underground Railroad Network to Freedom program."

Gordon smiled, basking in the flattery. "Yes. That's our goal."

Seeing his pleasure, Zoe decided that now

was the time to go for it. "I'm sure you can see, the slave tunnel at Shepherd's Point is a key element for my documentary, Professor Cox. I must get video of the tunnel where slaves ran from the sea to freedom, and I was hoping that you'd be able to help me."

"You mean take you to the tunnel?" Gordon's expression soured. "I'm afraid that would be impossible. Agatha Wagstaff has forbidden anyone from entering."

Zoe was not about to give up. "But perhaps if you appealed to Miss Wagstaff, she might make an exception, for the sake of education," she pleaded.

"I'm sorry, Zoe." Gordon was resolute. "I can't help you. Now, if you'll excuse me, I have some work to do."

Can't or won't? Zoe wondered angrily, as the professor limped away. She was even more piqued as she watched Gordon beckon to Grace Callahan.

CHAPTER 78

Grace tried to make small talk on the ride from Fort Adams to the limestone chateau on Bellevue Avenue. But her attempts to engage the professor in conversation were met with short answers.

As she stood in the cold kitchen of The Elms, Grace had the feeling that Professor Cox didn't want to be here. Maybe he thought she was beneath him. But she had her assignment, and tired or not, she was determined to carry it out. She scribbled notes on a yellow legal pad, gathering preliminary information for the segment scheduled to air Thursday morning on what it was like for the servants who worked behind the scenes at one of the fabulous mansions.

"There were forty-three in staff," Gordon recited. "Twenty-seven worked in the house, and sixteen worked outside: a head gardener, two greenhouse men, two gardeners, two grounds-keepers, a chauffeur, three grooms, a coachman, two footmen and a . . ." Gordon paused, searching his memory. "I've forgotten now who the last outside workers were. If you really need it, you can ask a docent."

They walked across the terrazzo floor, past a wooden trunk for storing silver that was big enough to hold a human body, and into the sprawling laundry room.

"This is where all the laundry was done for the Berwind family, their guests, and the staff. There were no dry-cleaning services, so all the linens and uniforms were also done here." Gordon motioned downward. "Maids scrubbed the floors, down on their hands and knees. The expression 'Elms' knees' came into the vernacular to describe the ruined knees that resulted."

"That's interesting," said Grace as she wrote on her pad.

"Now we'll go down to the furnace room."

They climbed down the metal steps into a cavernous, underground room. A giant cast-iron furnace dominated the space. But Grace's attention was drawn to the opening at the side of the room.

"That's the coal tunnel," said Gordon, following her gaze. "Mr. Berwind, like Mr. Vanderbilt, didn't want unsightly fuel deliveries made in full view of the residents. So the coal was dropped through a chute behind a fence on the road at the side of the mansion into the tunnel below. Forty tons of it could be stored here at a time. It was moved in five-ton batches, loaded onto that big cart on those mini-railroad tracks, and rolled into the boiler room."

Grace approached the tunnel opening, aware of the musty smell. Lit with electric lights, the tunnel's redbrick walls were damp to the touch.

"The Elms was one of the last cottages built during the Gilded Age," the professor continued. "The electrical system was so modern and expertly installed that it still functions today."

But Grace was more interested in the tunnel.

"If I go out to the side street, will I be able to still see the chute where the coal was dropped?"

"Yes," said Gordon, "but there's really not much to see. There are just metal doors set into the sidewalk, covering the chute. Eventually they had to alarm them to keep kids and vandals out." Gordon began his climb back up the stairs. "Come on," he said, wincing at the tightness in his knee. "We still have a drying room, an ice-making room, a root cellar, a wine cellar, a pastry kitchen, a cooking kitchen, and a butler's pantry to see—and, oh yes, there's also some china displayed in the mezzanine pantry."

"I'm right behind you," she said, still enthralled by the tunnel.

CHAPTER
79

When Grace arrived back at the hotel, she bumped into her daughter in the lobby.

"Lucy, honey, what are you doing down here all by yourself?" she asked, giving her girl a big hug.

"Dad and Jan are in the dining room finishing lunch. I wanted to check the gift shop to see if I could find a souvenir for Grandpa."

"Find anything?"

"Yeah." Lucy held up a paper bag and pulled a long, tissue-wrapped item from it. "I got him a letter opener, Mom. You know how Grandpa is always doing his bills and paper-work," she said, unwrapping the tissue and holding up the opener for Grace's inspec-tion. "It's scrimshaw," Lucy said proudly. "You know what that is, don't you? They carve de-signs on whale teeth. Newport used to be a whaling port."

"That was a great choice, Luce. Grandpa will absolutely love it." Grace couldn't bear to tell her excited child that her gift was made of plastic. Maybe someday she would show Lucy the scrimshaw test that she had just learned about, but this certainly wasn't the time.

"Are you having a good time, honey?"

"The best. Yesterday we took a tour of two mansions. It was really cool to see how the rich people lived. And we had lunch at the Tennis Hall of Fame. They had really good soup with clams in it. I didn't think I would like it, but Daddy made me try it, and I was glad I did. It's my new favorite now." The en-thusiasm dripped from Lucy, her face ani-mated and shining. But then it clouded as she looked at her mother, as if she suddenly felt she was being disloyal. "That's really all we did," she added hastily.

"Lucy, believe me, sweetheart, I'm so glad that you are having a great time. I want you to have a good time with your father."

"I know you do, Mom. But are you having any fun?"

Even if she weren't, Grace would have said she was. Fortunately, she didn't have to fib.

"Yes, I am. It's been really interesting, and I've met some great people and I'm learning a lot. As a matter of fact, I just came back from a mansion tour myself. The Elms." Grace went on to give a thumbnail sketch of what she'd seen, spending the most time on what was most memorable to her.

Lucy's face perked up again. "The tunnel sounds awesome, Mom. I sure wish I could see it."

"Ask Daddy if you can take the tour." Grace kissed her daughter on the forehead. "Well, all right, honey. I've got to get some lunch. You better go back now to Daddy and Jan."

Unfortunately, Grace missed her escape by moments. Frank and Jan arrived in the lobby as if on cue. Once again, Grace felt bedraggled when she observed Jan's immaculate appearance. She smiled politely and asked what the happy family's plans were for the rest of day.

"We're off to take a sailing tour of Newport Harbor and the Narragansett Bay on a seventy-two-foot schooner," Frank announced. "Then we have an appointment with a real estate agent later this afternoon."

"Daddy and Jan might buy a summer place in Newport, Mom." Again, there was that enthusiasm in Lucy's voice.

"Is that so?" Grace kept her expression pleasant, while inwardly she seethed. *You haven't sent your child support payment, you bum, but you can afford a second home.*

"Yeah, well, you know, things are going pretty well with the business," Frank boasted, oblivious to his insult. "And I've always liked it here. I came up here the summer that I was nineteen for my scuba-diving certification test. I took it right off the rocks out at Shepherd's Point."

Grace did the mental math. She was thirty-two, and Frank was a year older. He was nineteen years old and in Newport the summer that Charlotte Sloane disappeared.

CHAPTER
80

No one had seen Sam Watkins since Sunday night. The intern had not called. His room had not been entered, except by Grace yesterday morning, and then again this morning by security, at Beth Terry's request. His bed still hadn't been slept in, and none of his belongings seemed to have been touched.

Beth didn't care if Linus liked it or not. She was calling the police to report a missing person.

CHAPTER
81

In the Bellevue Ballroom, a buffet lunch was being served. Grace noticed with pleasure that it wasn't the usual sandwiches and potato chips. There were platters of hot pastas with seafood, primavera and marinara sauces, and big bowls of green salads sprinkled with cucumber, olives, and bright red tomatoes. Large loaves of crusty Italian bread were arranged, sliced on a wooden cutting board. Beside the board, a tiny card announced that the buffet had been prepared by Seasons Catering.

Grace got on the buffet line behind Beth Terry. "This looks great," Grace said. "And it smells even better."

Beth heaped a spoonful of the seafood pasta on her plate. "I'm so tired of ordering the same ol' deli stuff. So I got the name of the guy who did Joss Vickers's party, and it turns out he does more than just clambakes." Beth continued on to the pasta primavera and Italian bread, and piled some of that on her plate, too.

With her plate in hand, Grace looked around the newsroom, ostensibly searching for a place to sit down and eat. More important, she was hoping to find B.J. But he was nowhere to be seen. Grace sought out another intern as a lunch companion and spotted Zoe eating by herself at the side of the room.

"He went out to a winery to shoot for his piece tomorrow," Zoe announced, seeming to read Grace's mind.

"Who?" Grace felt herself blush.

"B.J.," Zoe said. "That's who you were looking for, wasn't it?"

Was she that obvious to everyone?

"And he took Joss along with him." Zoe delivered the stinger, spearing a ripe wedge of tomato with her plastic fork.

It was absolutely ridiculous to feel hurt or slighted in any way. After all, she hadn't been around this morning for B.J. to ask that she accompany him to the winery. He had every right, perhaps even a responsibility, to give another intern some field experience. Still, Grace was disappointed that he hadn't tracked her down or beeped her. Even worse, he had asked Joss instead.

She finished her lunch, unable to really enjoy it, and tossed the plate and utensils in the trash receptacle near the doorway. There was no point in brooding. There was nothing she could do about it.

Actually, this might work out well. She would skip the nap she had been hoping to catch. If no one in the newsroom had anything for her to do this afternoon, Grace could take the opportunity to go out to Shepherd's Point.

Maybe Agatha Wagstaff would be willing to see her, maybe the old recluse wouldn't. But Grace felt she had to make the attempt to tell the woman about her last conversation with Madeleine. If something happened to someone Grace loved, she would want to know what had occurred immediately before the person died. And if the loved one had spoken about Grace, she would want to know that, too.

Grace checked with the assignment desk, learned that she was free for the next few hours, and went out onto the porch of the hotel, asking the doorman to summon a cab.

CHAPTER
82

As Grace's cab pulled out of one side of the driveway, a police car pulled in the other. Officer James was driving. He was excited at the prospect of surprising Joss where she worked.

"This is all we need," groaned Detective Manzorella from the passenger seat. "The Sloane girl dead, now a student intern missing. If this one hits the local papers, we're going to have the mayor barking at us again. Crime doesn't foster summer tourism."

Inside the ballroom, Mickey oversaw the buffet cleanup. He wanted to make sure that, start to finish, this first job for the TV network went well.

KEY News was a prestigious client to add to his roster. Though the news team might not be in Newport again to order from Seasons for a long time, Mickey wanted them to be satisfied. He hoped to get a quote for the "Satisfied Customers" page in his brochure and website. That heavy woman who had placed the order had already offered to give him a rave. But Mickey was hoping for someone a little higher up the food chain than Beth Terry.

Constance Young hadn't touched the buffet, but Harry Granger looked like he had enjoyed it. He had gone up to the serving table twice. Mickey was about to approach the *KTA* host with his request when he noticed the tall policeman standing in the doorway. Mickey had a visceral urge to flee.

Be calm, he told himself. It was only Tommy James, and Al Manzorella along with him. *You've known these guys for years. They aren't even looking for you. They couldn't have known you'd be here.*

But when you had a guilty conscience, you feared that anyone could discover your secret.

*   *   *

The detective and patrolman crossed the newsroom to the assignment desk.

"We're looking for Beth Terry."

"That's me."

Al and Tommy identified themselves. "Thanks for calling in with the information, Miss Terry," said the detective. "We'd like to talk to anyone who might know anything about Sam Watkins. What he did that night, who he talked to."

Beth glanced nervously around the newsroom to make sure Linus wasn't there. "Well, I suppose the thing that stands out most for me is that Sam was scheduled to appear on *KTA* the next morning. His face had been shown on a promo, not identifying him by name but touting him as an eyewitness to Madeleine Sloane's murder."

So this was *that* kid, thought Tommy James with anger, recalling the resistance the night-shift guys had reported getting when they'd come here Sunday night. If they'd identified Sam Watkins then, they might not be in this mess now.

"We'd like a copy of that video of Sam, Miss Terry, so we can get a picture out of it for our investigation and search." Detective Manzorella made a notation in his book.

"Certainly," said Beth. "We have the equipment to isolate that picture for you here, Detective."

"Can you suggest anyone else we should talk to?" asked Al.

"Scott Huffman, the satellite truck operator, was the last one I know of who saw him. Scott's down at Bowen's Wharf getting the truck in position for the broadcast tomorrow morning." Beth bit her bottom lip, trying to think of who else might be able to help the police. "Maybe the other interns?" she offered, looking around the newsroom again. "But Joss Vickers is out on a shoot right now. I don't know where Zoe Quigley has gone off to. And you just missed Grace Callahan. I know Grace said that she bumped into Sam outside on the porch just before he left to go over to The Breakers Sunday night."

Hearing the name, Detective Manzorella made the connection. Grace Callahan had come to the station the day before with the story about the dream Madeleine Sloane had confided to her shortly before she died. The same Grace Callahan had been the one to talk to Sam Watkins right before he disappeared. Maybe Grace Callahan was more involved in this than was healthy for her.

CHAPTER 83

"You better let me off here," said Grace as the cab arrived at the gate to Shepherd's Point. She paid the driver, suddenly realizing she'd have no way back to the hotel once he drove away. "If I call you later, will you come to pick me up?"

"Sure, but it might take a while for me to get back out here."

"That's fine. Thank you very much."

Terence was not stationed at the entrance to the estate this afternoon, and Grace was glad. She didn't want to have to talk her way onto the grounds. The gate was slightly ajar, as if no one cared enough anymore to bother trying to keep intruders away. As Grace entered, she was reminded of that first meeting with Madeleine at this gate just a few short days ago.

The cats lying in the sun glanced disinterestedly at Grace as she walked up the long driveway. Heat waves shimmered above the overgrown shrubs and uncut grass. She felt a bead of perspiration trickle down her side.

The shade of the porte cochere was a relief. Grace walked up the steps, took a deep breath, and knocked on the peeling door. After a few moments, a glowering elderly woman appeared.

"Hello. My name is Grace Callahan. Are you Miss Wagstaff?"

"No. I'm her housekeeper."

"Oh. Well, I was hoping that Miss Wagstaff would be able to see me."

"About what?" The housekeeper eyed Grace with suspicion.

"Actually, this is a condolence call about her niece."

"Well, thank you very much for coming, but Miss Agatha isn't receiving anyone right now."

Grace had no intention of forcing herself on the grieving woman. "All right," she said. "But would you please tell Miss Wagstaff how sorry I am and that I was with her niece the night she died. Madeleine spoke of how much she loved her aunt. I hope Miss Wagstaff will find some comfort in that."

The housekeeper nodded and started to shut the door as Grace turned to leave. She had reached the bottom step when she heard the aristocratic voice.

"Let the young woman in, Finola."

The stench of cat urine was nauseating. As Grace followed Agatha into the darkened deck room, she stifled a gag. Didn't they smell it? If Grace stayed in this house, she was afraid she was going to vomit all over the worn carpet.

"I'm so sorry, Miss Wagstaff, but I have a cat dander allergy," Grace fibbed. "Is there any possibility that we could speak outside?"

If once Agatha would have balked, today she didn't care. "Finola," she called. "Please bring me my parasol."

"This was one of Madeleine's favorite spots," Agatha murmured as they walked down the fieldstone steps from the veranda into the terraced garden. "She loved to play here as a child. She'd sit on that bench over there and play with her dolls and sing songs by the hour. Madeleine was such a joy to have around. Such a comfort."

With sympathy, Grace gazed at the older woman. Despite the shade afforded by the faded parasol, the afternoon light was unforgiving. Agatha's wrinkles were etched deeply in her almost translucent skin. Grace marveled that, in spite of her grief, Agatha had still managed to apply her crimson lipstick.

"Should we sit on Madeleine's bench?" Agatha asked.

"Yes. That would be nice."

As they sat side by side, Grace began to recount her story, but found herself editing out the part about Madeleine's dream. She didn't want to upset the old lady further by bringing up her sister's murder.

"Madeleine told me that you had showered her with affection and that she loved you very, very much."

Agatha reached over and took hold of Grace's arm. "You don't know how much it means to me to hear that. I did my best to care for Madeleine, especially after her mother wasn't here anymore. I came to despise Oliver after Charlotte disappeared and all the talk was that he had killed my sister. But, to his credit, he didn't keep Madeleine from me. I'm so grateful for that."

Loosening her grasp on Grace's arm, Agatha got up from the bench. "I want to show you something."

On her spindly legs, Agatha stepped gingerly into the brambles at the center of the garden. She pulled back some overgrown brush. "Come look at this, Grace."

Beneath the weeds, Grace could make out the shape of an iron circle. A thin triangle projected from the face of a clock. A sundial.

"See the inscription? It says 'Time Flies, Love Stays.' That's what I will try to remember, Grace. Love stays."

"That's a beautiful sentiment," Grace whispered.

"I know it is. Madeleine's mother loved it, as did our mother before her. My father had earrings made for my mother, tiny versions of this sundial. I gave them to Charlotte. After everything happened, I asked Oliver for them back, but he said Charlotte was wearing them the night she disappeared."

Grace recalled the single earring Charlotte was wearing in Madeleine's dream. So, this was the design of that earring. What had happened to its mate? she wondered.

CHAPTER 84

Lifting the heavy iron seagull door knocker, Mickey was relieved to have gotten away from the hotel and the police, but he was not exactly looking forward to his meeting with Elsa Gravell to go over the last-minute details for the Ball Bleu. He thought her obsession with birds bordered on weird. It was one thing to have a hobby, but Elsa had taken her fascination to another level.

Elsa answered the door, wearing a pale green linen dress with a canary pin attached at the shoulder. "Mr. Hager, please come in."

He followed her into the parlor noticing, as he had the first time he had come here to make plans for the party, the pains to which Elsa had gone to implement her bird theme. The sofas and club chairs were covered with fabrics printed with parrots and cockatoos in vibrant colors. Antique brass cages, with tiny glass birds sitting on wooden perches, were displayed on tables and on the fireplace mantel. Every lamp had some sort of bird included in the motif on its porcelain base. The large round coffee table was stacked with heavy books on birding. Audubon prints of owls, seagulls, hawks, and woodpeckers hung from the walls. The place was bright enough, Mickey thought, taking a seat on top of a parrot-covered cushion, but it creeped him out.

"I have the final head count for you here," said Elsa, handing Mickey a sheet of paper. "The turnout is gratifying."

Mickey glanced at the sheet. "Fine. This is just about what we were expecting."

"I suppose you want the next-to-last payment now," said Elsa.

"Yes, ma'am."

Elsa went to the desk, took the checkbook from the drawer, and after writing out the agreed amount, handed the check to him. "I'll have the rest of it for you Thursday morning, provided, of course, all goes well."

"Oh, everything will go well, Miss Gravell. You can be assured of that." Mickey followed

Elsa back out to the spacious foyer, sure that she had no memory of him as the young kid waiting tables at the country club all those years ago. Those rich people never gave him the time of day.

Except for Charlotte Sloane. And the attention she gave him wasn't the kind he wanted. Mickey had been rewriting those deposit slips for over a year, and Oliver Sloane had never caught on, as a club treasurer should have. He had a drink in his hand whenever Mickey saw him, and Oliver had been glad to have Mickey do the grunt work of going to the bank and making the deposits. It was easy for Mickey to steal blank deposit slips from the office, rewrite them, and skim off the excess for himself. Oliver never even glanced at them when the slips came back from the bank.

It could have gone on forever. But Charlotte must have realized that Oliver wasn't paying attention. She went over the books herself and realized that there should have been more money in the account.

Thank God, Charlotte's first priority had been protecting her husband's reputation. She had added her own money to the account to shield Oliver. But she had demanded that Mickey resign. If he didn't, Charlotte was going to expose him.

For all its size and population, Newport was still, in so many respects, a small town. People knew one another's business. Mickey had no intention of leaving Newport and no intention of being disgraced.

How ironic, he thought as he heard Elsa close the door behind him. Charlotte had confronted him with her ultimatum, pulling him aside at that first, small Endangered Bird fund-raiser all those years ago. Now he was running one of Newport society's biggest summer bashes. He'd been a servant then, but a kid with much bigger plans for himself. Plans he wouldn't alter.

CHAPTER
85

Zoe was disappointed. She had slipped away from the KEY newsroom and taken the sixty-five-minute ferry ride all the way up to Providence, thinking she was going to get some video of the famous building. The Bethel Church, the oldest black church in Rhode Island, with its reputation as a monument to freedom, had served for many years as a destination on the Underground Railroad for fleeing southern slaves—the place at which Mariah had stopped on her way to Canada.

But the church was gone. There was only a plaque to mark the former site of the Bethel African Methodist Episcopal Church, the spot now a tree-lined walkway near the Brown University campus.

Zoe shot a minute of tape of the plaque anyway. Hardly exciting video. Hardly worth the effort and time it had taken away from her internship. But she supposed she'd be glad to have the video later as another vignette for her documentary.

She hadn't given up getting the most important video—of the slave tunnel at Shepherd's Point. Since Professor Cox wasn't going to help her, she had another plan. The video that B.J. and Grace had brought back that first day from their trip to Shepherd's Point sat on the file-tape shelves at the side of the ballroom. Tonight, she could sneak downstairs and dub off the video of the slave tunnel and nobody would be the wiser.

She retraced her steps to the trolley stop and boarded the green bus. The trolley dropped her off at the Point Street Landing, where the ferry going south to Newport was waiting.

Watching the steeples of the Newport shoreline come into view, Zoe pictured the beautiful town as it must have been when it was one of the major slave markets in the American colonies. Although the slave trade and plantations were considered southern ways of life, Zoe had learned that they had existed far beyond the South, right through the Revolutionary War.

The summer breeze blowing off the water felt soothing as the ferry pulled into the dock at Perrotti Park. Zoe picked up her knapsack from the bench and waited for the signal to disembark. A man was handing out flyers to the passengers who streamed off the ferry. He looked familiar to Zoe, but she couldn't quite place the face until she read the paper he handed to her.

Times must be tough, she thought, now recognizing the man who had entertained everyone with his body painting at the clambake. The flyer offered two tattoos for the price of one.

CHAPTER
86

The satellite truck operator didn't have too much to say when the police went to question him on Bowen's Wharf. Scott Huffman had left Sam Watkins to guard his precious trailer while he went to get a few things at the store. When he got back, Sam wasn't there.

"The kid said he had to take a whiz. I told him there was a bathroom in the gatekeeper's cottage. That's the last I spoke to him."

Tommy James had a hunch he thought was worth pursuing, if only to make sure that the Newport police were not caught with especially messy egg on their faces. Anyone who had ever taken a tour of The Breakers knew about the tunnel beneath the property. Ignoring the slave tunnel at Shepherd's Point for fourteen years had been a fiasco in the Charlotte Sloane case. Tommy reasoned that, since Sam Watkins had disappeared just outside the Vanderbilt estate, the first place to rule out was the tunnel that ran from the gatekeeper's cottage up to the mansion.

CHAPTER
87

Grace bumped into B.J. in the hotel lobby.

"I've been looking for you," he said. "Where you been?"

"I had some things to do," answered Grace, holding back telling him about her trip to Shepherd's Point to see Agatha, still smarting because B.J. had taken Joss with him on the winery shoot.

"I looked for you this morning after the broadcast to see if you wanted to go out on the shoot with me, Grace."

You didn't look very hard, did you? You didn't beep me, Grace thought.

"No problem," she lied.

"Well, a bunch of us are going out for drinks and something to eat in a little while. Want to come?"

Why not? What else was she going to do? Sit alone up in her room, watch a movie, and sulk?

"Sure," she said. "Sounds like fun."

The hostess told them it would be an hour before they'd be seated in Salas' dining room, but Joss assured everyone that the wait was worth it. "They have really good lobster, and the Oriental spaghetti is the best. Let's go down to the bar, and they'll let us know when our table is ready."

Grace was struck by the democratic camaraderie of their group. Constance and Harry, the cohosts, were right there along with the interns. B.J., Beth Terry, and Dominick O'Donnell completed the group.

The beers were icy cold, and the first ones were swallowed in short order.

"Here's to Sam," said B.J., raising his glass. "Let's hope he turns up soon."

"And in one piece," Beth added.

"This better not be some sort of crazy, attention-getting stunt," Harry growled.

"I doubt that," said Grace. "From the little I

know about Sam, I'd say he wouldn't do anything to jeopardize his internship."

They were on the third round when the hostess came to tell them their table for eight was ready. Grace noticed that Constance and Harry left their untouched bottles on the bar, but the others in the party carried theirs upstairs.

Grace broke off from the group to make a stop in the ladies' room. Zoe followed. In the cramped space in front of the sinks, they stood and washed their hands.

"I wasn't there when the police came this afternoon to inquire about Sam. Were you, Grace?"

"No," said Grace, ripping a paper towel from the wall dispenser.

"Actually, I think I may ring them up tomorrow. I might have something that could help."

"Really? What?"

"I was running near The Breakers Sunday night, and I saw an auto tear off on the street around the corner from the mansion. It almost ran me down. It might be nothing, but I think I should mention it."

"What kind of car was it?" asked Grace.

Zoe shrugged. "I don't know my American auto models and it was dark, so I couldn't even make out what color it was. But I did see a bit of the license plate. I noticed the first three letters, S-E-A."

"Zoe, you've got to tell the police."

Somewhere between the garlic bread and the lobster, amid raucous comments and laughter, the subject of tattoos came up.

"I have a tiny butterfly," Joss offered.

"Where?" asked B.J.

"I'm not telling." Joss smiled tauntingly.

Grace wanted to wipe the smirk off her competition's face.

"I don't have the guts to get one," said Beth. "It's so"—she searched for the word—"permanent."

"You could get the kind that Grace got," said Joss. "A henna one." She said it in a tone that Grace felt portrayed her as a sissy.

"Well, if you decide you want one, there's a special running at Broadway Tattoos," Zoe piped up. "The bloke was handing out flyers advertising 'two for one' today."

"Really?" asked Joss. "I was thinking of getting another one."

As if the special price mattered a hill of beans to you, thought Grace.

"Anyone else game?" asked Joss, looking directly at Grace as if daring her.

What the heck? Why shouldn't she get one? It would be a lifelong reminder of her mother, as well as a memento of her first trip with KEY News. The first of many, she hoped. Grace was determined to get the job and, now, with three beers under her belt, determined to beat out Joss Vickers.

"I will," she answered, picking up the gauntlet. "Let's go after dinner."

CHAPTER
88

Their group shrank. Constance and Harry begged off, citing the fact they had to be bright-eyed and bushy-tailed for their on-air performance in the morning. Beth and Dom said they were tired, and Zoe said she had something to care of back at the hotel. So it was only Grace, Joss, and B.J. who actually made it to Broadway Tattoos.

On the sidewalk out in front of the shop, Grace looked at the hot pink neon sign that blazed from the window and considered backing out. The guy who had painted the henna tattoo for her at the clambake had told her it would hurt like the dickens to have a real one engraved on the top of her foot. But she'd made it through childbirth. How bad could this be? Grace threw back her shoulders and led the way into the shop.

The proprietor sat reading a *Playboy* magazine. He looked up as the threesome entered and stared at the two women.

"You're the girls from the clambake the other night, aren't you?"

Grace nodded as Joss ignored the man and walked over to study the tattoo designs tacked along the wall.

"All three of you getting tattoos?" Rusty asked hopefully.

"Just the two ladies," B.J. answered.

"What'll it be?" asked Rusty.

"I don't know," said Joss, perusing the wall. "I was hoping for something a little different. I don't see anything here that turns me on."

Rusty pulled a ringed binder from behind the counter. "I have some other designs here. Some of my personal artwork. Take a look and see if there's anything you like."

Joss flipped the cellophane-covered pages while Grace stood beside her.

"I'd like an ivy leaf, just like the henna one you did for me at the party," she said as she watched Joss turn the pages. Toward the middle of the book, Joss stopped to study a particular design.

A circle with numbers around the edges, the face of a clock. "TIME FLIES, LOVE STAYS" engraved at top and bottom. Grace recognized it immediately as the design of the sundial at Shepherd's Point. How weird that it would appear in Rusty's "personal" art.

"Where did you get the idea for this one?" Joss asked, knowing full well that it was the design of the earring that had been found with Charlotte Sloane's body, the earring Tommy had shown her.

Rusty hesitated. "Oh, I don't know. It just came to me somehow."

Just then, B.J.'s beeper sounded. Reading the text message, he whistled through his teeth.

"What is it?" Grace asked.

"They've found Sam. Let's go."

CHAPTER
89

On the WPRI eleven o'clock news, the recovery of Sam Watkins from the coal tunnel at The Breakers was the lead story. There was no video to broadcast since there hadn't been enough time to get a reporter and camera crew down to the Vanderbilt estate. Instead, the local news anchor, with a "This just in" graphic over his left shoulder, read from the teleprompter above the camera lens.

"Tonight, Newport police found a KEY News intern who had been missing since Sunday lying unconscious in a tunnel at The Breakers. Twenty-one-year-old Sam Watkins, of Hollis, Oklahoma, and a senior at Northwestern University, was rushed to Newport Hospital, where he is in critical condition. Watkins was doing an internship with

Key to America in Newport, where the morning news program is broadcasting this week. The recovery of Watkins in the Vanderbilt tunnel comes on the heels of the discovery last week of the remains of Newport socialite Charlotte Sloane in a tunnel at Shepherd's Point after she had been missing for fourteen years. Charlotte Sloane's daughter, Madeleine, died Saturday after a fall down the steps at Newport's Cliff Walk. Police are investigating whether, or how, the incidents are related."

CHAPTER
90

With any luck, the intern wouldn't make it. Chances had to be good that he wouldn't survive. Sam Watkins had been cracked across the skull with a tire iron and left alone, beneath the ground, for two full days with no food, no water, no treatment for his head wound. That Sam had lived at all was only a testament to his youth and his attacker's stupidity.

"I should have made certain the kid was dead," the assailant muttered aloud, snapping off the television. The force of the blow to the head should have killed him, just as it had Charlotte. A tire iron from the trunk, a shovel from the playhouse hearth—they were basically the same. Deadly when wielded as weapons.

The report said that Sam was unconscious, and tomorrow, a trip to the hospital could ascertain if that remained true. If Sam came to, he would have to be permanently silenced. But there was still a chance that nature would take its course and, without anything more having to be done, Sam would just die on his own.

Right now, there was another, more immediate detail that had to be attended to. Now that Sam had been found in the tunnel at The Breakers, anyone in the neighborhood who had seen anything suspicious would be offering what they knew. If that black jogger came forward with details about the car she'd seen speeding away down the side street near the mansion, everyone would know exactly where to come looking.

How convenient of her to have supplied her own name on the T-shirt she wore that night. Quigley of KEY News.

WEDNESDAY

JULY 21

CHAPTER
91

"Hello. I'd like to leave a message for Zoe Quigley."

"If you don't want to wake her, I can connect you to her voice mail," offered the hotel's overnight operator.

"Actually, I was hoping that you could take the message down for me and deliver it to her yourself at three-thirty A.M. She's not expecting to have to get up this early, and I'm worried that she won't wake up. It's essential that she gets this message." *And it's essential that my voice is not on any recordings,* the killer thought.

"All right, go ahead, please."

"Great. Would you please tell Zoe that she's needed down at the wharf for the broadcast. She should be there by four A.M."

"Yes. I'll see that Miss Quigley gets the message."

"Thank you very much," said the killer, hanging up the phone.

CHAPTER
92

The hotel room was pitch dark when Zoe awoke to the screeching ring. She fumbled for the telephone receiver next to the bed and listened to the message the operator delivered.

All right, Zoe thought, as she rose. *Finally, they actually need me for something. Wouldn't you know, it would be this morning.* She had hoped to get up early and make that dub of the slave tunnel video. She hadn't been able to do it—not with all the hubbub in the newsroom about Sam Watkins last night. After coming back from the restaurant, she'd watched the local news reports along with the other *KTA* staffers clustered in the newsroom. Then, she'd gone directly to bed.

She had slept fitfully. That Oriental spaghetti hadn't set well with her. Zoe was tempted to call down to the newsroom and tell them that she was sick but then rejected the idea. She wanted to find out what was happening with Sam.

She took a quick rinse in the shower, grabbed some clean clothes from her suitcase, and dressed. Slipping her billfold and key card into the pocket of her cotton trousers, Zoe walked out the door.

It was still dark as she exited the hotel onto Bellevue Avenue and walked up the short block to Church Street. She turned right and started down the hill toward the harbor.

The car pulled slowly away from the curb and made the same right-hand turn. Church Street was deserted. No one was up yet.

In the darkness, the headlights had to be switched on. There she was on the sidewalk. Parked vehicles at the curb protected her.

She would have to cross the street soon. At the intersection, Zoe Quigley would be vulnerable.

The car slowed almost to a stop, waiting for Zoe to reach the trap. As the young woman reached the corner, she noticed the headlights, though the car itself was not visible behind the glare. The vehicle came to a complete standstill. Thinking it was waiting for her to cross the street, Zoe stepped from the curb.

The driver floored the accelerator pedal just as Zoe was able to read all six letters on the vanity license plate, a second before the full force of the vehicle knocked her to the ground. The driver shifted the car into reverse, rolled back over Zoe, and then forward again, for good measure, before speeding off.

CHAPTER
93

By habit, Izzie whisked the kettle from the top of the stove the instant it started to whistle. There was really no reason to act so quickly anymore. With Padraic gone, there was no one to wake with the noise.

She forced herself to put a slice of raisin bread into the toaster, though, as usual, Izzie wasn't hungry. Nothing tasted good to her anymore, and she no longer had the cravings for chocolate and sweets that had once been her downfall. Once, she had worried that she was too heavy; now she knew that she was way too thin.

Her clothes hung from her body, but Izzie had no desire to spend good money for new duds. She didn't go anywhere except to work at the hotel and to church. She had her chambermaid's uniform for the Viking, and God didn't care how she looked or what she wore. It wasn't like the old days, when she wanted to please Paddy. When they would go out dancing at the Hibernian. When they would save up for a lobster dinner at Christie's.

Those days were over. Two packs of cigarettes each day had seen to that for Paddy. And soon, cancer was going to take her, too.

The toast popped. Izzie spread a bit of butter on the bread and took an unenthusiastic bite. Sipping her tea, she braced herself for the morning ahead. If she could pace herself, she should be able to make it through another day of making beds and cleaning up other people's messes.

Izzie glanced disinterestedly at the stack of unopened mail which had accumulated on the kitchen table. Too bad God had never blessed her and Paddy with children, she thought. Then there would be a reason to fight on. But there just wasn't anymore.

CHAPTER
94

That little bastard didn't show up Monday morning, but this is even better, thought Linus as he shaved. The executive producer cared less about his intern's medical condition than he did about a potentially sensational story.

Linus had ordered a remote camera to be set up at Newport Hospital, and Lauren Adams would report live from there with the

Sam Watkins story. Lauren would, as much as possible, link the intern who had been found trapped in The Breakers' tunnel to the deaths of Charlotte and Madeleine Sloane. For Linus, that was killing several birds with one stone, not the least important of which was massaging Lauren's outsize ego. She had been nagging him all week for more time on the air.

He came out of the bathroom and glanced at the rumpled bed linens where Lauren had slept just an hour before. If Linus wanted to continue having a good time, he'd have to make certain that Lauren got more face time. This should satisfy her. She was scheduled for the top of the show, and he'd made sure she got B. J. D'Elia as her producer.

Linus finished dressing and went out to the car that was waiting for him in front of the hotel.

"Can't you make a right here down to the wharf?" he asked the driver as the car didn't slow down at the first turn.

"Yeah, usually you can. But they have the street blocked off. There's some sort of accident down there."

CHAPTER
95

"Check with the nurses' station again on Sam's condition, Grace, will you?" Lauren commanded rather than asked.

"All right," Grace answered, doubting that it would be any different from when she'd checked fifteen minutes ago. *Why not wait until just before the report began to make sure you had the most current news?* Instead, Grace felt she was bugging the nurses, who were already getting exasperated with the repeated questioning.

She left B.J. and Lauren to confer beside the satellite truck in the hospital parking lot. As she crossed to the entrance of the building, an ambulance sped past her, pulling into the emergency room bay.

"We've got a DOA," Grace heard the paramedic announce as he opened the double doors at the back of the ambulance. "We lost her on the ride over."

Grace watched as the stretcher was lifted out. The poor soul's face was already covered, but a dark-skinned hand with long, slender fingers dangled from the side. A female's hand. A young black female's hand.

"Any ID?" asked the nurse who had come out to meet the ambulance.

"Yeah," the attendant said. "The card in her wallet says her name is Zoe Quigley."

CHAPTER
96

Professor Cox limped across the cobblestones, aware that he was late. Late, at least, by that slave driver Linus Nazareth's standards. Linus wanted the historian to be on the set an hour before the broadcast actually went on air. Something about being available for any last-minute questions from the writers. So far, Gordon had not been asked a single one.

Showing up this early was another waste of his time, but he was being paid well, making enough this week to more than pay for a first-class vacation during the Christmas break. And Linus had mentioned something about working for *KTA* again, perhaps when they did a remote from Williamsburg. Gordon knew a good thing when he saw it. He didn't want to blow this consultancy.

Cursing as he tripped over one of the scores of electrical cables threaded across Bowen's Wharf, Gordon searched for Linus among the staffers preparing for the broadcast. There seemed to be extra activity on the deck of the sight-sailing vessel docked at the base of the wharf where technicians were busy adjusting equipment. Gordon wasn't particularly looking forward to the little cruise that he and the cohosts would be taking during *KTA*'s second hour this morning. In his hurry, he'd forgotten his sunglasses. The sun would be glaringly bright out on the water, even this early in the morning.

An enterprising vendor had gotten up early to provide coffee and muffins for the *KTA* staff. Gordon hobbled to the kiosk, looking forward to a steaming cup of caffeine. He'd had no time for breakfast.

Beth Terry stood at the counter, peeling back the paper on a huge chocolate-chip muffin.

"Good morning, Professor."

"Good morning."

"I guess you heard about our intern," she said, the statement more a question.

"What?"

"They found Sam in the tunnel at The Breakers last night. Alive, thank God, but in bad shape. He's in the hospital, still unconscious."

Gordon squinted as he took a sip of hot coffee. He felt no sympathy for the kid. If not for the intern's bragging that he'd been an eyewitness, Gordon would not have been put in the position of talking about Madeleine's death to an audience of millions.

Dominick O'Donnell took the call from B.J. over at Newport Hospital. Word spread quickly through the stunned staff.

"Zoe Quigley is dead."

Linus looked quizzically at his deputy.

"You know. Zoe. Our intern?" Dominick

guessed he shouldn't have been surprised. Linus lived in a world ruled by self-interest. In that world, it wasn't necessarily important to know the names of your underlings.

"The black one?"

Dominick winced as he nodded.

"What happened?"

"It looks like a hit-and-run. This morning when she was on her way down here."

"Jesus." Linus groaned. "I hope we don't get hit with a lawsuit."

As soon as Linus walked away, it struck him. Zoe Quigley's death could add further drama to this morning's show. Even the darkest cloud had a silver lining.

CHAPTER
97

Standing in the hospital parking lot, Grace found herself shaking as she listened to Lauren begin her report at the bottom of the first hour of the broadcast.

"Hello, Constance and Harry. Yes, it's a tense, sad morning here as one of our KEY News interns is dead and another fights for his life. Twenty-year-old exchange student Zoe Quigley of Richmond, England, died in the ambulance on her way to Newport Hospital this morning, the victim, it seems, of a hit-and-run driver. Details are sketchy at this point, but it appears that Zoe was walking, before dawn, on her way to work at our broadcast site at Bowen's Wharf. She was mowed down by a vehicle two blocks from the hotel where she and our news staff are staying while we're in Newport."

Grace found herself suddenly worried about Lucy. She hoped her daughter was still asleep, safe in her room at the Viking, oblivious to any of this.

Lauren was continuing. "At the same time, Constance and Harry, twenty-one-year-old Sam Watkins, another *KTA* intern, lies in the intensive care unit here. As you know, Sam had been missing since late Sunday. Newport police found him last night in a tunnel on the property of The Breakers, the Vanderbilt estate. He has head injuries and has not regained consciousness."

Grace knew that Lauren was being careful

with her wording here. In his instructions given minutes before the report began, Linus had been adamant that Lauren delete any mention that Sam had been scheduled to be interviewed about what he'd seen of Madeleine Sloane's death. *KTA* had provided Gordon Cox in Sam's stead when the intern had not shown up. There was no need, as far as the executive producer was concerned, to emphasize that. Grace still marveled that there had been no viewer phone calls, at least as far as she had heard, picking up on the discrepancy between the video of Sam in the promo and the image of Professor Cox that actually was served up.

"All of this, Constance and Harry, comes on the heels of other tragic and disturbing events that have been rocking this city by the sea. A fourteen-year-old missing persons case turned out to be a murder when socialite Charlotte Wagstaff Sloane's remains were discovered buried in a tunnel on another estate here and identified this past weekend. Also over the weekend, her daughter, Madeleine Sloane, fell to her death on a staircase from the cliffs to the Atlantic Ocean. The medical examiner's office has announced that they will be issuing their findings in that case later this morning, while police continue to investigate if and how these events are linked. Back to you, Constance and Harry."

Grace watched Lauren unclip her microphone and hurry over to B.J. to ask how she had done. As if it really mattered, thought Grace. Madeleine was dead; Sam, who said he was an eyewitness, was fighting for his life; and Zoe was never going to return to her family in England.

Despite the warming morning air, Grace felt a chill as she recalled what Zoe had told her in the restaurant ladies' room the night before. The car on the road near The Breakers speeding past the young intern, almost knocking her down, on the night Sam was last seen there. Had the driver finished the job this morning, thinking that Zoe could identify Sam's assailant? Had Zoe been intentionally run down and killed?

CHAPTER
98

The green Mercedes pulled up on Thames Street and parked directly at the opening to Bowen's Wharf.

"I don't give a rat's ass if I get a ticket," Mr. Vickers yelled at his wife. "I'm getting Joss and I'm getting her right now. I'm not going to let my daughter be exposed to this."

"What exactly is *this,* Howard?"

He looked at her, stunned by her seeming incomprehension. "*This* is danger, Vanessa. What's the matter with you? Don't you see what's happening?"

"What I see is a horrible accident. A young woman was hit by a car. It happens, Howard. It's very sad, but it happens."

"And what about the other intern, that boy in The Breakers' tunnel? What do you see there?"

"I don't see anything yet, Howard. We'll

have to see what the police turn up or what the young man says when he wakes up."

"*If* he wakes up, Vanessa. How can you be so naïve? Three people who were at our clambake Saturday night have been attacked. Two of them are dead and the other is near to it. Sam Watkins and Zoe Quigley have been interning with KEY News. So is our daughter, and I'm getting Joss out of here—out of the Viking and back home where she belongs."

He slammed the sedan door and marched to the end of Bowen's Wharf.

CHAPTER
99

At the close of the broadcast, after a water tour of the harbor and coast of Newport, the sightseeing vessel carrying Constance, Harry, and Professor Cox docked again at Bowen's Wharf. From the deck it was Harry, this time, who wrapped things up, teasing the audience about the next morning's show.

"Tonight there will a fabulous party, the Ball Bleu, held at The Elms, to raise funds to help the endangered birds of Rhode Island. *KEY to America* will be there, and we'll show you all the glamorous goings-on, along with a fascinating view of what it was like to be one of the servants in that Gilded Age mansion. That, and much more, tomorrow on *KEY to America*."

CHAPTER
100

Elsa walked away from the television set and out into the garden. She sat down in a chaise longue on the patio and listened to the energetic chirping of the birds. The little creatures were always busiest in the morning.

So they were finally going to issue the results of Madeleine's autopsy, Elsa thought. She wanted to be with Oliver when he got the news. He would need her by his side. It would be hard for him, no matter what the medical examiner found. Surely, if she were there for him in this, his hour of greatest need, the bond between them would be unbreakable. She just had to be patient.

In her mind, Elsa was already Mrs. Oliver Sloane. After some more time passed, Oliver would come around and marry her. He just didn't know it yet.

She thought of the swans, so graceful on the water, so awkward on land. Swans, it was said, mated for life. Just like swans, Oliver and she were meant to be united forever, sailing placidly through the rest of their lives together.

CHAPTER
101

His eyes burned after a sleepless night. Rusty stood under the shower spray, hoping the rushing water would relieve the tightness in his neck. He stood there for a long time, but the tension did not lessen.

That rich girl, Joss, the one whose parents had hosted the clambake, had recognized the tattoo design he had copied from Charlotte's earring. He was almost sure of it. He could tell Joss hadn't bought his lame explanation last night.

Idiot. You shouldn't have had it in the design book for anyone to see. What were you thinking?

Joss, and those other two with her, were with the news. They'd gone rushing out when they heard that the kid had been found in the tunnel but, when Joss had time to think about it, she could tell them about the design. They might come back, they might tell the police. Who knew what they might do?

Rusty's mind raced. He had to get rid of the earring. A design on paper was one thing. Having the real McCoy, the earring that Charlotte Sloane had been wearing on the last night anyone had seen her alive, was another. It would incriminate him, big time.

He knew he should have disposed of the earring earlier, but he hadn't been able to bring himself to part with it. It was so beautiful, unlike anything he had ever seen before. The earrings he used to buy his mother in the jewelry departments at the discount stores looked like the cheap imitations they were next to the richness and textures of Charlotte's earring. The gold more lustrous but less shiny. The diamonds exquisitely fine.

Exquisite. Just like the lady who wore it that warm summer evening. The damsel in distress, desperate to escape the country club and what had upset her inside its walls. The classy creature who'd had no idea, as she accepted his offer of a ride, that the night would be her last.

CHAPTER
102

Before she did anything else, Grace wanted to call Lucy. She needed to hear her daughter's voice. B.J. offered his cell phone, and she stepped away from the satellite truck to make the call. Hearing her own voice message on the cell phone she'd lent her daughter, Grace called the room directly.

Frank answered on the third ring.

"Hi, it's me. Grace."

"Hello."

"I'd like to talk with Lucy."

"She's not here. Jan just took her down to breakfast."

Grace's heart sank. "Is she all right, Frank?"

"Do you mean is she upset with all this craziness on your news show this morning, Grace? The answer to that question is yes."

"I'd hoped you would have kept Lucy from watching."

"That would have been impossible, Grace. Lucy has made it a point to watch *KEY to America* every morning this week. She wants to see what her mother is working on. So, no. I didn't keep her from watching. And frankly, I don't see why I should have. Lucy is old enough to see what her mother is choosing to get herself into."

"Getting myself into? What am I getting myself into, Frank?" Grace made a concerted effort not to raise her voice, mindful that B.J. could overhear.

"I don't know, Grace. You tell me. It seems

to me that those interns you pal around with are dropping like flies."

And you'd love to see me drop, too, wouldn't you, Frank? Grace wanted to yell it into the tiny phone, but she held herself in check.

"Just tell Lucy that I called, will you please? Tell her that I'm fine and that I love her and I'll see her later. Tell her there is nothing to worry about."

CHAPTER
103

From The Elms' rooftop, Newport Harbor could be seen in the distance. Mickey stood on the third-floor balustrade and looked out at the huge pale blue tent set up on the lush, green lawn. Several hundred guests would be dancing in the tent tonight, all of them expecting flowing liquor and fine food, all of them having the potential to be future clients.

He was exhausted but determined to summon the energy to ensure that the Ball Bleu was a resounding success. He had paid attention to every detail. The robin's egg–colored table linens, the flower center-piece arrangements of anemones, bluebon-nets, and forget-me-nots, the menu that began with Blue Point oysters and ended with blueberry cobbler. He'd even assem-bled a gaggle of blue toy swans to float in the bronze fountain. The guests would surely be impressed.

Thank God, it's going to be a beautiful day, thought Mickey, looking up at the crystal clear sky. A beautiful day and a gorgeous, memo-rable night. The night that would put Seasons Catering on Newport society's radar screen.

He'd come a long way from the days when he'd waited tables. But even then he'd known that he would be a success. All he'd needed was a boost to get started. It was easy to justify his actions. Those fat cats at the club had so much and he'd had so little. As far as Mickey knew, the members had never even noticed that the funds were gone.

Except for Charlotte Sloane. Somehow she had figured it out. She had pulled him aside that night at the club and confronted him, upset that he had cheated and lied to her husband. Telling him that, if he put the money back and resigned, she wouldn't tell anyone what he had done.

But Mickey couldn't do that.

CHAPTER
104

Once the broadcast was over and the updates for the West Coast were completed, Grace checked one more time on Sam's status before heading back to the Viking. Nothing had changed.

Driving to the hotel, Grace and B.J. didn't talk much. Both were shell-shocked and spent. B.J. waited for the valet to take his car while Grace went directly to the newsroom. The work space was unusually quiet.

"Hey, Grace. Your father called a couple of times," the assignment editor said when he saw her. "He wants you to call him back."

Grace went straight to a phone.

"Dad?"

"Gracie." She could almost hear the relief in her father's voice. "How are you, kiddo?"

"I don't know how I am, Dad. It's pretty sad up here. I guess you watched the show this morning?"

"Yes, I did. Do you think you should pull out and come home, honey?"

"Would *you,* Dad?"

There was a long pause at the other end of the line. Finally, her father answered. "I don't know, Gracie. I don't have all the facts. I don't know what I'd do."

"I'd feel like a quitter if I left, Dad. There are only a few more days up here."

"Well, if you decide to stick it out, Gracie, *please,* be careful. A lot can happen in a few days."

A lot can happen in a few seconds, thought Grace as images of Madeleine, Sam, and Zoe flashed through her mind.

CHAPTER
105

Camera crews from all the local outlets were at the news conference, ready to record their images and rush them back to their stations for the noon broadcasts. The assistant Rhode Island medical examiner strode to the podium and stood in front of the bank of microphones to announce the results of the autopsy. The notoriety this case was garnering had forced him to fast-track the process.

"Madeleine Sloane died from a fall resulting in a broken neck. Because of Ms. Sloane's elevated blood alcohol level and because there were no conclusive signs of a struggle, at this time we find her death to be a tragic accident."

CHAPTER
106

The phone conversation with her own dad reminded Grace that she wanted to see Madeleine Sloane's father. No matter what was going on, she didn't want to neglect paying that condolence call. If something happened to her, Grace knew that her own father would greatly appreciate having someone tell him the kind things his daughter had said about him. Oliver Sloane would most likely feel the same way.

But before visiting Mr. Sloane, she had to call Detective Manzorella and tell him about the car that had almost run Zoe down Sunday night near The Breakers. Was the car with the S-E-A tag the same car that had killed Zoe this morning?

Grace went up to her room to make the call.

* * *

"Detective Manzorella is not in at the moment. Would you care to leave a message for him?"

"Please, just have him call me when he gets back. I don't have a cell phone, but he can beep me and I'll call him right back." Grace found her beeper in her stuffed tote bag, checked the still unmemorized number, and recited it back to the dispatcher.

CHAPTER
107

Joss watched the WPRI noon news on the television set in her hotel room, skeptical of the medical examiner's findings. It was hard to believe that Madeleine Sloane's death had been an accident. Madeleine's fall down the Forty Steps, followed by the attack on Sam, who said he'd witnessed Madeleine's attack, and now Zoe's death—it all added up to more than coincidence.

Her parents might be right for once, Joss thought as she packed her bags. She didn't need this internship. It wasn't worth her life. If she decided she wanted to make a career for herself in broadcast journalism, she still could. It didn't have to be with KEY News. No other network news division need ever know that she had dropped out of her internship with KEY. And who cared if she lost the chance for the three measly academic credits? She'd easily pick up another course next semester or the one after that.

Tossing the copy of Charlotte Sloane's journal into the wastepaper basket next to the desk, Joss gave up her quest.

Let Grace Callahan win the competition. Let Grace be the only one left.

CHAPTER
108

It wasn't as grand as many of the mansions she had seen this week, but Oliver Sloane's home was impressive just the same, thought Grace as she walked up the gravel driveway.

The sprawling white clapboard colonial with dark green shutters was set well back from the road. Grace climbed the steps to the front door and pushed the doorbell that was affixed beneath a small brass plaque engraved with a single word, SEAVIEW.

Oliver Sloane himself answered. His face looked strained and tired.

"May I help you?"

"Yes, Mr. Sloane. My name is Grace Callahan, and I wanted to come and speak with you about Madeleine."

Oliver's head recoiled slightly.

"I'm sorry, Mr. Sloane. I didn't come here to upset you. But I was with your daughter the night she died. We spoke at some length, and I thought that it might be of some comfort to you to know what she said."

Oliver studied Grace as if trying to make up his mind. Then he pulled the door wide open.

"Won't you come in? A friend and I were just having some iced tea in my study."

Grace followed him, unprepared to have such a personal conversation with another person present. But there was no going back now.

The study was a beautiful, comfortable room lined with mahogany bookshelves stacked with leather-bound volumes. Along the front of the shelves, pieces of scrimshaw were interspersed. Based on the price tags she'd seen at Kyle Seaton's shop, Grace knew she was looking at a very valuable collection.

A middle-aged woman sat in a wing chair beside the fireplace. Grace searched her memory bank, knowing that the woman who was dabbing at her eyes with a handkerchief looked familiar but not being able to quite place her.

"Elsa Gravell, this is Grace Callahan."

Elsa did not rise from her chair, waiting, instead, for Grace to come to her. As Grace extended her hand, Elsa shook it limply. "Yes, Grace. I think we've met before. At the clambake. Madeleine introduced us."

It came back to Grace now. "Oh yes," she said, "you're Madeleine's godmother."

"That's right," Elsa said, her expression downcast. Grace had the distinct feeling that she was interrupting something, that Elsa would have preferred to be alone with Oliver. But Grace could understand that. By now, they had undoubtedly heard the autopsy findings.

"Won't you sit down, Grace?" Oliver indicated the matching wing chair on the other side of the unlit fireplace as he took a seat behind his desk.

"I'll only stay a few minutes," said Grace. "I don't want to bother you at a time like this. But I wanted to let you know, Mr. Sloane, that Madeleine spoke very lovingly of you that last night."

"She did? What did she say?" Grace read the hope in Oliver's eyes.

"She said you had done the best you could, under very hard circumstances, to raise her with great love and tenderness. Madeleine said she loved you very much, especially for what you had endured."

Oliver seemed to hang on every word. "I'm afraid it was Madeleine who had to endure too much, Grace. Losing her mother as a little girl, being left alone with a father who had been ostracized by society. A father who everyone believed had killed her mother." Oliver's voice cracked, and he looked down at the scrimshaw paperweight on his desk.

"Madeleine didn't believe you killed her mother, Mr. Sloane. I know she didn't."

Oliver looked up. "She told you that?"

"Yes. And she also told me of a dream she had been having about the night that her mother disappeared. She felt that she might be coming close to recalling something that would lead to your wife's murderer."

"Well, we'll never know now, will we, Grace? Madeleine isn't going to figure anything out now."

"I'm so very sorry, Mr. Sloane. I truly am." Grace rose. "I'll be going now," she said. "I don't want to take any more of your time."

Oliver Sloane stood up, visibly moved. "I can't tell you how much I appreciate that you took the time to come over. With the exception of Elsa here, you are the only one who has bothered to pay their respects."

He looked down at his desk and picked up the scrimshaw paperweight. He extended it toward Grace. "I would like you to have this."

Grace shook her head. "Oh, no, Mr. Sloane. I couldn't take that."

"Please, take it," he insisted. "As a memory of Madeleine and a token of my appreciation for your kindness. It will make me feel better if you accept it, Grace."

CHAPTER
109

An unscheduled checkout.

"Damn it," Izzie swore softly. She was in the habit of husbanding her strength, doling it out room by room, stretching it just long enough to finish her assignments. Even one extra room to clean made her despair.

Opening the door to 226 and walking inside, Izzie had all she could do not to weep. The occupant had been a real slob. Fast food and candy wrappers were strewn over the carpeting. The sheets were stained with lip gloss and mascara. In the bathroom, wet towels lay in heaps on the floor. The sink was crusted with globs of toothpaste, and bottles of shampoo and conditioner had been tossed carelessly in the tub, their contents oozing across the porcelain. Long, black hairs clogged the drain.

Taking a deep breath, Izzie began. *Just take it one step at a time,* she told herself. *One step at a time.* She stripped the linens from the bed and scooped up the towels from the bathroom floor. She bent to gather the discarded food wrappers from the rug, feeling light-headed as she rose again. Izzie stumbled over to the chair at the desk and sat down to wait for the dizziness to pass.

When she opened her eyes, she spotted the papers in the wastebasket. Funny that the pig who had stayed in this room had bothered to throw anything in the trash. Izzie reached for the basket and was about to dump the contents when she noticed the notation at the top of the cover page. "Original returned to Agatha Wagstaff, sister."

Izzie pulled the photocopied papers from the trash can and, folding them up, stashed them in the pocket of her uniform.

CHAPTER
110

She felt guilty going shopping when there was so much pain around her, but Grace had to take advantage of this bit of free time. B.J. had asked her if she wanted to come with him to shoot at the fund-raiser at The Elms, and she had nothing appropriate to wear. She didn't have to be dressed as formally as the guests, but nothing she had brought with her would do, either. On the way back to the hotel, she stopped at Talbots, encouraged by the sale signs in the window. A half hour later, she emerged with a sleeveless navy blue linen sheath that had been marked down, a black clutch bag, a pair of black patent leather high-heeled sandals, and the khaki slacks she'd been hoping to buy.

Back at the Viking, she avoided the newsroom and went directly to her room with her packages. She placed the scrimshaw paper-weight on the night table next to the tele-phone. As she was hanging her new dress in the closet, her beeper went off. Going to the phone, Grace punched the numbers she read from the tiny beeper screen.

"Detective Manzorella, please. Grace Cal-lahan calling."

Grace sat on the edge of the bed and waited, staring down at the henna tattoo on her foot. In all the commotion of rushing out of the tattoo parlor last night, she had forgot-ten, until now, the strange coincidence of the design in Rusty's book being a duplicate of the sundial in the garden at Shepherd's Point. He'd told Joss that the idea had just come to him, but Grace doubted that. How had Rusty known about the sundial?

As Grace studied her tattoo, it occurred to her. Agatha had told her that Charlotte had been wearing tiny versions of the sundial as earrings on the night she disappeared. Per-haps Rusty had never seen the sundial. Maybe he had seen Charlotte's earrings in-stead. But either scenario seemed unlikely. Rusty didn't look the type to be spending time at Shepherd's Point, or with Charlotte Sloane for that matter.

"Hello, Ms. Callahan. Al Manzorella speaking." The detective's voice diverted Grace from her thoughts.

"Oh, yes, Detective. I wanted to get back to you with something that I thought you should know. Something that Zoe Quigley told me just last night."

"What's that?"

"Zoe told me that she was jogging near The Breakers Sunday night and a car sped by her, almost running her down."

"What kind of car was it?"

"She wasn't sure. Zoe was from England, you know. She said she wasn't familiar with most American models. But she did see a partial license tag. Zoe said she saw the letters S-E-A."

"A vanity plate?" the detective asked.

"I don't know."

"Okay, Ms. Callahan. Thank you very much."

Grace didn't want to get off the phone. "Do you think that will be helpful in finding out what happened to Zoe and even to Sam Watkins? Maybe the driver of the car was the one who attacked Sam. The time frame would seem to fit."

"We'll look into it, Ms. Callahan, I promise. And keep this to yourself, will you? This could be crucial evidence. If it is, it's important that the suspect doesn't know we have it."

Grace hurried on. "You know, they could be connected. Like falling dominoes, one crashing against another. None of these events seems isolated. Maybe Zoe's hit-and-run wasn't an accident. Maybe she was run down because the killer thought Zoe could place him at The Breakers when Sam was attacked. Maybe Sam was attacked because he had seen the killer push Madeleine down the Forty Steps. Maybe Madeleine was killed because she was getting too close to discovering who had killed her mother."

"That's a lot of maybes, Ms. Callahan. But don't worry, we are checking every lead we get. Let us do our jobs. Thank you very much."

Grace heard the click at the end of the phone line and was frustrated. But perhaps it was all for the best that the detective had cut her short. It wouldn't be fair to implicate Rusty on the basis of a design in a tattoo sketchbook. She needed more before she could go to the police with that.

CHAPTER
111

Grace poked her head into the ballroom. Neither B.J. nor Joss was anywhere to be seen. But Beth Terry was sitting at the assignment desk, her brow furrowed. Grace walked over.

"Can I do anything for you, Beth?" she asked.

"Not unless you want to make arrangements to have a body shipped back to England."

"Oh, man." Grace shook her head. "Did someone call Zoe's parents?"

"Yours truly." Beth's expression was solemn. "I've never had to break news like that before. I hope I never have to do it again."

"I'm so sorry, Beth." Grace searched for some way to be helpful. "Can I get you something? A cup of tea? Something to eat?"

"No, thanks," Beth said glumly. "For once, I don't have any appetite."

"What's the latest on Sam?" Grace asked.

"The same. Nothing's changed."

Grace turned to walk away.

"Grace, wait," said Beth.

"Yes?"

"Just be careful, will you?"

Grace looked at her quizzically.

"I don't know, Grace. Just be careful. I'm not superstitious, but you're the last intern standing."

"What do you mean?"

"Haven't you heard?"

"What? Did something happen to Joss?" Grace's heartbeat quickened.

"Joss quit, Grace. You're the only working intern left."

There were still two hours before she had to meet B.J. to go to The Elms. Grace called upstairs to talk to Lucy, but there was no answer. She was actually happy that her daughter was out somewhere with Frank and Jan, safe and having a good time.

With nothing to do in the newsroom, Grace couldn't stand around and wait. Though there was no love lost between the two of them, Grace was shaken by Joss's resignation. She was about to call the Vickerses' house but thought better of it. What was there really to say?

It looked like she was going to win the job competition by default, and there was little joy in the victory. Grace didn't feel she had done much to distinguish herself from the other interns.

But if she could figure out the strand that connected Charlotte's, Madeleine's, and Zoe's deaths, and Sam's attack, that would make her feel she'd earned the job. More important, she wanted to do her part, if she could, to end the senseless violence and the heartbreak for all the people connected to the victims. This killer had to be stopped.

Of course, it would be foolhardy to take any unnecessary risks—and it would be irresponsible as a parent. Beth was right. She had to be careful.

But how dangerous would it be to go see Rusty at the tattoo parlor while the sun was still shining?

The first falling domino was Charlotte Sloane.

Grace theorized that from Charlotte's death came all the others.

She could see the police station up the block as she stood on the sidewalk in front of Broadway Tattoos. It was broad daylight, and she could run up the street to safety if she had to. Grace opened the door to the shop and walked inside.

Rusty was talking to a teenager at the counter, giving instructions on how to care for his freshly engraved tattoo. Grace stood back near the entrance and waited for the customer to pay and leave. Rusty came from behind the counter and approached her. Grace eyed the fine spattering of blood on his T-shirt.

"Don't mind this," Rusty said, pinching at the cotton and pulling it away from his chest. "Sometimes there can be a little blood spray. It's no big deal though. You ready to get that tattoo now?"

"No," said Grace. "I'm going to think about it a little more."

"Oh," Rusty looked disappointed. "Well, what can I do for you then?"

"I wanted to talk with you about the design we saw in your book last night."

"I was afraid of that." Rusty sighed deeply. "I could tell that friend of yours recognized it the moment she saw it."

Grace thought back to the night before.

Of course, Joss *had* asked about the design, but until this moment Grace hadn't thought to question that. She had only focused on the fact that the design was the same as the sundial at Shepherd's Point. Why had Joss been so curious about it?

"So you didn't come up with the design all by yourself?" Grace asked.

"I have the feeling you already know I didn't or you wouldn't be asking me about it. Look, I don't want no trouble. Can't you just leave it alone?"

The anxiety Grace was feeling lessened as she saw the defeated expression on Rusty's face. "Why don't you tell me?" she urged. "If you don't, I can go to the police and they'll come and ask you about it themselves." She took another step back toward the door.

"I have an explanation, but you have to promise you won't go to the police."

"That depends."

Rusty was in a bad position, and he knew it. But telling this woman and hoping she'd be satisfied was far better than having the cops traipsing in here. The police wouldn't believe him, but she might. He'd have to take the chance.

As Grace and Rusty stood near the doorway, he recounted his story of working as a driver for the admiral.

"I was outside that night, waiting for my boss, who was partying it up with all the other swells at that country club bash. I was staying to myself, sneaking a few cigarettes and thinking it must be nice to have the kind of dough that made it possible to donate wads of money to make sure that some birds kept flying, when I was having no success in saving anything out of my measly navy pay."

Grace nodded in sympathy.

"Anyway," Rusty continued, "Charlotte Sloane came out of the club, real worked up. She saw me and asked me if I could give her a ride. I knew I wasn't supposed to leave, but I couldn't say no. She was so beautiful in that shiny, gold gown. Like Cinderella at the ball.

"She had a photo in her hand, and I think it upset her very much. I kept looking in the rearview mirror and watching her in the backseat. She had flipped on the overhead light and was staring at the picture and mumbling something about someone lying and cheating. I asked her what happened, but she wouldn't tell me. She said she just wanted to get to her little girl.

"It wasn't far to Shepherd's Point. I dropped her off at the foot of the driveway and drove back to the country club. The admiral never even knew I left."

"But what about the design, Rusty?" Grace asked.

"When I was cleaning out the car the next morning, I found an earring on the floor. I was going to return it—honest, I was. But then I heard that Charlotte Sloane was missing. I couldn't give the earring back then. I couldn't take the chance that everyone would think I had something to do with her disappearance."

"So that's why you never went to the police," Grace mused aloud.

"Look at me," Rusty implored, holding out his hands. "I'm the sort of guy the cops love to pin things on. I'm an easy mark. I thought of telling them what had happened, many times. But I was afraid they'd turn it around to make me out to be the guilty one. They'd say I was the last person to see her alive."

"But you weren't the last one, Rusty," said Grace. "Charlotte's murderer was."

CHAPTER
112

Why had Joss been so curious about the earring design? Grace wondered again as she walked out of the tattoo parlor, hoping a cab would come her way. What did Joss know?

Determined now to find out, Grace gave the Vickerses' address to the taxi driver who picked her up at the curb.

A bikini-clad Joss answered the door.

"Grace. What are you doing here?" she asked, her face registering her surprise.

"I was hoping that we could talk about something, Joss."

"What? Did you come to gloat?" Joss sneered. "Well, I wouldn't if I were you. I walked away from the internship, Grace. You're not exactly winning fair and square, are you? The rest of your competition's been eliminated, too. How convenient for you."

Grace had a good mind to turn and walk away, but she held herself in check. *Swallow it. Find out what you want to know.*

"Who wins the competition isn't the important thing anymore, Joss," she said. "It's really scary what's been happening this week. Madeleine. Sam. And now, Zoe. I think that if we can do anything to help figure out what's going on, Joss, we have to do it."

Joss looked at Grace with skepticism. "Yeah, and score one for yourself and KEY News."

"No, Joss," Grace insisted. "Score one for being decent citizens."

Joss stared down at her bare feet, wriggling her pretty toes on the entry hall's ceramic tiles. When she looked up again at Grace, Joss invited her former competitor inside.

Grace chose the same seat that she had taken when she had been in this living room the night she came to the clambake. But Joss didn't sit beside her on the sofa as Madeleine had. She positioned herself in a wing chair across the living room.

"All right, Grace. What did you want to talk about?"

"I just came from Broadway Tattoos."

"And?"

"Rusty told me how he came to make that design," said Grace. "You know. The one you asked him about."

"What did he tell you?" Joss's foot bounced.

Grace decided that she should give something to get something. "He said he copied it from an earring. An earring that Charlotte Sloane lost in his car the night she disappeared."

"Jesus." Joss uncrossed her bare legs and leaned forward in her chair. "He could be the one who killed Charlotte."

"Let's not get ahead of ourselves, Joss. You were very interested in the design when you saw it in Rusty's book last night. I'm wondering why."

Grace could almost see the wheels spinning in the former intern's mind.

"All right. What the hell," Joss said, her decision made. "Wait a minute." She stood up and walked out of the living room. When she came back again, she was carrying her purse. She pulled a folded paper from it and handed it to Grace.

Unfolding the paper, Grace looked at the sketch. The sundial design.

"Rusty may have one of the earrings, Grace, but the police have its twin. It was found in the pocket of Charlotte's evening gown. The cops haven't made that information public though."

"How do you know?" Grace asked, still looking at the paper.

"I have a good source," Joss said in a tone that left no doubt she wouldn't be telling Grace who it was. "But, trust me, I saw the earring myself."

Grace was all for the principle of not revealing one's sources, so she didn't push Joss. But she was intrigued by the additional drawing at the bottom of the paper.

"What's this?" she asked, pointing to the penciled square.

"Oh, that's the other thing that was found in Charlotte's dress," Joss answered. "A lemon-yellow silk handkerchief."

As she watched Grace walk down the driveway, Joss remembered Charlotte's diary. She was about to call out to Grace but thought better of it. Joss worried she had already said too much.

What a colossal break.

Madeleine's autopsy results were another clear signal from the authorities that you really *could* get away with murder.

But the coast wasn't clear yet. If Sam Watkins came to, that would be a major problem. Still, it was best to wait and see, and hope that heaven would provide another blessing, taking the young man home.

Zoe Quigley, thank God, would never be able to tell anyone what she saw.

But Grace Callahan was a wild card. Was Grace getting too close?

CHAPTER
114

Grace showered and shampooed her hair, spending extra time to blow-dry the honey-colored strands into soft, fluffy curls. She applied her makeup, paying special attention to her eyes, shadowing the lids in smoky blue-gray and applying a thin liner to the bottoms and tops. As she whisked the mascara wand across her lashes, she noticed her bare fingernails. It was too late to get a manicure, but at least her nails could be shaped and buffed.

She rummaged through her cosmetics kit, finding an emery board at the bottom. Pulling her robe on, she went out into the bedroom, sat down on the bed, and began to file. After a few minutes she was satisfied that, while not glamorous, her nails were presentable.

There was still fifteen minutes before she

had to be ready for The Elms, and Grace didn't want to put on her dress until the very last second. Linen wrinkled so easily. So she decided to put her feet up, lie back, and close her eyes, hoping a short rest would refresh her. But she couldn't relax. Rusty's story kept running through her mind, along with the information she had gotten from Joss.

Grace sat up anxiously and thought of calling Lucy again. As she reached for the phone, she spotted the scrimshaw paperweight, Oliver's gift to her, sitting on the nightstand. She picked it up and ran her hand over the smooth, cool surface.

With the emery board right there, she decided, just out of curiosity, to try Kyle Seaton's test. Grace picked a spot on the underside of the paperweight and briskly pulled the emery board back and forth across the surface, fully expecting to smell the odor of burning bone.

Instead, her nostrils picked up the scent of smoldering plastic.

Oliver's paperweight was fakeshaw.

There was a knock at the door.

"Who's there?" called Grace.

"It's me. B.J."

"Just a minute. I'll be right there."

She had thought she would be meeting him in the lobby. Grace hurried to zip up her dress as she walked, barefoot, to the door.

B.J. stood there, tanned and freshly showered, wearing a navy blazer, crisp white shirt, and pale blue tie, his beige slacks pressed, his shoes polished. He held out a small, square, white box.

"For me? You brought flowers for me?" Grace was delighted. Not only had it been ages since she'd been given flowers, but it had been even longer since she had been given flowers by anyone who excited her.

B.J. grinned, pleased at her reaction. "I thought you might like them."

"Like them? I love them." Grace studied the soft blue blossoms. "They're exquisite, B.J. Thank you."

Carefully, she lifted the corsage from the box. "Where do you think I should wear them? On my dress or my wrist?"

B.J. reached out and pushed back a loose strand of Grace's hair. "How about here, in your hair?"

"All right. Have a seat for a minute while I go do it."

Grace went into the bathroom, where she stood before the mirror and gathered her hair up on one side, attaching the flowers with bobby pins.

"Nice scrimshaw," B.J. called from the outer room, picking up the paperweight from the night table.

"It's fake," Grace said. "I tried the scrimshaw test on it."

"You didn't expect it to be the real thing, did you?"

"Actually, I did, considering where it came from. Oliver Sloane gave it to me this afternoon."

"You're kidding. How did that happen?" B.J. asked.

"I went to pay a condolence call and he was touched. He insisted I take the paperweight in memory of Madeleine."

"Think Oliver knew it was a fake?"

Grace fastened the last bobby pin and stood back to observe the effect in the mirror. "I kind of doubt it," she called. "The way his study looked, I wouldn't think anything but the best is good enough for Oliver Sloane."

"Are you gonna tell him?"

"Maybe I should. Kyle Seaton told me at the clambake that Oliver and Charlotte had been great customers. I wonder if Kyle sold Oliver that paperweight."

She gave her hair one last primp. "How do I look?" she asked, coming back into the bedroom.

B.J. looked at her with appreciation. "Dynamite. You look great, Grace."

Too bad Lauren Adams was going with them in the car.

Grace knew that they would be working tonight, but it felt like she and B.J. were going out on a date. Fake scrimshaw and sundial earrings were forgotten for a while as she slipped on her new sandals and gathered up her clutch bag. "Shall we go?"

CHAPTER
115

Izzie lit the candle next to the tiny holy statue perched on the tub's edge and eased herself into the warm water.

"Ahhhh," she moaned in relief. She was going to have to give her notice at the Viking. She'd clean those rooms until the end of the week and then no more.

Izzie stared at the statue of the young maiden dressed in blue and pink robes. Her expression was so serene, though Izzie knew she had endured the tortures of the damned. Young, beautiful, and rich, she had lived a life consecrated to God and had been beaten, imprisoned, and tortured by her enemies, her breasts crushed and cut off before she was finally dragged on burning coals until she died.

"Saint Agatha," Izzie prayed, "please help me." The patron saint of nurses, firefighters, and women suffering from breast cancer silently stared back at the chambermaid. Izzie knew the Christian faith taught that the pain and affliction of this world would be surpassed by the spiritual bliss of the next. She was counting on that and was eager to be with her Padraic again. *It shouldn't be too long now, Paddy, my love.*

Dipping a washcloth in the water, Izzie gently rubbed it across her scarred chest, all the while staring at the statue. How strange it was that her adult life had started out with one Agatha and was ending with another. She had learned the skills of making a bed the way Miss Agatha liked it and polishing porcelain tubs and basins until they shone under Finola's strict tutelage at Shepherd's

Point. She might have worked there still had she and Paddy not been in the playhouse the night Miss Charlotte was murdered. After that terrifying time in the old slave tunnel, crouched beside Miss Charlotte's lifeless body, and the threatening letter that had come afterward, Izzie had wanted to escape from Shepherd's Point and the horrific memories.

She struggled to lift herself from the tub. She dried herself off, patting at the pink V-shaped scars on her chest, and took her thin cotton nightgown from the hook on the back of the bathroom door. Then she padded to the kitchen, put the kettle on to boil, and steeled herself to tackle the pile of mail that had been accumulating, unexamined, all week.

Bill. Bill. Junk mail. Bill. The next envelope caused Izzie to take a deep, troubled breath. She recognized the exaggerated handwriting that she had studied hundreds of times before. Another letter from the same person who had threatened Paddy so effectively all those years ago, threatening to place him at Charlotte Sloane's murder scene. But this time, the letter was addressed to her.

The kettle whistled, making her jump. Izzie

turned off the stove but didn't bother to pour the water over the tea bag. She went back to the table, her hands quivering as she opened the letter.

I WARNED YOUR HUSBAND FOURTEEN YEARS AGO AND I'M WARNING YOU NOW. DON'T THINK BECAUSE THE BONES IN THE SLAVE TUNNEL WERE FOUND THAT THIS IS AN OPPORTUNITY TO REVEAL WHAT YOU KNOW OR WHAT YOU *THINK* YOU KNOW.

I STILL HAVE THE WALLET LEFT BEHIND IN THE PLAYHOUSE THE NIGHT CHARLOTTE SLOANE DIED. IF YOU GO TO THE POLICE WITH THE PHOTO, I'LL PRODUCE THE WALLET. WHO DO YOU THINK THE POLICE WILL BELIEVE? YOU OR ME?

As Izzie read the letter over again, the fear she felt began to turn to anger. She had done nothing wrong except to love Paddy in the wrong place at the wrong time. Yet they had worried themselves sick over the years that they would be accused of murdering Charlotte should her body, and Padraic's wallet, ever turn up. Izzie had wept many nights, wanting to do the right thing and tell the police what had happened that night. But as she and Paddy had studied the photo-graph that had come spiraling down from the playhouse to rest on Charlotte Sloane's body, they agreed over and over again that there was nothing in it that could really incriminate anybody. They were never quite sure what the murderer was so worried about, but they were certain that they would look guilty if the story of Padraic's wallet being found in the playhouse were ever told.

Izzie stood and opened the cupboard door, pulled out the cookbooks at the front, and felt for the cellophane envelope. Her hands still shook, but now with rage, as she carefully slid out the contents. Enough was enough.

She had little time left in this world, but she was going to go to the next one with a guiltless conscience. And if, in the process, she helped another hardworking young woman who could use a boost, so much the better. She had this old photograph and Miss Charlotte's photocopied diary she had pulled from the wastebasket today. She was going to give them both to that kind Grace Callahan and maybe help her with that career of hers.

CHAPTER
116

The chauffeured town car waited in the driveway as Oliver, dressed in a dinner jacket, got out and knocked on Elsa's door. A golden cuff link glistened against his bright white shirt cuff as he impatiently lifted the seagull door knocker. The last time he'd worn the sundial cuff links was at the country club party the night Charlotte disappeared. For all these years, he hadn't been able to bring himself to use the last anniversary gift from his missing wife. But now, knowing Charlotte was truly gone, it seemed appropriate to wear the links in her memory.

Elsa opened the door, resplendent in a form-fitting, marine blue evening gown, a diamond brooch in the shape of a seabird on her breast. Her hair was piled high on her head, just as she and Charlotte had both been coiffed the night of the first fund-raiser.

Though never beautiful, Elsa had held up amazingly well, thought Oliver. She didn't look terribly different in her forties than she had in her twenties.

"You look lovely, Elsa."

"Thank you, Oliver, dear. Come in and we'll have a drink."

Oliver didn't move from the entryway. "I don't think I should. I've already had a cocktail, and the last thing I want to do is appear inebriated at the party. I've no doubt people will be watching me more closely than ever."

"All right, dear," Elsa agreed, not wanting to upset him in any way. "I'll get my purse."

CHAPTER
117

Grace watched as the photographer had each arriving couple pose for a picture. Already, the photographer's assistant was arranging developed photos on a large easel. Apparently, in addition to forking over substantial bucks to attend the Ball Bleu, the guests could shell out a few more for their souvenirs.

The partygoers chatted amiably, almost everyone apparently knowing one another. But as the new couple arrived, the small talk ceased.

Grace felt sorry for Oliver Sloane as she watched him hold his head high and put his arm around Elsa Gravell, his gold cuff link sparkling in the photographer's flash. Grace inched close enough to see that it had the same design as the Shepherd's Point sundial and Charlotte's earrings.

CHAPTER
118

KEY News is in my way, thought Mickey, as he glared at the satellite truck parked near the canopy of leaves at the service entrance to the mansion. The damned truck was making the path for the waiters going from the kitchen with silver trays of hors d'oeuvres to the guests on the lawn harder than it had to be.

He cursed as he watched one uniformed waiter bump into another. "That's it." He spat. "They have to move that truck."

Mickey stalked over to the truck and knocked persistently on the cab door, getting the attention of the driver who snoozed inside. "You have to move this thing right away."

Scott Huffman looked at the caterer without concern. "I'm not moving this rig anywhere, buddy, unless one of my bosses tells me to."

Mickey scanned the beautiful grounds, searching among the carefully clipped ginkgo, maple, and linden trees. Between a massed rhododendron and an enormous weeping birch, he spotted the guy with a video camera. Mickey made a beeline to him and got right to the point. "You guys have to move. Your truck's interfering with my waiters."

B.J. looked in the direction Mickey indicated. "All right, pal. Calm down. I'll see what we can do."

CHAPTER
119

Her high heels kept sinking into the lawn, the mosquitoes were starting to bite, and now she was left alone while B.J. worked out the satellite truck problem. So far, the evening wasn't turning out to be the romantic interlude Grace had found herself hoping for. From a professional stance, it wasn't much better. Lauren seemed more interested in flirting and making connections with Newport's society men than with shooting interviews for tomorrow morning's package.

Grace decided to tour the grounds on her own. Trying to avoid dirtying her patent leather heels further, she put her weight on the balls of her feet as she walked to the western edge of the property. Two small marble teahouses with copper roofs marked the entrance to a formal sunken garden with hundreds of pink and white begonias. Grace turned to look back up at the mansion and take in the view of all the partygoers against that impressive backdrop when she heard a giggle.

At the side of the teahouse, away from the sight of the guests but plainly visible to Grace, was her ex-husband. Frank was kissing a dark-haired woman. A brunette, not a blonde.

It wasn't Jan.

Grace paused, not sure how to proceed. Finally, she cleared her throat, loud enough to make the lip-locked pair look her way. Grace wished she had a camera to capture the expression on her former husband's face.

"Oh my God! Grace."

She couldn't help but smirk. "Nice evening, isn't it, Frank?"

Frank turned to his companion. "Will you excuse me? I'll meet up with you a little later."

The brunette departed, walking across the lawn toward the tent and not looking particularly upset. *She might be married, too,* thought Grace. *This is probably a big game to her.*

Grace looked at her former husband and shook her head. "Tsk, tsk, tsk. And I thought you had such a fabulous thing going with Jan."

"Cut it out, Grace. It's none of your business."

"Oh? Isn't it? You want our daughter to come live with you in that perfect little home of yours and it's none of my business? Let's see." Grace crooked her finger to her chin. "I wonder how a judge will feel about placing a child in a home where the father is a philanderer. In fact, I wonder what Jan would think of all this. Maybe I can go tell her now. After she finds this out, you may not have any home at all."

Frank touched at the corners of his mouth with his handkerchief and held it out to inspect the lipstick he'd wiped away. She had him and he knew it. "All right, Grace. You win."

"You'll drop the custody suit?"

"Yes, as long as you don't tell Jan."

"And you'll get caught up with the child support payments and start paying me on time from now on?"

He looked at her with contempt. "What choice do I have?"

"None, really. And by the way, what are you doing here anyway?"

"Jan had a bee in her bonnet about attending a Newport social event."

Grace searched the crowd. "I don't see her. Where is she?"

"I don't know. I left her talking to some society matrons."

"And where's Lucy, Frank?"

"She's back at the hotel."

"By herself?" Grace was angry now.

"She's old enough to be left alone, Grace. After all, we let her travel up to see me on the train all alone."

"That was different, Frank. That was only for one hour, in broad daylight—not for an entire evening in a hotel room in a city reeling from a wave of murders."

CHAPTER
120

Grace's stomach twisted in knots as she strode away from the teahouse and Frank. It was debatable that Lucy was old enough to be left alone in a hotel room, but as far as Grace was concerned, there was no question that leaving her daughter by herself under the current circumstances was unthinkable. She'd never forgive herself if something were to happen to Lucy.

Grace noticed Detective Manzorella, snappily dressed in a dark suit with a striped tie and matching pocket square, positioned near the northeast corner of the massive blue tent, his dark eyes scanning the crowd, his expression solemn. She didn't go over to him. She was in a hurry.

She found B.J. standing in the driveway, watching the satellite truck be repositioned.

"B.J., I'm sorry, but I have to go back to the hotel," she said.

He looked at her with incomprehension. "What's wrong? Are you sick?"

"No. It's Lucy. My husband—I mean my former husband—left her alone. I don't feel good about it, B.J.," she apologized. "I have to go and make sure she's all right."

"Sure, I understand," said B.J., though his face registered disappointment. He pulled the keys from his pocket. "Take the car. Lauren and I will find a way home. Don't worry about it, Grace. We'll be fine here."

"I know you will be." That was true enough.

B.J. and Lauren could get done what they needed to without her. Grace pushed aside her own disappointment over not spending the evening with B.J., over not being part of covering the extravagant event. Maybe there was a lesson for her here. She was always going to put her child before her career. Yet, these were extraordinary conditions, Grace reasoned. If she knew Lucy was safe and secure, she would feel comfortable leaving her daughter to go to work. It was just that, right now, she couldn't be sure about Lucy's safety.

For Grace, there was no question what she had to do.

"Lucy, it's me. Open up." Grace rapped on the hotel room door. She could hear the *Law & Order* theme blaring from the television set inside.

She knocked again, louder this time. "Lucy, it's Mom. Open the door, honey."

Where was she? Grace felt her pulse quicken. *Don't panic,* she told herself. Maybe Lucy had fallen asleep, maybe she was taking a shower.

Grace walked down the hall and grabbed

the house phone from the wall near the elevator, her knuckles whitening as she gripped the receiver. After a dozen rings, Lucy still hadn't picked up. Grace's adrenaline pumped. She could wring Frank's neck for leaving their child alone. Her mind began running through terrifying scenarios.

Just as Grace was trying to figure out what to do next, the elevator doors opened. Lucy strolled out, a package of Twizzlers in her hand.

"Hi, Mom. What are you doing here?"

"Oh God, Lucy." Grace exhaled, wrapping her arms around her daughter. "I was so worried."

Lucy looked at Grace, puzzled. "I just went downstairs to get some candy. No big deal."

The last thing Grace wanted to do was raise a worried, insecure child. There was no use in berating Lucy. She hadn't done anything wrong.

"What are you doing here?" Lucy asked again.

Grace didn't want to lie to her daughter either. "A lot's been going on around here, Luce. I didn't think you should be left by yourself."

"Dad said it was all right." Lucy bit the end off a red licorice stick.

"Well, I don't." Grace spoke firmly. "Come on. Let's go to my room so I can get out of these new shoes. They're killing me."

"You look great, Mom," observed Lucy as they waited for the elevator doors to open again.

"Thanks, honey."

"How did you know I was by myself anyway?"

"Dad told me."

"Oh. You saw him at that party him and Jan went to?"

"*He* and Jan," Grace corrected her daughter. "Yes. I saw him there."

Man, did I see him there, Grace thought, smiling to herself and appreciating for the first time that Lucy would be staying with her—full time, forever.

CHAPTER
121

Detective Manzorella continued studying the faces of the guests and listening to snippets of conversations. But the call that came through on his cell phone excited him far more than anything the Ball Bleu had offered.

Sam Watkins had regained consciousness.

The detective hurried to his car and headed to Newport Hospital.

CHAPTER
122

The other chambermaids had long since gone, their morning and afternoon shifts completed. Izzie came in through the rear entrance, hoping she wouldn't see any of the skeletal evening maintenance staff. She didn't want to get into a conversation with anyone.

With her envelope tucked inside her handbag, she took the elevator to the second floor and walked down the hallway to Grace Callahan's room. If she wasn't there, Izzie planned to slide the envelope under the door and leave her phone number for Grace to call her. But Grace answered right away.

"Yes?" Grace almost didn't recognize the woman dressed not in a maid's uniform but in a cotton shirt and slacks. But the short, feathery hair was the reminder.

"Hello. I'm Izzie O'Malley." Izzie's voice

trailed upward at the end of the statement, making it sound more like a question.

"Of course, Izzie. How are you feeling?"

"Better," Izzie lied.

"I'm glad to hear that," said Grace, looking at her expectantly. "Can I help you with something?"

"Actually, I was hoping we could help each other," Izzie answered.

Lucy sat on the love seat, munching on her Twizzlers, her eyes trained on the television set in the Queen Anne–style armoire as Grace stood over Izzie. The chambermaid sat at the desk and spread out the contents of her purse.

"I was at Shepherd's Point the night that Charlotte Sloane was murdered," Izzie said softly.

"Come again?"

"Padraic—he was my boyfriend then," Izzie confessed, "Padraic and I were in the playhouse doing something we shouldn't have been when we heard Miss Charlotte coming. We knew about the tunnel, so we sneaked out that way."

Grace made no judgment on Izzie's pre-marital behavior. But she held her breath as she asked the question, "Who was Charlotte with?"

"I don't know," said Izzie. "But I do know that whoever it was didn't want *this* to come to light." She held out the cellophane envelope to Grace. "I've stared at this for fourteen years. See if *you* see something. Paddy and I never did. Be careful not to touch it, though. It's evidence, Grace. Except for me and Paddy, the last one to handle it was Charlotte's murderer."

Holding the photo by the edges, Grace brought it up to the lamplight and stared at it. It was similar in size to the ones she had just seen being posted on the easel at The Elms. The shot was taken from the back of the room, where people in formal attire stood watching a woman speaking from a podium. The faces of the people listening to the speaker weren't visible, but as Grace studied it more closely, she was fairly certain that the woman at the podium was Charlotte Sloane.

"Why would a murderer be worried about this picture?" she murmured.

"I don't know," said Izzie. "But whoever it is blackmailed Paddy and me for all these years. You see, in our hurry to get out of the playhouse, Paddy left his wallet behind. The murderer wrote and told us that we'd be turned in to the police if we came forward with the picture and that the police would think we were the guilty ones. Just today, I opened another letter warning me to keep quiet." Izzie handed both letters to Grace, one fresh, the other yellowed with age. "And I have something else to give you. I think this is a copy of Charlotte's diary."

Grace looked at all the evidence, paying special attention to the last entry in the photocopied journal.

Fool. Why am I so naïve? People lie and cheat all the time. I can't let this go on one more minute. Tonight's disappointment at the country club was enough.

"Why are you coming to *me* with this, Izzie?"

"It's time to let the chips fall where they may. I've lived with this secret for all these years, and as you can see, I'm not well. Even if the police turn around and blame me, I'm not going to rot in jail for long. I don't have much time left. But when I meet my Maker, I don't want him asking me why I never came forward with what I knew."

"But why not go to the police?" Grace asked, still looking at the documents.

"I was hoping that I'd be sort of killing two birds with one stone. Telling the truth but also helping you. Maybe you could use this to impress your bosses. You were kind to me; now I'm repaying the favor."

"Honestly, Izzie, the police have to have this information." Grace was adamant. She wasn't prepared to live with the consequences if she sat on this evidence while the killer struck again.

"That's up to you, my dear. Do with it as you will. I'm too tired to care anymore."

Grace glanced at the clock. It was only nine o'clock. Detective Manzorella would still be at The Elms. She could take the photo and the papers to him and tell him Izzie's story.

"I could take these to the police now, Izzie. I don't think we should waste any time."

"Whatever you think is best."

Grace looked at Lucy sitting on the love seat. Should she bring her daughter with her?

It was as if Izzie had read her mind. "I could stay here with your daughter, if you'd like, and if she doesn't mind."

But Lucy had been listening to the conversation instead of the television show, and she was excited at the prospect of real-life suspense. "No way, Mom," she insisted. "I'm going with you."

Tonight's disappointment at the country club was enough.

Grace reread Charlotte Sloane's last journal entry. What happened at that fund-raiser on the night Charlotte disappeared? Rusty had told her that Charlotte had been upset by the photo. Somehow, the answer must be in the photograph.

Before she and Lucy left the hotel to head back to The Elms, they stopped in the newsroom and searched the file-tape shelves. Finding the dub of the WPRI material shot at the first endangered bird fund-raiser, Grace asked an editor to insert the tape into a playback deck.

The same video that she had hurriedly screened with B.J. Sunday night looked different to her now, just three days later. As Grace studied the footage, she actually recognized some of the faces, younger versions of the people she had met this week. There was Professor Cox with dark hair before it went silver, and Kyle Seaton before he went bald, both in tuxedos. Was that Mickey, the catering guy, waiting tables?

Grace squinted as she watched the rolling tape and smiled at her discovery. She recognized the profile of a youthful Detective Manzorella, holding a walkie-talkie to his mouth. His navy blazer suggested he wasn't a guest. He must have been working security for the party.

"Come on, Mom. I'm bored," Lucy interrupted her.

"Cut it out, Luce. This is important. It'll just take a few more minutes."

The guests swirled and gyrated on the dance floor. There were Charlotte and Oliver and Elsa Gravell.

"You don't, by any chance, have a magnifying glass?" Grace asked the editor after she viewed the file tape.

"No, but my eyeglasses are pretty damn strong. Would they work for you?" He offered the glasses to Grace.

She held them over Izzie's photo and squinted. After viewing the old file tape, Grace recognized two things in the old photograph.

CHAPTER
123

On the drive to The Elms, Grace tried to rein in Lucy's enthusiasm. "This is no game, honey. We're not playing cops and robbers here. People have really died."

"I know, Mom, but it's totally cool to be in the middle of something, just like on TV."

"It's not cool, Luce. It's dangerous." Grace was adamant. "When we get there, you are going to stay where I tell you to stay. No fooling around. There's too much at stake here. I don't want you getting involved in this."

"Can I at least see that tunnel? We're going to the mansion with the tunnel, right?" Lucy was determined to squeeze some fun out of this.

"If there's time, Lucy, but don't count on anything tonight."

*   *   *

Grace searched for a spot to leave Lucy, a place where she would be not only safe but not in anyone's way. Her daughter couldn't be left to wander around the party; nor was it right to have Lucy accompanying her as she talked with Detective Manzorella. Grace thought about leaving her at the satellite truck but rejected that as an option. It didn't seem appropriate to ask Scott Huffman to babysit.

"Maybe I could hang out with Daddy and Jan," Lucy suggested.

Grace didn't love the idea but, as she quickly thought about it, decided to go along. Frank was supposed to be responsible for their daughter tonight anyway. He wouldn't dare let Lucy out of his sight now that Grace had the goods on him.

"All right, Luce. I see Daddy and Jan down there." Grace pointed down the sloping lawn. "I'll wait here and watch until you get to them."

CHAPTER
124

Grace walked to the blue tent and searched the faces there. The revelers danced beneath the swirling white birds that were projected on the ceiling, but Detective Manzorella was not among them. Nor was he anywhere else on the grounds that she could see.

Concluding that the detective had left already, Grace decided to call him. She was about to go find B.J. to borrow his cell phone when she noticed Kyle Seaton standing by himself on the lawn. It figured the scrimshander would be here, Grace reasoned; these people were probably some of his best customers. She walked over to him and opened the conversation.

"I tried your scrimshaw test today," she said.

"Pardon?"

"You know, the one with the emery board

that you talked about on the show yesterday morning?"

"Oh." He sniffed dismissively. "What did you do? Try it on one of those pieces of garbage you can get at a souvenir shop?"

"Actually, no," she said. "I tried it on a handsome piece, a paperweight that was given to me by Oliver Sloane from his personal collection." Grace studied the scrimshander's face in the torchlight as she dropped her bomb. "Funny thing, though; it smelled of plastic instead of bone."

Kyle said absolutely nothing as Grace excused herself to go find that phone.

CHAPTER
125

It was interesting, from an anthropological point of view, thought Professor Cox, as he danced with his newest coed. Females of the human species didn't seem to care if their partners were much older than they were. In fact, sometimes they went out of their way to find older men; human males were, for the most part, just the opposite. Gordon was glad for this fact as he danced, trying to ignore the pain in his knee, with Susie Gonzalez, another redhead he had met in his academic world. Judy didn't know about Susie, and Susie didn't know about Judy. As long as he could keep things that way, his summer was going to be a great one.

This week with KEY News, though, hadn't turned out to be as enjoyable as he had hoped. He'd be glad to collect his fat paycheck and say good-bye when the week was over. If KEY did call him back when they went to Williamsburg in the fall, he wasn't sure if he was going to say yes. Money was important, but so was the pursuit of his dreams.

Gordon had devoted years of his life to getting that slave tunnel opened. He would never give up on the quest.

CHAPTER
126

B.J.'s face lit up when he saw her. "You came back?"

"Yes." Grace nodded. "I had to." She pulled out the papers from her purse. "Let's go somewhere where the light is better." She grabbed his hand. "I've got to show you something."

They went into the mansion through the service entrance that led to the Preservation Society's gift shop and on to the kitchen. Grace found an unused table in the corner of the spacious, busy room and spread out the photograph, the letters, and the diary. She explained to B.J. about her visit from Izzie and the story the chambermaid had told her.

"There's not much to see in this photo, Grace," said B.J., as he studied it.

"Look closer," Grace instructed. "See that man's hand? The one that's caressing the woman's rear end?"

"Yeah. Big deal."

"Well, if you had a magnifying glass, you'd see the man's cuff link is in the shape of a sundial. That's the same sundial design that sits in the garden at Shepherd's Point, the same sundial design of Charlotte Sloane's earrings. Those are the same cuff links that Oliver Sloane is wearing tonight."

"And you know all this how?" B.J. asked.

"It's a long story, B.J.," Grace hurried on. "But you can go outside and see the cuff links on Oliver yourself if you don't believe me."

"I believe you, Grace. Of course, I believe you." B.J. looked at the photo again. "Fine, this is Oliver's Sloane's cuff link I'm looking at. It doesn't mean he killed his wife."

"Yes," said Grace, "but that's his wife at the front of the room at the podium. So his hand is on another woman's backside."

B.J. smiled. "Okay, so Oliver fooled around.

That doesn't make him a killer, either. It's too easy to divorce your wife—he wouldn't have had to murder Charlotte."

"I know who the other woman is, B.J."

He looked at Grace expectantly. "Well?"

"See that large bow on the back of the dress in the photograph?"

"Uh-huh."

"I just looked at the video that was taken at the fund-raiser fourteen years ago. The woman wearing that dress was a young Elsa Gravell."

"The woman chairing this event tonight?" B.J. asked, already knowing the answer.

"Exactly," said Grace. "And Charlotte Sloane's best friend."

B.J. shrugged. "Okay, so Elsa's a louse and Oliver's a cheat, but that still doesn't mean either one of them killed Charlotte. And it's certainly hard to believe that Oliver would go on to murder his own daughter—if Madeleine's death *was* a murder, that is."

"I still think I should go to the police with this," said Grace, undeterred. "Can I borrow your cell phone, please?"

The mansion's thick limestone walls made a phone connection difficult, so Grace went outside.

*   *   *

Beneath the canopy of leaves, Grace called the police station.

"Detective Manzorella is at another location."

"But I have something important to tell him."

"I can take a message for you, ma'am."

Grace hesitated, but she wanted to get the information off her chest. "All right," she agreed. "Tell him that Grace Callahan called. Tell him that I have an old photograph that I think could help him identify who killed Charlotte Sloane and the others. Here's my beeper number."

CHAPTER
127

When Detective Manzorella arrived at the hospital, the nurse forewarned him. "He's quite groggy. He doesn't remember anything after arriving at The Breakers on Sunday night," she said. "He doesn't remember being struck on the head, much less if he saw anyone attack him."

"Think it'll come back to him?" the detective asked with impatience.

"It's hard to say. His mind has blocked it out. Sam is protecting himself."

The inconclusive answer didn't satisfy Al. "I want to see him for myself."

CHAPTER
128

The lifestyle correspondent had pulled herself away from her flirting and socializing long enough to conduct the interviews they needed for the piece in the morning. B.J. had audio and video of the fund-raiser's chairwoman, Elsa Gravell, talking about the importance of the effort to save Rhode Island's endangered seabirds, along with shots of the caterers serving the sumptuous feast and sound bites from their boss, Mickey Hager, the proud owner of Seasons Catering.

Several party guests had been interviewed as well, but B.J. thought it a good idea to get one or two more before they headed back to the Viking to cut the piece. As luck would have it, he approached a couple named Frank and Jan Callahan and asked if they would be willing to be interviewed by Lauren Adams. They readily agreed.

"This will be on tomorrow morning?" Jan asked with enthusiasm as the interview was completed.

"Yes. I can't promise that your sound bites will be picked, though," said B.J.

"Oh, I hope you'll use us." Jan pouted.

Her husband intervened. "You know, my ex-wife works on your show," he boasted. "Grace Callahan. Does she hold any sway?"

B.J. instantly paid more attention to this interview subject, sweeping Frank's muscular physique with his eyes. So this was the man Grace had chosen to marry and have a child with. Physically impressive but instantly unlikable as far as B.J. was concerned. And that was Grace's daughter standing to the side watching, thought B.J., recognizing the girl who had come into the newsroom to greet Grace the other day. Cute kid. She looked a lot like her mother, though B.J. could see the father's genes there, too.

"Grace holds more sway than you can imagine," B.J. answered.

As the newsman asked Frank and Jan to spell their names for the identifying supers that would be flashed beneath their pictures if their images were chosen, the girl grew bored. With the adults engrossed in their tasks, it was easy for Lucy to slip away.

CHAPTER
129

"Elsa, can we go home now? I've had enough."

"But I'm the chair of the event, Oliver. I really should stay until the very end."

"Well, I'm leaving." He was firm. "I'll send the driver back for you."

Elsa looked at her beloved's strained face.

He had been brave to come here tonight. She mustn't let him down.

"No, dear, don't do that. I'll leave with you in a few minutes. You just go ahead to the car. I'll finish saying my good nights and be right behind you."

CHAPTER
130

Detective Manzorella cursed the dispatcher for not getting Grace Callahan's message to him sooner. He beeped Grace from his cell phone as he raced back to The Elms. If she had evidence that could solve the Charlotte Sloane case, he wasn't going to wait until morning to get it.

CHAPTER
131

The party was breaking up. Grace gazed from the top of the lawn as the guests strolled up the gentle slope to the mansion and the cars waiting for them out front. B.J. was having a last exchange with the satellite operator about tomorrow morning's broadcast. Lauren was engrossed in conversation with a handsome male. It was time to call it a night.

As she turned to find Lucy, she heard the faint beeping coming from her clutch bag. She took out the beeper and checked the number but didn't recognize it.

Grace still had B.J.'s cell phone. She flipped it open and tapped the numbers on the keypad.

The deep voice answered. "Manzorella."

"Oh, great, it's you, Detective. I wasn't sure about the number on my beeper."

"I'm using the phone in my wife's car," he

explained. "What's up? The dispatcher gave me your message. Something about a photograph?"

"Yes. It was taken at the country club the night Charlotte Sloane disappeared. I've compared it to some old videotape of the fund-raising event, and between the two, I think it will help identify Charlotte's murderer."

"Where are you?" Grace heard the urgency in the detective's voice.

"At the top of the lawn, near the service entrance."

"I'll be there in a few minutes, Grace. Wait right where you are."

CHAPTER
132

It was amazing how careless people were on their cell phones. Holding private conversations right out in the open. Just because they didn't see you listening didn't mean you hadn't heard every word they said.

Mickey stood beneath the canopy of leaves that sheltered the path into the service entrance and waited for the tightness in his chest to lessen.

Tonight had been a triumph, the Ball Bleu a resounding success. Some of the guests had taken his business card, raving about the evening and inquiring about his availability for future events. Elsa Gravell was so pleased that she had stopped on her way out to tell him that she would be using Seasons Catering for the fund-raiser next year.

He should have been ecstatic, but he wasn't. His history with Charlotte Sloane continued to haunt him. There was no getting away from it. No matter how successful he became, the victory was bitter.

CHAPTER
133

Something was wrong.

As she waited for Detective Manzorella to arrive, Grace spotted Frank and Jan walking up the lawn together. Lucy wasn't with them.

Grace walked the few yards down to meet the couple.

"Where's Lucy, Frank?"

Her former husband looked at her with confusion.

"Isn't she with you? I thought she had wandered off to be with you."

"No! Damn it, Frank. You were supposed to be watching her." Grace wanted to slap him.

"What's the problem?" Detective Manzorella asked, trying not to show that he was out of breath after his run from the parking lot.

Grace turned to the detective, feeling a bit of relief. "My daughter is missing."

"*Our* daughter," Frank corrected her. "And don't be so dramatic, Grace. Lucy isn't missing. I'm sure she's around here somewhere. She's probably just exploring the place."

"She better be, Frank," Grace said, trying to hold her anger in check. "If anything happens to her . . ." Her voice trailed off. The thought was too much to even allow herself to consider now.

They were only wasting time bickering.

They had to find Lucy.

They fanned out to search the property, enlisting B.J. and Lauren to help. Grace's instincts told her that Lucy would head for the mansion. Her daughter would be curious about a home like The Elms, so unlike anything Lucy had been exposed to before this week in Newport, and she'd been especially interested in the tunnel. Still, the property was expansive, with lush plantings, providing places for Lucy to hide or, in a worst-case scenario, places for a murderer to stash a young body.

Every foot of the grounds had to be inspected. They needed more help.

It was as if Detective Manzorella had read her mind. Grace was profoundly thankful as

she heard him take control, giving assignments, telling each of them where they
should search.

"I'm going to call for backup, Grace," he reassured her. "Don't worry. We'll find your
daughter."

She heard them calling her name.

Lucy peeked over the third-floor balustrade
into the lamplit darkness, looking down at
people scattered around the edges of the
property. The search party was busily peering behind bushes along the fence that
edged the lawn.

"Lucy. Lucy." She recognized her father's
voice calling out to her.

Man, she was going to be in big trouble
now. She had just wanted to see what this
mansion was like. She'd found the tunnel
first, and then it had been fun to climb the
stairs and poke her head in the big rooms,
pretending that the home was her own, that
she was a daughter with rich parents and
lots of servants to make her bed, pick up her
room, and anything else she told them to do.

She never thought this would happen.

Her mother was going to be really ticked
off. She had told her to stay with her father

and Lucy had disobeyed. Maybe, if she just kept out of sight a little longer, her mother would be so relieved to see her that she wouldn't be mad when she finally came out.

Lucy crouched down behind the balustrade to wait it out awhile.

CHAPTER
134

The dark-clad figure kept close to the wall, careful to maintain a safe distance, following Grace into the house. Inside the kitchen, the caterer's carving knives rested on the counter, available for the picking.

Grace walked through the spacious laundry area, her heels clicking across the hard floor. She clutched her purse, hoping to hear her beeper go off, signaling that Lucy had been found. As she reached the end of the long space, she paused at the top of the stairs to the boiler room. Sensing movement behind her, she looked back over her shoulder. She saw nothing.

The new sandals were killing her. Blisters had formed where the straps rubbed against the sides of her feet. Grace slipped the shoes off, climbed down the stairs, and went directly to the mouth of the coal tunnel. The coal truck stood right where it had when she'd been there with Professor Cox yesterday morning. Electric lights, affixed to the brick walls, dimly illuminated the dark passageway.

"Lucy. Lucy," she called. When she heard no response, Grace's heart sank. She had been hoping to find her daughter here.

Dear God, let Lucy be all right.

With desperation, Grace turned around to continue her search. She was met by a figure looming at the top of the stairs, blocking her way out.

Frank was finally getting worried now. He didn't want to think about what his life would be like if something had happened to his daughter.

It was worth a shot. Maybe Lucy had gone out to the car in the parking lot. Maybe she was sound asleep in the backseat.

He jogged across the crushed gravel, noticing, with no particular interest, the vanity plate on a dark sedan.

SEANNA.

"Oh. Detective Manzorella. You scared me." Grace put her hand over her chest.

"Find anything?" he asked as he started downward.

Grace watched as the long legs navigated the stairs. The detective held his left arm behind him, gripping the railing with his right hand.

"No. She's not here," Grace answered.

Why was he continuing down the steps? He should turn around. They had to keep looking for Lucy.

"I need that photograph, Grace."

"Sure. Of course, I'll give it to you. But let's not stop for that now. We have to find Lucy first. Then I'll tell you everything I suspect." Where the hell were his priorities? Didn't he see she couldn't focus on anything else until she was certain her daughter was safe?

"Give it to me, Grace. Now."

She was taken aback by the fury she saw in his dark eyes.

*   *   *

Lucy had to face them sometime.

She got up from her hiding place, went back inside the mansion, walked slowly down the flights of stairs, came out at the service entrance, and braced herself.

"I guess you never called for that police backup," Grace said softly as she saw Manzorella switch the knife from his left hand to his right.

As Manzorella took another step closer, she backed up against the coal truck and tried to scream. Instantly, his one hand was upon her mouth, the other holding the knife to her neck.

"You should have stayed out of this, Grace."

His palm blocked her answer. He had to find out what she knew so he could ascertain whether there was any danger of being found out after he killed her.

"I'll take my hand down, but if you try to scream again, this blade slits your throat."

Grace nodded, her eyes bulging.

"Now, tell me what you know."

If she told him everything, he would surely kill her. If she refused, he would kill her as well. Grace knew she had to buy time.

"I know about the sundial earrings. I know that the police found one in Charlotte's gown." Even now she wasn't going to tell about the other one that Rusty had. She wasn't going to drag him into this.

"Fine. That's no big deal," Manzorella muttered. "What else?"

"And I know about Charlotte's diary. I've read the entry from the night she died."

Manzorella was impressed. "Where did you get that?"

"Someone gave it to me."

"Who?"

"The same person who gave me the photograph. So you see, I'm not the only one who could piece this together, Detective. You'd be better off letting me go and turning yourself in."

"Nice try, but don't make me laugh." Manzorella sneered. "So Izzie O'Malley finally turned over the picture. She and her husband held on to that damned thing for all these years, terrified that the wallet he left in the playhouse would make them look guilty. No problem. I can take care of Izzie. As for the diary, that doesn't worry me either. I've read it again and again. Charlotte wrote her last diary entry before I came to Shepherd's

Point to see her that night. There's nothing in the diary that points to me as her killer."

"But, why *did* you kill Charlotte?" Grace asked point-blank.

Manzorella had to admire the woman for having the moxie to put the question directly to him. Grace was brave and she was smart, too smart for her own good. But he could tell her now, since she wasn't going to have a chance to tell anyone else.

"I didn't mean to kill Charlotte, I really didn't. I loved her. I knew we could have been happy together in a world where it didn't matter what your social or economic status was."

"That's not this world, Detective."

"Charlotte agreed with you. That was the problem. She wouldn't consider leaving that cheating husband of hers, even when the evidence of his infidelity was right in front of her in that photograph. I had noticed the same thing myself at the country club that night. Oliver was all over Elsa Gravell, whenever they thought Charlotte couldn't see them.

"But I was glad. It meant there was hope for me with Charlotte. When no one answered at Seaview, I called Shepherd's

Point and went there after I got off duty. I had to tell Charlotte that I still loved her, would always love her. I begged her to leave Oliver and be with me. She spurned me and I snapped. It's as simple as that."

Manzorella's eyes welled up.

Grace felt the cool steel blade pressed against her neck and prayed that he wouldn't snap again.

"But why kill Madeleine?"

"I heard the two of you talking at the Vickerses' house. Madeleine was getting too close. I couldn't take the chance that she would remember seeing me at the gate at Shepherd's Point that night."

"And when Sam was advertised as an eyewitness to Madeleine's murder," Grace reasoned aloud, "you had to get rid of him."

"Yep. And that Quigley woman happened to run by as I was leaving the scene. She had to go, too. It was just as you said, Grace. Dominoes."

"And the s-e-a license tag?" Grace asked.

"Only Zoe, you, and I know about that. I never did anything with the information you gave me on that, never ordered the DMV to do a search."

Grace knew where this was going. Manzorella was making sure there wasn't some bit of incriminating evidence floating out there that he didn't know about. After he had pumped her for everything she knew, he was going to kill her.

The group clustered around Lucy were visibly relieved as they listened to the girl's explanation of where she had been. There was none of the scolding that Lucy had feared.

"Where's my mother?" she asked, knowing she still had to face the final judge.

"Good question," said B.J. "She's probably still inside looking for you. Let's beep her."

B.J. entered a text message. LUCY SAFE. SERVICE ENTRANCE.

She heard the beeper go off in her purse.

"There's one more thing," said Grace, clinging to the hope of still getting out of this and being able to tell the authorities what she knew. "The yellow silk handkerchief. I know that it was found in Charlotte's dress, too."

"Ah, yes. Finally we do come to a problem." Manzorella nodded. "I couldn't take that from the evidence room because it had already been logged in, and if it disappeared, it would look like an inside job and might lead to me."

"Your DNA is on it," Grace pointed out.

"True. But nobody's going to think of trying to match it to me. And I'm certainly not going to order that test."

Grace cast about in desperation, trying to think of something else that could make Manzorella see he couldn't get away with this. "You can see you're wearing the yellow handkerchief in the file tape we have," she said, averting her eyes as she lied.

Manzorella laughed. "You may be smart, Grace, but you're not a good liar. The pocket square doesn't appear in the videotape, does it?" He didn't wait for her affirmation. "Not to worry, though. Even if I do appear wearing it in the video, it's highly unlikely that anyone is going to think anything of it if they haven't so far.

"No, the photo is the only link, and if I hadn't been so crazed that night, I never would have dropped it down over Charlotte's body. I should have taken it with me and destroyed it. Instead, I left my fingerprints all over it.

"Fingerprints can last for years and years,

Grace. Did you know that?" His eyes narrowed with menace. "Now give it to me, like a good girl. Drop your purse," he commanded.

Where was Grace?

Why hadn't she come running after he paged her?

Something must be terribly wrong. Nothing would keep Grace from her daughter.

B.J. ran into the mansion, his video camera still on his shoulder, shouting her name. Frank grudgingly followed.

Manzorella instinctively shielded his face against the hurled purse as Grace struggled out of his grasp, putting the coal truck between herself and her attacker. She stood at the opening of the tunnel, wanting to run through to the hatch and the street above. But she remembered what the professor had told her. The coal hatch was locked now and alarmed. She couldn't get out that way.

But maybe she could set off the alarm.

Grace ran barefoot over the cool bricks on the tunnel floor, hearing Manzorella behind her. She came to the tunnel's end, and there it was, overhead. But she couldn't reach it. She looked around in desperation for something to knock at the hatch. From a pile of coal, left for the benefit of tourists, a shovel protruded. Grace lifted it and smashed it at the double iron doors above her.

B.J. and Frank were in the ballroom when the alarm sounded in the distance.

"It's coming from downstairs somewhere," called B.J., as he sprinted across the polished floor.

Grace felt the searing pain as the knife pierced her back. Using all her energy, she spun around to face her attacker, swinging the coal shovel as hard as she could into Manzorella's head. Both of them fell to the ground, one unconscious, the other bleeding.

Grace lay there, staring at the detective's motionless body for what seemed like an eternity until she heard the voices at the end of the tunnel calling her name. It was only then that she let herself slip away.

EPILOGUE

Grace felt the gentle lips that kissed her forehead. Slowly, she opened her lids to find a pair of brown eyes peering intensely into hers. They were B.J.'s.

"What time is it?" she whispered groggily. They must have given her some sort of sedative.

"Almost seven o'clock," he answered, taking her hand.

"At night?"

"No. In the morning."

When she tried to sit up in the hospital bed, the soreness in her back brought the rushing memories. Detective Manzorella, the tunnel, the knife. She had focused on Elsa and Oliver because that was where her personal outrage lay. That had been a mistake.

"Easy," said B.J., helping her up. "You're going to be fine, but take it easy. You were lucky, Grace. No internal organs were affected. They say you might be able to leave later today, tomorrow for sure."

Grace scanned B.J.'s rumpled shirt, the one he'd worn at the party.

"Have you been here all night?"

"Yep," he answered. "Believe it or not, Linus assigned someone else to finish Lauren's piece on the Ball Bleu. He was all for me staying here with you."

"That was nice of him," Grace said. "Maybe he has a heart after all."

"Maybe. Or maybe he's worried about you suing or something." B.J. smiled at her tenderly. "I'm so relieved that you are all right, Grace. I couldn't take it if someone else I cared about so much died so violently."

Grace looked at him questioningly.

"It's a long story, honey," he said. "I'll tell you all about it sometime. We'll have lots of time to talk about my past and anything else you want." He bent over and kissed her on the lips.

Grace closed her eyes and kissed him back, her wound, for the moment, forgotten.

"Lucy. I need to call Lucy." Grace reached for the phone on the table next to the bed. She was suddenly frantic as she remembered. What kind of mother was she? Making out with her new boyfriend before giving a thought to her child.

"Lucy is fine, Grace. She's with Frank. He's going to bring her over later."

Again, Grace looked at him in puzzlement. "How do you know Frank's name? I never mentioned it to you."

"I have my ways." He grinned as he glanced at his watch. "Could you stand watching the show?" he asked, changing the subject.

"Okay," Grace agreed as she lay back gingerly in the bed.

Constance and Harry made their introductions, opening the Thursday morning edition of *KEY to America* from The Elms—not from the mansion's lawn, as had been originally planned, but from the coal tunnel.

"A fourteen-year-old murder mystery has seemingly been solved," announced Constance, "a mystery that began in one tunnel and culminated in another, this one beneath The Elms, one of Newport's most renowned mansions."

As Grace listened to Constance describe

what had happened, she marveled at the dark video that appeared on the television screen. The images of the tunnel were shaky, as if the cameraman had been running.

"KEY News has this exclusive footage of the scene last night."

Grace watched as the camera zoomed closer to the tunnel's end, recording the video of the two figures who lay on the floor. She shivered as she recognized herself lying alongside the murderer.

"Forty-two-year-old Albert Manzorella, a detective with the Newport Police Department, was taken to Newport Hospital to be treated for injuries sustained in a confrontation with *KTA* employee Grace Callahan. Early this morning, Manzorella confessed to the murders of Charlotte Wagstaff Sloane, her daughter, Madeleine Sloane, and *KTA* intern Zoe Quigley. Manzorella also admitted attacking Sam Watkins, another *KTA* intern. Grace Callahan is also in Newport Hospital, recovering from a stabbing wound inflicted by Manzorella."

"Thank God I didn't kill him," Grace murmured. But the thought that the disgraced detective might be in a nearby room unsettled her.

B.J. turned from the television to look at her. "Did you hear that, Grace? Constance said '*KTA employee* Grace Callahan.' You got the job, baby!"

The phone rang almost immediately following the news report. It was her father, frantic with worry.

"I'm fine, Dad. Really, I'm fine. You don't have to worry."

"I'm getting in the car and driving up there," Walter Wiley said.

"You don't have to do that, Dad."

"I'll be there by lunchtime."

Grace replaced the receiver in the cradle, not unhappy, despite her protestations, that her father would be with her soon. Maybe, with her newfound leverage, she could talk Frank into letting Lucy go home with her early and they could all go back to New Jersey together. Maybe B.J. would want to drive along with them.

When B.J. had gone down to the coffee shop to get them something decent to eat, the attending physician came in, checked her, and reiterated what B.J. had already told her.

Grace could leave the hospital later in the day as long as she took it easy. She should see her own doctor at home.

A nurse came in with a comb, washcloth, and toothbrush. Grace walked carefully to the small bathroom and freshened up. When she came out again, Oliver Sloane was sitting in the vinyl-covered chair next to the bed, a bouquet of yellow roses in his lap.

He stood up. "Oh, Grace. Thank the good Lord you are all right."

Grace smiled, touched that this man who had been through so much, lost so much, had come to see her. "I'm fine, Mr. Sloane. The doctor says I'm going to be fine."

"I wanted to thank you, Grace. For everything you've done. Manzorella would have gotten away with everything if not for you. Charlotte, my sweet Madeleine, and those other poor young people."

Grace sat back on the bed and pulled the thin cotton blanket over her legs. "I don't know about that. I think the police would have figured things out sooner or later."

Oliver grimaced. "Maybe, maybe not. They hadn't figured anything out in fourteen years—why should we think they were going to do any better now? Who knows how many traitors they have in their midst?" he asked with bitterness in his voice.

She felt sorry for the man as she watched him. His wife and daughter dead, murdered by someone who wanted Oliver's wife but could not have her. As a man who had dallied while married, even as his wife was trying to make things work out between them, Oliver had to be carrying around a great deal of guilt. That was for him to reconcile, if he possibly could, thought Grace. He was going to have some tough days ahead.

He handed her the flowers, and she thanked him. As he started for the door, she stopped him.

"I hesitate to tell you this," Grace began, "but I think you'd want to know. The scrimshaw paperweight you gave me?"

"Yes?"

"It isn't authentic, Mr. Sloane."

"I don't understand," said Oliver.

"I tested it. It's plastic of some sort."

"How could that be?" asked Oliver, perplexed. "I purchased that piece from Kyle Seaton. He's a very reputable dealer."

"I don't know, Mr. Sloane, but you might

want to check the other pieces in your collection."

The hospital had no problem allowing Lucy
to be with her mother. At first the girl was
solemn, her brown eyes frightened, but she
relaxed after just a little while, reassured that
Grace was all right. Fifteen minutes into the
visit, Lucy was clicking the remote control,
searching for a *Law & Order* rerun on the
room's television set.

"You like *Law & Order?*" B.J. asked.

"I *love Law & Order,*" Lucy corrected him.

"Me, too."

Lucy looked at B.J. with interest, taking
this tall guy's measure. He might be all right.
She couldn't tell yet. But she did know one
thing. Her mother didn't seem like a sick person as she sat in that hospital bed. Her
mother looked happy. Real happy.